# Return to Willow Creek

by

## Roberta C. M. DeCaprio

*Between the Rifle and the Spear
Series*

**Return to Willow Creek**

Cover Art by *Diana Carlile*

The Wild Rose Press, Inc.
PO Box 708
Adams Basin, NY 14410-0708
Visit us at www.thewildrosepress.com

Publishing History
First American Rose Edition, 2014
Print ISBN 978-1-62830-485-5
Digital ISBN 978-1-62830-486-2

*Between the Rifle and the Spear Series*
Published in the United States of America

## Dedication

During the writing of this book I lost a few family
members, a dear friend, and a beloved cat.
So I dedicate this book to the memories of:
Aunt Jane Formichelli Bohunicky,
Cousin Madeline Guarino DiCaprio,
Richard H. Stoffels Sr.,
and my cat, Ginger.

Also to my editor, Allison Byers.
Her encouragement, patience, and professionalism
has been extremely appreciated.

Chapter One

*Willow Creek, Arizona*
*February 1895*

Amanda gently, as not to awaken her sister-in-law, peeled back the quilt and crept out of bed. For many months, the two of them, since fleeing the reservation, had shared a room at the parsonage. Softly she made her way to the window and gazed out to the dark, quiet street below. The darkness had come on early, as the skies wept with a chilled rain...much like her, opening forth to deluge all with her sorrow. A tremendous hollowness bore into her and grew larger with each passing moment, until the loneliness became too much for her to bear. She belonged for so long beside him— where could she go—where did she belong now?

She remembered standing here once before, on this very spot, thirty-one years ago, to be exact. She was eighteen and a young bride...a white woman married to an Apache warrior, when she got word of Proud Eagle's death. Now she mourned him again. But this would be the last time she'd bid him farewell...in truth he was gone from her forever.

She had stood outside of their home, the wickiup they shared all these loving years, and watched it burn. The flames danced high, seeming to reach the sky and licking the full moon that had shone brightly down upon her sorrow. His body lay inside, as was the Apache death ritual and custom. After the embers had cooled, and before she was made to leave the reservation, she found a clay pot and with a slate, managed to fill it with ashes...her husband's remains mingled with the life they shared in the wickiup. This was her custom, to bury some remnants of him. And until she decided on a final resting place, the small clay pot, its opening stuffed with sweet grass, was housed in the church, behind the pulpit...safe from harm. So, this time there was no mistake, as there was before. Proud Eagle's spirit now dwelled with his ancestors. He would finally sit beside those gray-hairs he honored, in the counsel of the afterlife. And Amanda had no doubt they'd welcome him with respect, as he tried desperately to uphold their traditions in spite of the white agent's intrusion upon their village.

"You are gone, really gone, my husband," she whispered, tears welling in her eyes. "And I have no clue as to what I'll do without you."

The room suddenly filled with light, and she turned to see Rising Sun adjusting the wick of the bedside lantern.

"I'm sorry to wake you," Amanda apologized.

Rising Sun threw her legs off the bed and made her way to her. "You must sleep now, my sister." Gently she caressed Amanda's brow. "The weariness is etched upon your face."

Her sister-in-law's display of affection unleashed the sorrow she harbored, and tears streamed uncontrollably down her cheeks. "How can I rest? How can I...can I..." She placed a hand over her broken heart. "How can I possibly go on alone, without him?"

Rising Sun, with her own tears flowing, embraced her. "You are not alone, Golden Lady. We are family still, even though my brother is no longer with us. He would want it no other way." Rising Sun pulled back to search her face. "I want it no other way."

"I am thankful to have you, all of you," she whispered. Though there were only thirteen tribespeople left, they still honored her as the chief's wife...came with her to the parsonage.

"Come." Rising Sun took her hand and led her to the bed, where they sat in silence.

Amanda's gaze wandered to a nearby chair, where her husband's ceremonial headdress sat. She took it for Gabriel, her son. He would be chief now. Upon the dresser was her mother's Bible, and on the floor sat her father's violin. These belongings, along with a quilt; Duke, her dog; Todd, her horse; and her mother's wedding dress were all she took when she left her life to become Proud Eagle's wife.

Duke and Todd had gone long ago to their reward, the wedding dress went with her daughters to England, and she used the quilt to wrap her husband's body. Also in her possession was her father's pocket knife—the one his father had given him. The handle was made of silver, with tiny inlaid abalone chips along the side. She kept it in the bed side table's drawer.

"Golden Lady, you must rest now," Rising Sun urged.

"Each day the sun rises, each night it sets, just as it has always done before...when he was alive." She turned round and round the gold wedding ring she wore. It belonged to her mother, and the one on her thumb belonged to her father...and her husband, as she gave it to him when they wed. Now, it too, would be given to Gabriel. "Shouldn't something change? Shouldn't the world be different, now that he's gone?"

Rising Sun sighed. "It is only our world that has crumbled, my sister. Because we loved Proud Eagle and he meant so much to us, we cannot understand how life can be the same." Placing an arm around Amanda's shoulders, Rising Sun pulled her close. "Do you remember the story of how I became Proud Eagle's sister?"

She nodded. "Your own mother was his mother's sister. And after both your parents died, White Dove and Cunning Eagle adopted you."

"Because my mother died giving me life, I never knew her. To me she was just a beautiful and kind woman I learned about through the stories White Dove told me. But to White Dove, she was flesh and blood, laughter and tears. Her voice could still be heard and would never be silent until the day White Dove joined her. When we know and love the one who passes, everything changes...but only for us, not for everyone. You will always feel Proud Eagle sleeping deep in your heart—so will I. But for others life goes on. A new day dawns, another night falls, and life goes on," Rising Sun repeated softly. "It is good that it does, for the new lives joining us must have the same chance at life and love."

"Yes, for all of the new lives and those they'll love." She thought again of her three children, Gabriel, Raven, and Sunny. As far as she knew, the girls were both married. Raven had a son of her own, and both she and Sunny expected another. These babies Amanda didn't know and had yet to hold. England was so far away, but it was necessary for her girls to go to live with Kaylena Bentley, Amanda's aunt.

The white agents had compromised many of the women in their village, and she had worried for Raven and Sunny's safety. As it was, she feared she was too late; suspecting Raven had been taken against her will while returning after sundown to their wickiup. It happened when Rising Sun's daughter-in-law, Water Lily gave birth. Raven had helped Water Lily to her wickiup, and then went for the midwife. By the time she made her way to her own dwelling, it was dark.

Denton Hall was the white agent on duty. He always agitated Amanda and her daughters. He called them half-breed, white-trash, but lust was in his eyes even though he spat at them in disgust. And he took Raven that night. Her daughter showed the signs, withdrawn and fearful, shamed and sullen. She could say nothing to Proud Eagle or Gabriel, for fear they'd be killed defending Raven's honor. So she had no choice but to send them away from their home, from her, from their father who they'll never see again.

Rising Sun's soft voice broke through her thoughts. "It grows late now, Golden Lady. It is time for sleep."

She nodded, standing, reluctant to climb back into bed. Rising Sun lay beside her, covering them both with the quilt.

"You should be sleeping next to your own husband," she whispered.

Rising Sun sighed. "Falling Star knows we must be apart while we take refuge here. The holy man, Ben, and his wife, Sylvie, have been very kind. But there are only enough bedrooms for the women and children. The men must sleep for now in the stable."

"I know Reverend Newcomb has sent word to Reverend Holmes in England," she said, thinking of how much she needed to see Josh's face. He was there for her when her parents died, and again when she thought she'd lost Proud Eagle those many long years ago. "When he returns to Willow Creek, he will know what to do."

"Are you so sure he will come, Golden Lady?"

She reached for Rising Sun's hand and gave it an encouraging squeeze. "Yes, I am sure. As soon as he learns of Proud Eagle's death he will come." She sighed heavily. "In fact, I am most certain he won't be able to stay away."

Chapter Two

Joshua Holmes was awakened by the coach's sudden halt. He blinked his weary eyes into focus and glanced out the window. The main street of Willow Creek had changed in thirty years. There were taller buildings, more stores, a postal and telegraph office, a bank, a physician, a sheriff's office, jail, and several different eateries. A large hotel lined one side of the double sized causeway, replacing the small boarding house, as well as a huge livery stable and saloon. Downtown Willow Creek was not as refined as the bustling, pedestrian streets of London, with all its glass and glitz, but it was no longer as rural and desolate as he left it either.

The world was a waking giant, filling with new innovations, like the horseless carriage. American passengers he met aboard the ship he sailed upon talked with much enthusiasm and at great length about this new mode of travel. To hear them speak, one would be certain in a matter of a decade traveling by horse and buggy would become obsolete.

He opened the coach door, stood, and stretched his bones. His gaze immediately found the parsonage. It almost appeared dwarfed against its new surroundings. It was in bad need of a coat of paint, as was the small church. But it radiated warmth, a shelter in the storm, its doors ready to receive anyone who needed a helping hand. He thought back to the time it sheltered children orphaned by Indian attacks. Now it housed Amanda and a few of the Western Apache people that swore their loyalty to her.

A mixture of anticipation and anxiety washed over him. He remembered the last words she'd said to him...*may we live to meet again.*

"God willing," he whispered, as that was his thought at the time. It appears God *was* willing, for they were both still alive. Yet it was under the sad circumstance of Proud Eagle's death that they would meet again...truly a bitter-sweet reunion.

He sighed. *How* would this all culminate? How will she react to seeing him again? After all, she had been widowed only a few months and still heavy in her grief. No doubt, knowing her as well as he once did, she was fearful for the welfare of her Apache family...and rightly so. Other than Ben and Sylvie Newcomb, he didn't imagine many more doors opening to these folks. But he had a plan, one that would please her...please them all.

The wagon master approached with Josh's luggage. "Hope your stay's a nice one, Reverend."

"Thank you, Mr. Stone." He retrieved his bags and made his way to the parsonage.

Sylvie Newcomb opened the door. Her round face, with a no-nonsense expression and sparkling brown eyes, reminded him of Grace Thomas, Sylvie's aunt. Grace was another feisty lady, spared him no words or diplomacy when she had something to say. He cherished those days, her kind heart and extraordinary way she kept house for him when he was the vicar at the parsonage.

"Well, ain't ya a sight for sore eyes," Sylvie boomed, welcoming him with a wave of a hand into the parsonage and shutting the door behind him. "Can't tell ya how much we've all been waitin' on ya, especially Golden Lady...I mean, Amanda."

Golden Lady was the name Proud Eagle had given to Amanda, because of all her golden curls. He thought of the many nights he wished he could touch those tresses, bringing them to his face, and feel the softness.

Before he could question Sylvie further about Amanda, Ben entered the foyer. He was a little rounder, due to Sylvie's cooking no doubt, but otherwise still the cheerful chap he knew from days gone by.

"It is vith great pleasure to see you, Josh." Ben smiled, his Dutch accent still thick after all these years.

Josh smiled in return and shook the hand Ben offered. "I am glad to finally be here myself, though the circumstances are of great sorrow."

Ben's smile faded. "There has been so much sadness vithin these valls, Josh. If they could talk, vhat a story they vould tell." He shook his head. "And Golden La...Amanda," he quickly revised, "has so much despair in her heart. She doesn't sleep...just cries."

"Poor thing doesn't eat much to boot." Sylvie placed her hands on hips. "I tell ya, she can't go on like this, Reverend, else we'll be buryin' her next."

A chill ran down his spine at the thought of Amanda dead and buried.

"I hope you can help her, help them all in some vay," Ben said, his expression turning grim. "One too many have died already."

"That's why I've come. Gabriel and his wife will

be here in a matter of weeks, as well."

"What the devil's wrong with me, lettin' ya stand all this time holdin' these here bags, and not offerin' ya a place to sit and somethin' to drink," Sylvie said.

"Here, let me take them." Ben reached for the luggage. "I've got you in the den. Your old den," he added, heading for the other room.

"Wherever there's room," he called after him.

"The others are out and about, busyin' themselves with chores...got to say there's not a one in the bunch with a lazy streak. All hard workers and mighty grateful for whatever's given to them," Sylvie explained.

"How many all total have taken refuge here?"

Sylvie narrowed her eyes. "My count is fourteen, and that's includin' Amanda."

He frowned. "Ben's letter said there were perhaps less than a dozen."

"A few more arrived last week." She shrugged. "Only the good Lord knows where they went after all of them was run off the reservation, but somehow they found their way to us." She tilted her head sideways. "And I suppose you'll be wantin' to see her directly?"

Josh arched a brow. "Like your aunt, you don't waste words."

"Nope, ain't got time for wastin' anythin'." Sylvie headed for the stairs.

Standing alone in the foyer, he took a moment to look around. Outside of a different color paint upon the walls and throw carpets here and there covering the hardwood floor, the place looked the same. He inhaled the scent of homemade bread and lemon cleaner. The aromas filled his nostrils and bombarded him with memories.

The tiny town of Willow Creek was the first congregation he led...this parsonage his first home away from home. And he had loved it here...the climate, the people, and Amanda.

He closed his eyes with the thought of it all...with the thought of her...what she would be like, look like now, after all these years.

"Josh," a soft voice called.

He opened his eyes to find her standing at the top of the stairway. In spite of her grief and exhaustion, she was as ever beautiful. She wore a white blouse and a long flowered skirt that draped her slim figure attractively. Her full lips, the perfectly shaped nose, high cheek-bones, and long, golden curls gracing her shoulders quenched his hunger. He was like a man starved of food and then suddenly given a feast, as he devoured every inch of her in a matter of seconds.

"I knew you would come," she said, her almond-shaped, sapphire blue eyes locking with his.

His heart raced.

*God help me, I love her even more than I realized.*

She took the stairs two at a time and ran into his waiting embrace. Wrapping her arms around his waist, she buried her face beneath his chin. "Thank God you're finally here."

He held her close, stroking her thick hair as he always wished he could, marveling in the scent of her jasmine flesh. She felt fragile and frail, yet she filled him with glorious warmth. Pressed against his chest, his heart merged with the beat of hers. And he knew he was home, was finally where he belonged.

"I'm so sorry for your loss," he choked out, unable to say anything more.

Her whisper warmed his neck. "Me too."

For a while they stood in deep silence within each other's embrace. Though he wanted to say more to ease her grief, no words came. Perhaps there were none that needed to be spoken. Did it not say in Job 2, verse 13 *that his friends gathered to mourn with him for all he lost, and so the three sat down with Job upon the ground for seven days and seven nights...and none spoke a word unto him for they saw that his grief was great.*

Trembling, her voice caught in a sob. "Oh, Josh, you being here means everything to me. I've been so frightened...so worried."

"You need not be any longer; I am here now, and I'll take care of everything. And soon Gabriel and his wife will arrive as well."

She pulled back, eyes wide. "Gabriel is married?"

"Aye, the nuptial took place two weeks ago, just before..." he hesitated. "Just before we learned of Proud Eagle's death."

She frowned. "It took so long for word to reach you."

"Aye, mail delivery across the sea is slow." He brushed aside a strand of flaxen hair from her cheek. Still she wore it down, as he remembered a married woman by Apache tradition was required to do. But now that she was widowed...

She sighed. "Then why have Gabriel and..."

"Riley...her name is Riley," he supplied.

"Then why have Gabriel and Riley not arrived with you?"

"They have traveled to Ireland first, to tell Raven the news, and to see Riley's family."

"Ah, it is best he tell Raven face to face, and be there for her," she said with motherly approval.

"It was what we all thought as well, and that I venture on to America ahead of him," he explained.

"And so Gabriel's wife is Irish, then?"

"Aye, in part. She has family living not far from Raven," he said.

Her voice quivered. "And then, after they arrive, will you be returning to England?"

"Nay." He sighed and tightened his embrace. "I will never leave you again."

She nodded. "I have so much to ask you about my children."

He searched her face. "And I will be glad to answer those questions, as well as tell you of the plans Gabriel and I have for you and the tribespeople."

Hope radiated in her eyes. "Then come." She grabbed his hand. "Let's sit in the parlor and talk."

"Nay, not just yet." He brought her hand to rest on his heart. "First you must eat something."

"Oh, Josh, I'm fine and don't need anything..."

"Well, I believe you do," he interrupted. "And I'll not tell you a thing more until you are fed."

She stared up at him glumly. "You want me to eat right now?"

"Aye, now." He grasped her hand and led her toward the kitchen.

Chapter Three

Amanda took another spoonful of the chicken soup Sylvie had prepared. "Now tell me everything."

"Not until you finish the entire bowl," Josh diplomatically responded. "You need your strength."

She was bemused at his condescending tone. "You act as though I was a child." With a frown she added. "What comes next, tanning my hide if I refuse?"

"That might not be such a bad idea. I always thought your father allowed you to get away with way more than you should have." He raised a brow. "A swat to the bum now and then definitely would not have hurt."

Her cheeks warmed, and she dropped her gaze to the bowl set before her. "That is old news," she mumbled, taking another spoonful of soup.

He chuckled. "Well, I'm an old man—with several aches and pains to prove it."

"You are nothing of the sort." Surveying his handsome face, she smiled. "I'd say you are still quite well into your prime."

He only grunted at that remark.

Granted, his dark hair had grayed a bit at the temples, but she always thought this was a distinguished look for a man. His shoulders were still broad, waistline trim, arms well-muscled, and a twinkle still gleamed in his light blue eyes.

"You're probably not moving about properly or eating enough roughage," she offered.

He frowned. "I get around just fine, and my roughage intake has nay a thing whatsoever to do with the problem."

"Have you tried rubbing bear grease into your joints before bed?"

His frown deepened. "Nay, for obvious reasons." He pointed to the bowl. "And while we're having this riveting exchange of words, your soup grows cold."

She popped another spoonful into her mouth to please him. "I sometimes think as soon as a person turns fifty..."

"I am well over fifty, my dear."

She cleared her throat and continued. "As a person turns fifty, they suddenly believe they are old, and that they must start acting old, whether they feel old or not."

"Are you insinuating my morning ailments are all in my head?"

She shrugged. "The Apaches believe a person's age only applies to the number of years they've lived on this earth...nothing else or nothing more. You could have aching limbs at five or fifty. It doesn't mean because you ache that you are old. I've seen warriors older than you go out each morning to hunt, and bring back quite impressive game."

"Aye, well, I suppose one does what they must to survive," he shot back.

"I think it has more to do with not being slothful. When you lie back and become pampered, your body betrays you."

He crossed his arms over his chest. "Are you now insinuating I am lazy?"

She giggled...it was the first bit of mirth escaping her since Proud Eagle's death. "Perhaps settled would be more accurate."

"Eat your soup," he quipped, stifling a grin.

She finished the last of her meal, and then placed the spoon aside. "There...all gone." She wiped her mouth on the white linen napkin and sat back in her seat. "Now, tell me everything."

He cleared his throat. "Where should I begin?"

"The last word I heard from my daughters was that each was with child." She settled herself comfortably in her seat.

He frowned. "They all sent word to you of the births."

She sighed. "As you said, mail delivery across the sea is slow."

"Well, let me see then, the matter of the mites," he teased.

She frowned. "Mites?"

"Aye, the babes," he explained. "Truth be told, Sunny was with more than one child, as she soon learned when she gave birth to twins."

"Twins," she gasped.

"Aye, they're in my family. And since Sunny married my nephew, Rafe, it was inevitable they'd pop out somewhere."

"That's right, Sunny wed your sister's son," she recollected. "Was her wedding day wonderful?"

"Aye, that it was. And Sunny wore your bridal gown. She reminded me so much of you, the way you looked when..."

Tears welled in her eyes, and she swallowed hard the lump growing in her throat. She remembered wearing her mother's gown to marry Proud Eagle. They had already been married by his customs, but Josh urged Proud Eagle to honor her wedding tradition, too. "I wish I could have been there to see her for myself. Raven and Gabriel as well. I've missed all my children's weddings. And the babies, my grandchildren, to think I might not..."

"Let me tell you more about them, then," he broke in softly.

She nodded, wiping a tear from her eye.

"Rafe and Sunny have a daughter and a son. The girl is light-haired like Sunny, and the boy is a spitting image of his father."

She smiled. "How nice, one of each. And what are their names?"

He narrowed his eyes. "If I recall, the little girl is Amelia Dove."

She gasped. "Sunny's named her daughter after my mother, Amelia and Proud Eagle's mother, White Dove."

He nodded. "I believe it was Sunny's intent to honor her grandmothers in spite of Gabriel reminding her it was the Apache tradition not to name a child after those who have passed on."

"That's true, but I'm glad Sunny decided to do it her way. And the boy?" she inquired, suddenly picturing herself holding the two angels lovingly in her arms.

"His name is Peter Jerome," Josh said. "Jerome being his paternal grandfather," he explained further.

"And Peter being his maternal grandfather, as that was the Christian name Proud Eagle was given by his white grandfather, and the name he chose when he finally decided to be baptized. Reverend Newcomb performed the ceremony." She clasped her hands and brought them to her heart. "I'm sure he would have been so happy and honored, regardless of his tradition."

Josh reached out to her, his large, warm hand covering hers. And in that moment, she felt safe, safer than she had in a long time. Thank the heavens for this man, always around when she needed him. Affectionately she squeezed his fingers, provoking a smile that brightened his entire face.

"And mother and babies are doing well?"

"Aye, all is fine," he replied.

"What of Raven's family?" She kept her hand in his.

"You knew she had a son?"

"Yes, she wrote me after he was born. Casey Broderick is his name," she said.

"Aye, and now she has a daughter," he said. "I believe I heard they are calling her, Amanda Maureen...after her grandmothers."

Her heart soared with love. "Raven has named her daughter after me?"

"Aye," he said. "And I can't think of a lovelier name."

Her cheeks warmed to his compliment, as she was not accustomed to receiving any from a man other than her husband. Again tears threatened to come. They stung the back of her throat as she thought of all the endearments Proud Eagle had bestowed upon her. His look of love, his touch, and his kisses were all reminiscences of him still moistening the chamber walls of her mind. How will she ever carry on without him?

"Would you like me to tell you about Gabriel's wife?"

"Yes," she said, suddenly feeling awkward holding his hand. If any of Proud Eagle's people saw them, what would they think of her...newly widowed, still grieving. The disrespect she was displaying for her husband's memory suddenly sickened her stomach. Slowly she pulled away from his grasp and cleared her throat. "Please, continue."

His expression fell. "What's wrong, Amanda?"

"Nothing, nothing at all," she lied, forcing a smile. "I'm just a bit tired. You see, I haven't been sleeping well, with all that's happened."

"I understand completely," he said softly. "Perhaps we could continue our conversation after we've both had time to rest and refresh ourselves."

She nodded and stood. "Then I shall see you later."

He rose from his chair. "You will at that."

She took an audible breath, exhaustion weighing on her. "Thank you again, Josh, for coming." She blinked back the tears threatening to come.

Gently he placed a hand on each of her shoulders and looked deep into her eyes. "Take hope in knowing there is no further need for you to fear or worry," his tone most adamant. "And as I said before, Amanda, I'm never leaving you again."

Chapter Four

Josh lay upon the cot Sylvie made up for him in the den and surveyed his surroundings. The room hadn't changed much. The old tapestry of Daniel in the lion's den still hung over the fireplace mantel, a good reminder true faith can conquer fear. However, the mantel clock ticking beneath was new, as were the lanterns ensconced upon the wall.

The carpet remained the same, though more worn. On a pastor's wages anything serviceable continues to be useful. Even though he arrived only hours ago, he could spot many of Sylvie's frugal endeavors...like the homemade window treatments. They were fashioned from heavier material and were much longer than the light-weight curtains covering the casements before. No doubt to keep the rooms heated longer on cold nights, thus saving on firewood or coal.

The old mahogany desk still sat near the window, which offered him a perfect view of the garden. He remembered the days he'd gaze out at the many colorful blooms swaying in the breeze while trying to compose a worthy sermon. All times are challenging, but the years he pastored here were even more so, with the Indian attacks and so many orphaned children. What would he have done without Grace Thomas and Amanda to help him with his duties?

And when Amanda's father was a victim of one of

those attacks, Josh rested his elbow upon this very desk, head in his hands, and prayed she'd accept his marriage proposal. All he ever wanted to do was protect and care for her, love her and spend his life with her. And those hopes were dashed when she fell in love with Proud Eagle. But now that Amanda was alone, would he stand a chance at those hopes again? Did he dare try to win her heart?

Throwing his legs off the cot, he stood and made his way to the window. Suddenly Gabriel's words came back to haunt him.

*"You have been waiting for this moment for a long time," Gabriel accused. "It is no secret how you felt...how you continue to feel about my mother. I would say my father's death has made everything convenient for you."*

Josh still felt the bite of those words. Though he didn't deny his feelings for Amanda, he never wished any ill will to befall Proud Eagle. The Apache was his friend as well. Learning of his death brought him great sorrow. And even though they didn't see eye to eye on many things, the one thing they did agree upon was Amanda's wellbeing. She was their common bond, and because of her, the two of them respected each other. Proud Eagle sent word to Josh through Ben Newcomb. He had Gabriel read Ben's words for himself. Proud Eagle's last request was for Josh to return to Willow Creek and wed Amanda.

And he had done what he was asked to do. But a small part of him knew he would have come to be by her side whether he was asked to or not.

A knock at the door brought him from his thoughts.

"Enter." He turned from the window.

Ben came into the room. "Is all vell vith you in here, my friend?"

He nodded. "I am very comfortable, thank you. In fact, I'd like to thank you for all you and Sylvie have done for Amanda and the Apache people."

"They are all good souls and deserve so much better than they receive," Ben said softly.

"When I left Willow Creek, I asked you to watch out for Amanda..."

"Ja, I remember the conversation clearly," Ben broke in.

"I just want you to know how much I appreciate you keeping your word. You've done a splendid job. I couldn't have done better myself," Josh said.

Ben's face flushed. "Is that not vhat ve are called to do, as followers of Christ...are ve not used as His earthly instruments to help others in need?"

"Aye, but I believe you and Sylvie have gone above and beyond your duties." He neared the other man and gave him a friendly pat upon a shoulder. "Your kindness, I'm sure, has made a big difference to these folks. I wouldn't be surprised if you've even saved them from great harm on many occasions."

Ben sighed. "I couldn't save Proud Eagle. I tried to get him the medical help he needed, but the doctor in town vould not come vith me to the reservation." He rubbed a hand over his eyes. "I rode to the next county, sought help there, and finally I came upon a man that once practiced medicine. His vife died, and he couldn't save her, so he left his profession. But he agreed to ride vith me to the reservation. In the vind and rain ve traveled, and I prayed all the vay ve vould not be too late. But ve vere...by this time the infection had spread throughout Proud Eagle's body. He burned vith fever. And nothing anyone did vould cool his flesh." Ben cleared the emotion from his throat. "All that vas left for me to do vas give him the last rites."

"You couldn't save his body, but you saved his soul." He squeezed the other man's shoulder encouragingly.

"Ja, if nothing else, I managed that," he whispered.

"As you were called to do," he said. "And kindness brings forth trust." He smiled. "It is not hard to see, by their presence here, how much they trust in you."

His lips thinned. "Ja, they do, but now, Josh, ve are at a crossroad." Ben combed his fingers through his hair. "As much as I vant to shelter these folks, there is too many of them and not enough of the parsonage. And my vages cannot continue to feed all the hungry mouths. I am afraid the time is coming for them to find other accommodations." He sighed. "They cannot stay here much longer."

"I am aware of this, and be rest assured a plan is already in the works," he said.

Ben's despair lifted. "Vhat plan is this that you have?"

"I will tell everyone at dinner," he said. "As for now, what can I do to help out around here?"

Ben smiled. "Can you peel potatoes?"

He nodded. "I have done my share to scrape bare a spud or two."

"Then perhaps, if you are so inclined, you vouldn't mind helping Rising Sun vith such a task?"

He raised a brow. "Rising Sun and not Sylvie?"

"Ja, Rising Sun has been preparing all the meals since she's been staying here. At first my beloved vife was put out...you know a voman's kitchen is alvays off limits to another vomen. But then Sylvie began to see the vay of it...the joy of having more time to spend tinkering in the garden, or to vatch the sunset, and just enjoy some leisure time," he added. "And all of a sudden, Rising Sun in the kitchen set just fine vith Sylvie."

He chuckled lightly. "I don't doubt, but how has this happened?"

Ben scratched his head. "I believe Rising Sun is quite taken vith the convenience a vhite vomen's kitchen holds. No longer does she have to bring the dirty laundry to the river, or beat it upon a rock to clean. Ve have a scrub board and a vringer...much easier and faster devices to accomplish the task. The indoor tub holds varm vater for bathing, the private stall used for relieving one's self is...vell, more private than any bush could be. The stove, the ice box, the pump that expels vater into a sink vith just a push of a handle has suddenly put a fresh meaning to the daily routine of preparing a meal. And a calling-out of gladness has overtaken the dear voman, so much so, I think it vill be extremely hard for her to cook, to bathe, to function in any other vay from this point on."

He chuckled again. "Well, Ben, I am here to tell you, there is an excellent possibility she won't have to."

If Josh didn't already know the way to the kitchen, he would have been drawn to it by the sweet song Rising Sun hummed as she worked. Soon enough he discovered Ben wasn't exaggerating. The gladness radiating from Rising Sun, with every move she made, was a picture to behold. A woman's life in this room had become far easier than anything she'd endured on the reservation.

Taking in Rising Sun's joy brought a smile to his own lips, as did the memories this room of the house held. It was here while sitting at this very table, he proposed marriage to Amanda. He remembered the day like it was yesterday. Ethan Gregory, Amanda's father had just been murdered by Indians...they later would learn the attacks were done by the Chiricahua tribe and not Proud Eagle's...and she ran to the orphanage for refuge. But then, after she got her bearings, she wanted to return home to take care of her farm. One afternoon, while sitting at the kitchen table, they argued about her foolish decision. He couldn't bear for her to leave. The thought of her out there, alone and on her own, sitting prey to the danger lurking in every corner, was bloody nonsense.

But she raised her chin defiantly...always so independent, so willful, and challenged him. That stubborn streak had somehow made her even more appealing, and he found himself proposing.

He cringed now, as he did then, at his untimely, unromantic response. For the longest time thereafter he regretted being so frank at an inopportune time. Perhaps if he had waited, bided his time, given her a chance to heal...clearly he had made a shambles out of the whole situation.

In the end, she had asked for some time to think it over. To save face, he agreed.

But she never did think further on the matter, and when Proud Eagle entered her world, his proposal was forgotten. Her warrior carried her off to his village and made her his wife, and Josh returned to his home in England.

Rising Sun, dropping the lid to a pot on the worn, wooden floor, brought him back to the present. Stepping further into the kitchen, he could still hear Grace's high-top, brown heeled shoes clicking back and forth across those very boards with busy determination, as she went about preparing his meals.

And how could he forget the day Proud Eagle came knocking upon the back door to invite them, in courtesy of Amanda's traditions, to the first Apache Thanksgiving dinner? Grace took one look at the tall, imposing man and sank into a dead faint.

Aye, the kitchen brought many pictures to mind, and now one more was being created right before his eyes...that of an Apache woman cooking in her bare feet, wearing white women's clothes, in front of the cast iron stove.

Rising Sun's hair, long, ebony strands of silk, hung to her hips; hands moving efficiently as she went about making their dinner.

He cleared his throat to grab her attention.

She turned to meet his gaze, her round, bronzed face breaking into a welcoming smile as she caught sight of him standing in the doorway.

He inclined his head politely. "I've come to peel the potatoes."

Unexpectedly she ran to him, wrapping her arms around his waist. "I am so glad to see you, holy man."

She was short, only coming to his ribs, yet she could be a force to reckon with—as he remembered. He smiled and brought his arms around her tiny shoulders, briefly returning the affection. "And I, you, Rising Sun."

She stepped back, instantly becoming shy with her

boldness and made her way back to the stove. "Sit." She reached for a pot and paring knife.

He obeyed and she placed the items before him on the table, before turning to gather potatoes from a burlap satchel sitting on the floor. After filling her apron skirt with the desired amount for the evening meal, she brought them over to where he sat.

Reaching for a cloth hanging upon a hook nearby, she spread it out upon the table. "For the skins," she said, and then added, "Sylvie will not be happy if they land upon the floor."

He stifled a smile, as he had a good feeling Rising Sun wouldn't be too pleased about the mess either. "I'll do my best to be careful."

Satisfied, she nodded and carried herself proudly to finish her work at the stove.

"Golden Lady knew you would come." She cast him a glance over her shoulder. "She said you would not be able to stay away once you heard about my brother's death."

He set knife to spud and began to peel away the brownish skin. "And she was right." He cleared his throat. "I'm sorry for your loss, Rising Sun."

She sighed. "These past few moons have been the hardest of all to live through." She turned to face him, wiping her hands on the apron. "My heart cries out for Proud Eagle, as I loved him strong and miss him much, but he is now with our ancestors and no longer must worry about the things of this land." She shook her head. "This is not the way for all of us who are left."

He searched her face, knowing it would not take long to extract from her all he wished to know. He and Rising Sun always had a good rapport between them.

She was the first to welcome him on his maiden visit to their village, and set the premise for the others in the tribe to follow. "Who are those that are here?"

She pulled out a chair opposite him and sat. "Let me see—there is Falling Star, my *shikaa*, husband and Rising Star, my son. Then there is his wife, Water Lily. They have a son." The corner of her mouth curled. "I am a grandmother."

He returned her smile. "Congratulations."

She inclined her head in polite response. "He is a fine boy, strong like his father. That is why his name is *Kuruk,* which means bear."

"And the rest that have followed you?"

"My daughter, *Udaya*...her name means dawn. I named her so because that was when she took her first breath...at dawn of a very cold day. Along with Udaya there is her *shikaa*, Messai and their daughter, *Prita*...her name means dear one. Do you remember Little Elk?"

"Aye, I do," he said.

"He is here, with his wife, *Nascha*, Owl Woman. She is as wise as an owl. And so she is the midwife and shaman of the tribe..." She paused, her face saddening. "Or what is left of our tribe." Taking an audible breath, she continued. "And then there is Little Elk's son, Night Wolf." She smiled. "At one time we all thought my brother's youngest daughter, Sunny Eagle, and Night Wolf would marry. But she has found her heart with another, across the great waters."

"Aye, Sunny's husband is my nephew, Rafe," he explained.

Rising Sun nodded and continued. "And Night Wolf is now the *shikaa* of *Ela*...her name meaning earth. Their son, Micah, was born only ten days before you came."

"When Ben wrote to me he said there were only about a dozen tribespeople that left with Amanda to come to the parsonage," he said.

Rising Sun frowned.

"A dozen is the number..." he began to explain.

"Twelve," she cut in. A quick intelligence sparkled in her large, brown eyes. "The same number as those who followed the Christ God."

"Aye," he said. "There were twelve apostles."

"Holy man, Ben wrote you the truth, as that was how many of us first came to this house with Golden Lady. Night Wolf and his family came later, after word had already been sent to you."

He frowned. "Why did he wait?"

"Earth would not leave at first. She wanted to give birth to her baby in her own home." Rising Sun's face darkened. "But the white agents stripped and beat Night Wolf, threw them out of their wickiup, and set it on fire. I hear they set fire to everything...all of our homes are gone. Everything we ever worked for and saved...the memories, the heirlooms, even the clothes are all gone. We just have what was upon our back. That is the reason for us dressing in the white men's garments. And now only the scorched land is left, dark, dead blades of grass heaped with the ashes of all our lives." She sighed. "So, you can see why Night Wolf and Earth had no other choice but to follow the rest of us...coming in the black of night...Night Wolf's nakedness only covered by a blanket Earth saved and wrapped about his waist."

"Are they all well now...Earth and the baby?"

She nodded. Waving a hand in the air, she added, "Since they are safely housed here."

His heart bled for the sorrow and cruelty these good people endured. "I am so sorry."

She nodded again and then stood to resume her duties at the stove.

Quietly the two worked for a long time preparing dinner.

Then it was Rising Sun who broke the silence. "When I was just a maiden, my people talked about the young widows of the tribe." She paused as she continued to stir whatever was cooking and smelling so delicious on the stove. "It was said if a warrior died, his brother was to marry his wife. In this way, she would always have food to eat and be protected from harm."

"And what if the warrior's brother was already married or he had no sibling to ask this favor of, who then came to the widow's aide?"

"The tribe's chief would then choose a warrior best suited...a man loyal, brave, caring, and honest." She turned to face him. "This man chosen would be greatly honored to take this position, and do his best to fulfill his duty to the widow." She searched his face. "Proud Eagle did not have a brother, but as chief he did choose the man he would want Golden Lady to marry if he were no longer on this earth to love and protect her."

He swallowed hard, his heart racing. "What are you trying to say, Rising Sun?"

"Proud Eagle asked the holy man, Ben, to send for you because he knew you would be the only man to do right by his wife...the only one he could trust to love and protect her the way she deserves." Her eyes welled with tears. "He knew you loved her and would never see harm come to her."

"Nay, I would sooner die than to see her hurt in any way," he whispered.

"And so now it is you who must carry out my brother's last wish, and bring him peace."

As soon as his mind gave birth to the thought he was to wed Amanda, a hope he had entertained for over thirty years, it flew away...Gabriel's words returning once more to haunt him. He placed aside the paring knife, wiped his hands on a corner of the towel catching the potato peels, and stood. "Amanda is newly widowed and still very much enveloped within her grief." He paced the floor, just as he'd done when faced with his first proposal to her. "A marriage offer right now would certainly be refused."

"Then you must hold onto the thought a while longer, until she is ready," Rising Sun advised.

He combed his fingers through his hair. Amanda hadn't wanted to marry him the first time. "And what is to say she will accept my proposal?"

"What is to say she will not?" Rising Sun countered.

He halted his steps and turned to face Rising Sun. "Amanda is a willful minded woman."

"This I already know to be true," Rising Sun said in a dry tone.

"And she'll always be in control of her own destiny. She alone will be the one to choose her own mate, if ever she will again. An Apache custom isn't going to change her mind."

"Do you still love her?" Rising Sun clasped her hands in front of her.

"Aye, I do, thus the reason I never married," he

admitted. "I could not have her, and I did not want another."

"Then you must change her mind for her," Rising Sun urged. "This time is the right time to ask her, and my brother knew this as he lay dying upon his bed," she added with conviction. "You must ask her again." Quickly she wiped a tear away with the back of her hand. "Now you are the man who must marry Golden Lady."

Chapter Five

Amanda tossed upon her bed. Though she was bone tired, rest eluded her. After leaving Josh in the kitchen, she had come upstairs to think...to refresh herself. Seeing him again after all these years brought back bittersweet memories. He had shared so much with her...the time spent with her parents, Grace Thomas, and Proud Eagle. Their faces all flashed around in her head. Now, all of them were gone, left her to go it without them. But Josh was still here and promised he would never leave again. What did that mean to him, what would it mean for her?

She ran her hands over her eyes. Just newly widowed, grief still so thick around her heart, it was too soon to think further.

*And yet I am!*

From the moment she spotted him standing in the foyer, the breath she'd been holding cleared from her lungs. Just his presence lifted the weight pressing down upon her shoulders since her husband's death. And when Josh embraced her, she felt like she had finally come home after a long, exhausting journey. His concern was comforting...familiar. And she knew instantly she did not want to live without him again. But what exactly did that mean? What was she hoping for?

She threw her legs off the bed, and stood.

"Am I such a fickle woman?" She paced the tiny room. "My husband is not gone from this world more than three months, and I'm already looking ahead."

But this was what she and Proud Eagle had discussed, three nights prior to him taking his last breath. He was awake, and in pain...his body on fire, yet his mind still clear. She sat at the edge of their bed with a cool mug of water...helping him to take frequent sips. It was then he gently caressed her face and told her he asked Ben to send word to Josh.

*"When I go on to be with my ancestors, you are to be with the holy man, Josh," he had said. "You are to be his wife."*

*Tears welled in her eyes*

*"If he asks me, then I will accept. And that is all I will agree to, as I certainly do not plan on breeching the subject with him myself."*

*He smiled satisfied. "Ah, he will ask."*

That night he fell into delirium. The next day Ben arrived with the doctor, but as she feared, help came too late. She sat by his side throughout the night, holding his hand, wiping his brow, and greeting the tribespeople coming to the wickiup to bid farewell to their chief. Owl Woman prayed her shaman prayers, chanted her song, and sprinkled him with sacred pollen while Rising Sun and her daughter sat weeping in a corner of the wickiup. And just before sunrise, he opened his eyes a final time, the large brown orbs straining to focus upon her face, and smiled at her before breathing his last. In that second all of her joy was ripped from her heart, her world crumpled, and she knew her life would never be the same.

It not only hurt her emotionally to say goodbye to

him, but spiritually and physically as well. To never again feel his kisses, hear his voice, be surrounded with the love and energy of such a vibrant and intelligent man, was just too much to ask anyone to endure...and yet this horrible burden was placed upon her heart, crushing the very core of her being.

She hadn't really thought further about the promise she had made to Proud Eagle, with her sorrow so acute and the loss so great, until she looked into Josh's eyes. There she saw all she needed to know...he was still in love with her. And his declaration to never leave her made it all the more clear he was thinking ahead for her welfare, as her husband had done. They were two exceptional men, so very different from each other...their cultures worlds apart. And yet they shared the same feelings for her. Both thought of her wellbeing, wanted to love and care for her all the days of her life...of their lives. How fortunate could one woman be?

A knock at the door sounded.

"My dear aunt," Dawn called through the door. "My mother has sent me to tell you dinner is ready."

"Tell Rising Sun I will be down momentarily."

"Is all well with you?" Dawn said.

"Yes, I just want to fix my hair." She retrieved a brush from the dresser.

Standing before the mirror, she pulled the brush through her long curls. Married Apache women wore their hair down; maidens tied their tresses up into a device called a *nah-leen*. She supposed she fell somewhere in between, now that she was widowed.

She opened the drawer and searched for a piece of ribbon or cord...finally finding a strip of lace.

"This will have to do," she muttered.

It only took a few moments for her to remember how to braid her hair. Memories of watching her mother's long, thin fingers fashioning Amanda's golden strands into such a manner guided her task. In no time a thick, neat braid restrained her curls, tied off at the end with the strip of lace.

After splashing a bit of water upon her face from the basin, she smoothed the wrinkles of her skirt, straightened her collar, squared her shoulders, and made her way to the door. Reaching for the knob, she hesitated, her fingers gripping tight the round, black handle. From this moment on, she will be embarking on a new life...or would it be the second half of the old one? At any point, the time had come to begin again.

"Yes, it's time, Proud Eagle...time for me to move ahead, just as you wished," she whispered. "And just as I promised you I would do."

Chapter Six

The minute Amanda entered the dining room, Josh noticed her hair...not up, but no longer falling loose around her shoulders. One thick, golden braid hung down over her right breast...a very full breast, at that. Her body, still as perfect as he remembered, suddenly made his throat go dry. How many times had he dreamt of loving that body...kissing every part of her warm, wonderful flesh? And the thought of her loving him in return...he shook his head to clear it and forced his focus on what this hair-change meant. He was sure it was a silent message to him that she had decided a new way of life would now be hers to embark on. His heart lit with hope. Perhaps she would agree to embark on that new chapter with him? And if she declined his intentions, he was still proud of her. She wasn't going to let her sorrow, the tragedy befallen her family, define her. Instead, the hardships were going to refine her, give her the courage to move ahead...for herself, her children, grandchildren, and the Apache people.

Their gazes met across the room. With a slight smile and a nod of her head, Amanda confirmed his conclusion. He acknowledged her by returning the smile, then made his way to her. Taking her by the hand, he escorted her to a chair and took a seat beside her at the dining room table.

Ben and Sylvie sat at each end, remaining ever the

gracious hosts in the middle of a difficult situation. Rising Sun, her daughter, Dawn, and daughter-in-law, Water Lily, along with Owl Woman and her daughter-in-law, Earth, joined them. Of course, the younger women held the smaller babies, like Dear One and Micah, in their arms, while toddler Bear Star sat upon pillows in a chair in order to reach the table.

The men, Little Elk, Falling Star, Rising Star, Messai, and Night Wolf ate their meal at the kitchen table. He would have joined them to show unity if his first priority hadn't been to Amanda...and out of respect for Ben and Sylvie. They had put themselves in jeopardy with the townspeople and the congregation when they took in the remaining tribe members. Showing loyalty to Ben was the least he could do, as well as finding new lodging for the houseguests. And the sooner he and Gabriel could get them all settled elsewhere, the better.

From the corner of his eyes, he watched as Amanda bowed her head when Ben recited the meal prayer. Then sighing, she reached for her napkin and placed it upon her lap.

He leaned nearer and lowered his voice for only her to hear. "Have faith, Amanda. The Lord is close to the brokenhearted and saves those who are crushed in spirit."

She nodded. "It would seem brokenness is a part of life. More so, I tend to believe, for these people."

He glanced around the table himself this time. "Aye, their challenges do appear never ending. But I assure you, the sun will eventually shine down upon them as well."

She sighed again. "The world's wounds of hatred

and despair are vast and run deep. I fear, until they are healed, things will remain the same. The Apache are outcast amongst those of Willow Creek, as well as anywhere else they roam. A shining sun seems very far away."

He smiled encouragingly. "Then let me assure you, it is not as far away as you might imagine. But until that favorable time dawns upon them, we must trust in God to arm us in strength and keep our way secure." Briefly he placed his hand over hers. "After the evening meal, I will speak to you further about a plan for the future." He pointed to her plate. "But for now, eat your dinner."

She nodded again, looking down at her plate. Then, before picking up a fork, she flipped the braid aside, leaving it to hang down her back.

Without thinking, he reached over and stroked the bound tresses. A soft, silky texture met his caress. In that mere touch, he was lost in the insurmountable love he had for her and would always have until he drew his last breath.

She raised her gaze to meet his, and for a moment he froze. Had he overstepped his position? But then a small smile played at the corner of her mouth. "It is good to have you home."

He rested his hand for a moment on her shoulder. "It is good to be home."

After dinner, the others scattered to their own destinations...he and Amanda retired to the parlor.

She made her way to the fireplace, sat cross-legged in front of it, and silently stared into the flames.

He stifled a smile and sat beside her, grimacing inside as his bones met the hard, wood floor.

"You needn't sit here with me." She kept her eyes

on the wood-burning fire.

"I don't mind," he lied, shifting to find a more comfortable position.

She shrugged. "I'm told old habits die hard."

"And some needn't die at all."

"True," she agreed. "Then there are those habits, with the passing years, that turn only into memories."

"Which have their place as well," he added. "Some of my happiest moments are when I call upon fond memories."

"Or those that are not so fond." She glanced his way. "Do you remember the last time we sat in this room?"

He took an audible breath. "Aye, and I will never forgive myself for the way I presented you with such horrendous information. I apologize for the manner in which I explained, in graphic detail, General Carleton's plan for the Apache people, the atrocities of his minions, and the frame of mind from the general population. Purposely I spared you nothing. But I had no right to frighten you into listening to what I had to say."

Her gentle hand upon his arm brought warmth throughout his being. "You were only trying to save my life," she whispered.

"Aye, I was, but I got more than a bit carried away...gruesome to tell it correctly." He frowned. "I hoped, if I shocked you enough, repulsed you with the unconventional and brutal tactics the government planned on using, you'd see how dangerous it was for you to remain with Proud Eagle."

"And I was wrong to not listen," she said. "And so foolish not to heed your words and do something more about it all."

His frown deepened. "What are you saying?"

"I'm saying I was wrong to turn a blind eye and a deaf ear to the facts." She sighed. "Granted, to hear such abominable maneuvers by the white man were too much to tolerate, but they were the cold, hard truth that wasn't going to go away."

"And what would you have done differently?"

"I don't rightly know, Josh. But I shouldn't have ignored your warnings." She glanced back to the fire. "Or perhaps I should have insisted Proud Eagle and some of his family leave with me, to England. Aunt Kaylena's wealth could have easily housed us all without trouble. Maybe then, all the persecution the tribe has suffered would have never happened. And now, Proud Eagle would still be alive."

He reached for her hand. "You shouldn't second guess yourself. At the time, you did what you believed to be right. And besides, Proud Eagle would have never agreed to leave his village, his people. He was the chief; his notion was all about stepping into his father's role of keeping the Apache traditions alive, passing them onto his children."

She bit her bottom lip. "In the long run, that notion was completely destroyed. When the white agents infiltrated the village, all the ways of the Apache were squelched anyway. Upholding traditions meant facing starvation, torture, and death. They were stronger in number, much tougher than any of us. They had no scruples. And we knew the consequences of our actions, if we rebelled, would turn detrimental. So, we had no choice but to be stripped of our dignity, independence, and the right to live as humans. I saw women taken against their will, babies crying from hunger, the old dying of sickness that could have been prevented." She turned to look at him, sapphire eyes welling with tears. "If Proud Eagle thought I would leave without him, he would have changed his mind. But I feared if I forced him to do as I wished, his spirit would eventually suffer, his pride destroyed. And I didn't want him, in the years to come, to resent me, or regret his love for me." She choked back a sob. "How selfish was that, Josh? I thought only of myself...worried about my husband resenting me, falling out of love for me, when I could have prevented all that has happened. I had, in the very palm of my hand, the means to bypass all of this pain, and I let it slip through my fingers."

"I mean not to speak ill of the dead, but let me remind you of your sacrifice to live Proud Eagle's way." He arched a brow. "Did you ever resent your husband for asking you to renounce all you knew?"

She shook her head. "I'd been conditioned to believe it is the way of marriage...for the woman to follow her husband, since I was old enough to realize one day I would marry and have a family of my own." She frowned. "Then it all became so dangerous to live his way...to grow children in such an atmosphere. And now, looking back, I am so ashamed I kept silent. I had a way to get us out of that danger. But I didn't...I didn't to preserve his pride, his love for me as the perfect, supportive wife. And it cost us all dearly."

He tightened his hold on her hand. "Amanda, don't do this. If anyone is to blame here, it is me. I should never have gone back to England...left you here to deal with all this by yourself. Perhaps if I'd been around, someone for you to confide in...a safe haven to go to, you would have been able—stronger to make a different decision."

"No, all of what has happened is my fault," she protested. "And because of my stupidity, my indiscretions, God has turned away...forgotten us."

He brought her hand to his heart, holding it there as he spoke. "God forgets no one. He has good reason for doing the things He does...for allowing things to happen as they did. Our problem lies in not understanding His timing."

Tears cascaded down her cheeks. "What is there to understand? God gave us a free will, and I used mine wrong."

"Nay, you were not wrong. It was the way it had to be. I believe God, after we work through our plight, wants us to learn a lesson from the end result. Or perhaps He wants us to give time to someone else, so they can have enough of a chance to set their life right. Look how much you've impacted the Apache people with your ways, with friends like Ben and Sylvie...and me," he added. "And then it just might be God needed to show us the enormous power He has over man. Either way"—he pulled her close to him so she could rest her head upon his shoulder—"I've seen if I cling to my trust in the Lord, His way always turns out to be in my best interest."

She buried her face beneath his chin. "How is any of what's happened...all of us homeless, tormented by unbearable grief, frightened to face another day of persecution, and poverty stricken, be in our best interest." She moaned, before breaking down and weeping.

Her tears moistened his neck, and his heart broke into a thousand pieces. If he could just pick her up, put her upon his lap, and comfort her with his kisses, he would. But again he feared to overstep his position, so he held himself in reserve. Patience was essential. Any other move would be ridiculous at this point and would only manage to do two things: frighten or anger her to the point of pushing herself further from his arms than ever before. His patience had gotten him this close to her, as it is. She allowed him to caress and hold her. He dared not do anything more in the chance he'd upset or confuse her so she was forced to make any sort of premature decision about him...about them.

"If there was no sorrow, there would have been no need to send Gabriel and your daughters to England. And they would have never discovered the inheritances due them, which now can help you and the others," he said.

She pulled back to look at him. "What good are those riches if loved ones are dead?"

"They would have been called home to heaven no matter what the circumstance. When our time is through upon this earth, the celestial trumpets blare and we are to go...no questions asked...His will be done." He wiped her tears with a sweep of his thumb. The brief contact with her soft flesh brought waves of desire through him. Forcing himself to stay at bay with his affections, he continued. "But you see, Amanda, now those riches can help the ones who still live."

"Tell me how this will happen," she whispered.

"Do you remember the day you gave me the deed to your father's land?"

She nodded. "I had no further use for it, living in

44

the village, and I didn't want it to fall into ruin. My father gave his life's blood for that property, worked the land day after day to make a home for my mother and me." She suddenly got a far-away look in her eyes. "I remember the day I found him slain by the Chiricahua, lying bludgeoned to death in the forest surrounding the farm. It was so unnatural to see him that still, especially his hands. I never saw my father's hands do anything but work...provide sustenance and care for Mama and me...whether to milk the cow, plow the field, or build my mother a cupboard. So the thought of poachers setting a claim to the land he labored over would have dishonored his efforts. And I knew, somehow," she added softly, returning from her memories to gaze fully into his eyes, "you wouldn't let that happen."

"Nay, I wouldn't...I didn't," he corrected. "And if you'll come and sit upon the sofa with me, as my body can no longer take sitting here on this floor, I will explain what I have done all these years with that land...and how it can now be used to your advantage."

After rising to a stand, he reached out to help her to her feet, and then escorted her to the settee. To his delight, she kept her hand within his when they sat and again rested her head upon his shoulder. His heart raced, the joy of her nearness warming every ounce of his flesh. And for a moment, he envisioned nights spent like this together after the evening meal, having a spot of tea in the parlor of the home they shared as husband and wife, sitting close upon the settee before he led her upstairs to the bedchamber where the two would...

"Tell me then what you've done all these years with the land," she prodded at his silent hesitation. "And how can that property be used to our advantage?"

45

He cleared his throat and his mind once again from the horror of the past, as well as the delicious day dreaming of what he hoped for the future.

## Chapter Seven

Josh's embrace spread warmth and comfort through Amanda. Sitting so near to him on the settee left her feeling safe and protected. She made no attempt to move; in fact, she purposely kept her head upon his shoulder, relaxing against him. It was easy to be in his presence, as he made people feel comfortable. Closing her eyes, she inhaled his scent. The soft aroma of sandalwood and musk pleased her senses, filling her with a calmness she hadn't known in a long time.

In all her years living with the Apache people, only a handful of times did she actually feel secure enough to allow herself to enjoy the peace and contentment she experienced now. The discontent was not in the mate she'd chosen, or the people surrounding her...but instead in the ever looming dread of Carleton's men sweeping down upon the village to destroy its inhabitants. She feared for her life, as well as that of her husband and children. Most nights she slept with one eye open and an ear to the wind. After the white men infiltrated the village, turning it into a reservation, she didn't sleep at all at night. And by day she played hide and seek with danger. Every turn, behind any tree, trouble lurked. Daily she was hounded and tormented by the agent's cruel words, inappropriate advances, and hostel stares. Never could she tell her husband or go to him for comfort. If he knew what she endured, he would have come to her defense. And that alone could have cost him his life. So, she suffered the humiliation, the terror and uncertainties by herself. She felt alone as she feared for her safety, and that of her children. But sitting here now, with Josh so near, comforting and strong, she could feel a heavy weight lifting from her heart.

"Is everything, so far, fine with you, Amanda?"

"Yes, things seem to be slowly getting better. Thanks to you being here I don't feel so displaced."

"Everything will fall into order again; you just need to give it time." He gave her shoulder a gentle, affectionate squeeze. "All new challenges are hard at first. But once there is time to readjust to them, they become easier."

"It appears I just can't see how to get from the hard to the easy right now," she confessed. "I remember, right after losing each of my parents, feeling nothing would ever be right again. I looked around at everyone, able to go on about their lives...working, sleeping, eating, laughing, and I felt as though there was an invisible wall separating me from them."

"Do you still feel that way?"

"There are times, yes, I feel so lonely...so all alone in my grief. And then there are the times I know I'm not. My emotions are so scrambled, so confused. But all this pain is inevitable, wouldn't you agree?" She continued without giving him a chance to answer. "I mean, at some point loving someone truly carries the seeds of sorrow, when either one of the two die."

"Or only one truly loves the other," he added.

"Yes, there's that sort of sorrow as well. It wears on you for sure, as it is so hard to make any sense out of it."

"There's no need for you to make sense out of it all overnight. Just remember not to allow your heart to turn you bitter. Sometimes, after the grieving stage, comes the anger."

She frowned. "How does being angry play a part?"

"Well, the one left is forced to carry on without the other, and when it becomes difficult, the survivor becomes angered. But anger will only eat at you, take away and keep away your joy. So, I beg you not to choose anger in dealing with your sorrows. Instead, choose to focus on those who still live that surround you. Let their love dissolve the hatred and pain. Let a positive light guide you, the grace of the Divine, and soon you will see all else dims compared to such glory."

Though she was still enveloped in her sorrow, Josh's efforts to soothe them meant everything to her and talk of her father's property gave her hope. "All this time I thought the land once owned by my family had been abandoned, left to rats and the spirits buried there after you left for England." She pulled back to look at him. "Tell me of your plan."

He looked deep into her eyes, reaching out to push a wayward tendril of hair from her cheek. For a moment his touch lingered, ever so gently. "Before I went overseas, I had the burnt mess of what was left of the farm, cleaned out and hauled away. As I took the time to survey the land, I discovered it consisted of fifty-seven acres. The soil was rich for farming, and a stream and hunting grounds were nearby. It was an excellent investment, and I knew it had to be maintained if it were to remain prime property. So, I hired a young chap by the name of Vernon Washburn to be overseer in my absence. The deal I made with him was I pay for a cottage to be built in the woods, for him, his wife, and two sons, as well as allow him half of the profits the farm produces and a monthly stipend. Washburn has done a remarkable job throughout the years. Besides his home, upon the land there sits a large barn housing chickens and two cows, plus a stable with a few horses. He even maintains the family burial plot, where your parents rest in peace."

Hearing this news had special meaning to her, as she knew where she could lay Proud Eagle's remains to rest. "What of Mrs. Washburn and the sons?"

"Sadly, Mrs. Washburn passed away about five years ago, and the two sons live in Boston. But Vernon remains steadfast, and I am sure he will welcome company."

She frowned. "Even if the company was a small band of Apaches?"

"I have dealt with the chap for over thirty years. He is a sound and fair individual who respects my word and will be fine with whatever I decide." He shrugged. "And if not, then he can find a new place to live."

"The riches, the inheritance Gabriel has to his name, will then pay for homes to be built for the others?"

"Aye, that is the plan, although I have given Gabriel the deed to the land. It was his grandfather's farm, and therefore his legacy to have. So, he will rebuild a new village for his people," Josh explained.

She smiled. "I'm not surprised at his intentions. When he was younger, his favorite passage in the Bible was Isaiah 58:12." She shook her head. "He'd read and reread the piece of scripture."

Josh returned her smile and recited the passage, *"Some of you will rebuild the deserted ruins of your cities. Then you will be known as a rebuilder of walls and a restorer of homes."*

She nodded. "And with the Bentley fortune...an inheritance from my mother, he is doing just that."

He arched a brow. "Not just from the Bentley fortune, but from the Collins wealth as well."

Her eyes widened, and she sat forward in her seat. "That's right. Letters I received from Sunny said they were welcomed by Lady Lucinda Collins as long-lost relatives."

"It seems Lucinda Collins, a very dear friend of your mother by the way, had an uncle named Silas Collins. The chap, an adventurer, left England to take his chances in America and wound up in Mexico, whereby he fell in love with an Apache woman. And by her he had a daughter..."

"They named White Dove," she interrupted and then concluded. "Who turned out to be Proud Eagle's mother."

He smiled. "Precisely, and did you know Silas Collins was Amelia Bentley's inspiration to travel to America for her own adventure?"

She gasped. "So, it all comes full circle, in a matter of speaking. Silas Collins comes to America, weds an Apache woman, and has a daughter who then has a son...Proud Eagle. In the meantime Silas inspires Amelia Bentley to seek out new lands; she comes to America, meets and marries Ethan Gregory and gives birth to me. And I marry Proud Eagle."

"I can add to that," Josh said. "You and Proud

Eagle have a son, who travels back to England with his two sisters. But one sibling, Raven Eagle gets sidetracked to Ireland where she marries the Lord of Limerick. Gabriel, Raven, and Sunny then inherit both their maternal and paternal family's fortune. Along the way Gabriel meets and marries Lucinda Collins' ward, Riley Flanders." He held up a finger for her to listen further. "And the sister who made it to England with him, Sunny Eagle, marries my nephew, Rafe, who was the captain of the ship that brought them to England in the first place...and wasn't supposed to be onboard, but filled in for his brother, Simon."

She threw her head back and laughed. It was the first burst of joy and mirth she's had in a long time. "It was destiny...pure destiny...all of it."

"And there's another bit of happy news," he said. "Your Aunt Kaylena has set up an account for you at the Willow Creek bank whereby a monthly stipend will be deposited for your wellbeing. In that way you will also share your mother's inheritance." He pulled from his vest pocket a slip of paper and handed it to her. "This document is all the proof you'll need to be able to draw from the account each month."

She held the bank note close to her heart. "Oh, Josh. What wonderful news. Now, with my own birthright, I can also help with the building of this new village."

"*We* will build the village, Amanda...together," he corrected. "As I told you before, I'm not ever leaving you again."

"Do you think tomorrow we can take a ride out to the farm? I'd like to meet Mr. Washburn."

"Aye, I was about to suggest we do just that."

"But before anything else is accomplished, something important has to be done first." She took him by the hand and stood, pulling him to his feet. "Come, follow me, and I'll show you."

Chapter Eight

With their fingers intertwined, Josh allowed Amanda to pull him through the foyer, to the kitchen, and out the back door. Down the familiar brick path they walked, past the rose bush, and to the side entrance of the chapel. He had journeyed down this trail numerous times when he pastored the small flock at Willow Creek, his own footsteps instrumental in wearing away the pavement. But what could Amanda, at this hour, possibly need to show him in the tiny sanctuary?

She shivered as she reached the door. He stopped her hand from turning the knob long enough to remove his jacket. As he placed it around her shoulders, she leaned in to him.

Slowly she raised her gaze to meet his, her delicate features illuminated by the light of a full moon. "Joshua," she whispered.

He pulled her close...close enough for him to feel her racing heart against his own and returned her glance with feverish intensity. He would have liked nothing more than to join her lush, full lips with his. But decency demanded he remember his place, show her respect at all cost. Nervously he cleared his throat. "Amanda, you know that I..."

"Be patient with me." She hushed his words with a tip of a finger upon his lips. "I can't hear your declaration with a pure conscience at this moment. But I know what will happen...what is inevitable between us. I just need a little more time...the chance to set to rest one love before giving my heart to another."

He stared down at her, too amazed at her candor to manage saying a word.

"Come." She turned from him to open the door. "Help me bury my husband."

An uncertain frown creased his brow. He knew it was Apache custom for the chief, after death, to be burned in his dwelling. How then could he help her bury Proud Eagle?

She answered his question, as though she read his mind, while she made her way to the pulpit. "After the embers cooled, I entered the burial site, and with a piece of shale I scooped a pile of ashes into a clay pot. Then I stuffed the opening with sweet grass to keep the remains from spilling out."

The small, clapboard church was warmed by an iron woodstove...which was well-stocked to keep out the night chill. Several lanterns lit the dais, but the rest of the building rested in scattered, peaceful light. He was pleased to see Ben left the chapel comfortable and available for anyone to come and pray should they desire. He glanced at the large wooden cross above the pulpit. It was worn, even cracked along the side, yet still it remained. How many times had he knelt before it, baring his soul, pleading his heart, and praying for an answer to his petitions?

She bent to retrieve the urn from behind the podium. "It's nothing but a simple piece of pottery." She sighed, holding the clay vessel close to her heart. "But there was nothing else available at the time to use," she explained. "And since he had been baptized, I felt he needed to have a Christian burial as well as the traditional Apache." Briefly she glanced at the receptacle she held. "I didn't know where to bury him, though, until..."

"Until I mentioned the farm and Washburn caring for your family's plot," he finished for her.

She nodded, meeting his gaze. "It seems only fitting, for Proud Eagle to rest alongside my parents. He is...was my family, too."

"Aye, he was at that."

"So, then tomorrow, when we ride out to the farm, we can lay him to rest," she concluded. "And you will give the eulogy and prayers."

"Aye, if that's what you wish, but shouldn't you wait for your son to arrive?"

"No, he will have enough sorrow to bear," she whispered, handing him the urn. "It will be better for Gabriel to already have a place to go to honor his father. And the tribespeople said their farewells at the traditional ceremony. I'd like this time...this last one to be just us."

He nodded and glanced down at the clay pot, fingering the texture of the modest retainer holding his friend's remains. His heart filled with sorrow. "He was a good man."

"Yes, he was. And he thought the same about you," she added. "That's why he sent for you when he lay dying. He knew you would...you would..." she stammered.

"I would not disappoint him," he supplied.

She nodded, her eyes moistening with unshed tears.

He swallowed hard and inclined his head politely.

"Then I am honored to have been chosen to perform the last ceremony."

She neared him and gently placed a hand over his. Her soft touch warmed his flesh. "So am I," she whispered, forcing a smile. "So am I."

****

Amanda rose early from her bed, ate a quick breakfast of tea and toast, and then hurried out the door on her errand. The brisk morning air stung her nose and eyelids, causing her to wrap her woolen shawl higher and tighter around her shoulders, as she walked the two blocks to the Willow Creek bank. It had rained throughout the night, but now the late winter sun worked its best to dry up the puddles and soggy soil she dodged here in there to save her only pair of shoes from ruin.

Mr. Cargraves, the bank's manager, was a short, slender man. After she showed him the document Josh had given her the night before, he was more than eager to help her with inquiries about the new account. And to her pleasant surprise, the first stipend of her inheritance had already been deposited.

"I just need your signature and an address, and your account will be at your disposal," Cargraves said.

She cast him a warm smile. "That is very good news to hear."

He returned the pleasantry, his thin face flushing a bit in the process, and fixed his specs higher up upon his nose. "Then let us get to the business at hand."

"Reverend Benjamin Newcomb and his wife Sylvie are the dear friends I am lodging with at this time, so all correspondence concerning this account should be sent to the parsonage," she explained as she wrote down the address.

Aunt Kaylena had been very generous with a monthly distribution of fifty dollars wired for her use. Mr. Cargraves explained the benefit of leaving a running balance and helped Amanda to decide what amount would be wise to withdraw. In the end she saw fit to remove a total of fifteen dollars, five for her own monthly allowance and what personal items she might need, and ten to contribute toward the bills at the parsonage.

As she stowed the currency into a small leather pouch hanging from her belt, she thought of how Ben and Sylvie's generosity stretched well beyond what she hoped when they agreed to house so many at one time. But then to impose upon them to feed all of those mouths and clothe everyone was something that greatly troubled her. Now, with her inheritance, she could at least remove some of the burden placed upon such eager-to-help shoulders, by paying for the food, as well as bolts of fabric and thread.

After Proud Eagle's death, most of them fled with only a few buckskin tunics, breeches, and dresses...some with only the clothes on their backs. But in the months following the hurried departure, those items needed to be replaced with shirts, blouses, skirts, and trousers. Sylvie worked her fingers to the bone sewing for them on a foot-treadle operated sewing machine.

Rising Sun took a fancy to the process and eagerly learned the technique, as well as helping Sylvie in the kitchen. And although none of the Apache people were lazy or ungrateful, the men working outside as well as the women helping inside, Amanda could presently pay for everything they needed for the remainder of the time they all lived at the parsonage. And hopefully that wouldn't be much longer. Gabriel and his wife were set to arrive within another two weeks with the deed, whereby showing proof he owned the property. Then a claim would be filed and building on the land could commence.

Excitement rose within her, a gleam of anticipation so joyous it put a bounce in her step. For the first time since her husband had passed away, a ray of light shone upon them. She was equally terrified as she was delighted for what lie ahead. But to fret like a horse with a saddle that chafes was just plain silly. In truth, the second chance they had all been given was a lot better than she could have ever hoped for or imagined in her fondest dreams.

The thought of traveling with Josh back to her old farm today made her walk faster, holding her shawl tightly around her shoulders. Soon the Gregory land would once more be her home, housing them all without the threat of fear and danger.

"Home, sweet home," she muttered, breaking into a run when she spotted the parsonage.

Hurrying up the steps and entering through the front door, she found Josh waiting for her in the foyer. "I'll only be another moment." She rushed past him to the kitchen. There she found Sylvie and Rising Sun preparing dough for apple pie. "Sylvie, I have something for you." She reached for the pouch. Pulling open the drawstring, she grabbed the allotted funds she had set aside as payment for their keep and placed the cash into Sylvie's hand.

The other woman gazed down at the money resting

in the palm of her hand with a slight frown. "What in tarnation is this for, Amanda?"

"To pay for the food and clothing you and Ben have so generously given us, as well as room and board."

Sylvie shook her head. "I can't be takin' nothin' from ya," she protested. "Ya all will be needin' every morsel ya can scrape together as it is."

She smiled, reaching out to close Sylvie's fingers over the monetary gift. "It is fine, my dear friend. My Aunt Kaylena has decided to bestow upon me my mother's inheritance. I've just come from the bank, and already the monthly stipend has been wired to an account in my name." She squeezed Sylvie's hand affectionately. "So, take it...please."

Sylvie's eyes moistened. "I can't begin to tell ya..."

"No need," she interrupted. "I know you and Ben don't have a lot, and yet you would give us the last bit of food you had in the cupboard, or the clothes right off your backs. But there's no longer a reason you have to suffer to help us. Until we find other lodging, we will need to stay here. And as long as we're your guests, you can count on a monthly payment for the accommodations." Then she gave Sylvie a quick hug and whispered, "There's a little something extra there just for you. Buy yourself something nice, you deserve it," before she left the kitchen to meet Josh.

She sat quietly in the wagon, holding the urn housing her husband's remains in her lap. The good feeling she had given Sylvie payment for their lodging still buzzed around in her heart.

"It was a generous thing you did back there," Josh commented.

"No, the generosity belongs to Sylvie and Ben. I just did what should have been done months ago when we all showed up homeless and frightened on their doorstep."

He turned his gaze from watching the road ahead to look her way. "They were glad to do it for you all, it's how they are."

"I know. They're good, kind, and caring folks. But there's no need to continue to take from them. Now that I have my own funds available, I do not need their charity," she explained.

"Ah, pride," he muttered softly.

She met his gaze while raising a defiant chin. "There's nothing wrong with being proud, to be able to maintain dignity...hold your head high and not feel shamed by all eyes cast your way. The Apache people certainly didn't put themselves in the mess they're in. They didn't suddenly wake one morning and decide it was easier to get hand-outs rather than work hard and be independent.

"All the tragedy and discord brought upon them was done by others who couldn't mind their own business and let a peaceful tribe live the way they have for generations. Their greed took from these people all they had in life...all their forefathers before them worked for and created.

"Each day I look upon their faces I see their shame, their unhappiness in having to accept what Ben and Sylvie give them because they have no other choice. If they are to survive, feed their children, then they have to accept the help. And through it all, they've tried their best not to be a burden, using their skills to help in any way they can...whether it be to hunt game, fix a barn

Roberta C. M. DeCaprio

door, cook a meal or two, clean the house, milk a cow, do the wash...whatever they can do, they do. So, if my inheritance can buy back some of their self-esteem, then so be it."

Josh blinked, astonished at her straightforward and concise reply. "I meant no disrespect, Amanda. I was merely reflecting aloud." Turning back to look at the road ahead, he added, "My apologies."

She sighed, flexing her shoulders. How was it she'd become so irritated after feeling so hopeful? Certainly Josh didn't mean her any harm. Hadn't he, after all, come all this way to help her? She glanced down at the urn of ashes she held and realized she so needed this day to run smooth, as it would be the last farewell she was to give Proud Eagle. To avoid becoming embroiled by negative feelings or a further disagreement, she placed a hand upon his arm. Beneath her touch she could feel his muscles working the reins, controlling the horse.

"It is I who should apologize," she reasoned.

He seemed to be mulling over her words, as he hesitated with an answer. Then finally, "The thing I admire most about you, Amanda, is you're strong and unbending, though at times I will admit your willfulness can be exasperating as well."

"I would say, in regard to what I've lived through all of these years..." She paused to steady her voice. "Being defensive, not trusting others, and suspicious of their motives was how I was able to cope with the danger surrounding me."

"And I won't dare to object that your frame of mind was probably the only way you survived," he said. "But circumstances are not as they were, and very

62

soon your defiance will only bring you more grief than you've already endured."

"I won't argue the fact my attitude needs improvement," she reflected with a scowl. "But in our conversation just now I only spoke the truth."

"Aye, that you have, but speaking it so harshly will never allow it to set you free," he countered. "I am fully aware of your dignity, as I am of the Apache people. Such characteristics did not need to be slammed into my face."

She felt the tears of humiliation sting the back of her throat. Swallowing hard she conceded. "You're correct, of course. Such an approach to your comment was not called for. And in the future I will try to squelch my defiance, when the situation demands diplomacy."

He turned once more to look her way and arched a brow. "How about when it asks for sincerity?"

She nodded and dropped her gaze.

They rode the rest of the way to the farm in silence. Soon the lay of the land held an accustomed echo of her childhood. The forest sprouting around them, tangled and thick, gave way to a narrow road still visible through the dank density. And then the trees thinned around them in a way she remembered, as the carriage made its way down the familiar path.

The focus of her mind began to ripple and shift with thoughts of another time when her only problem was to pick enough berries for a pie. Carefree moments of extreme bliss surrounded her by the parents who loved and cared for her needs. Her scrapes were tended to, her flesh bathed, and tears were wiped away with kisses. And she was held close to their hearts as the promise of a bright new day lay on the horizon. Wrapped within their embrace, she was protected from the hurts and sorrows life held. She felt no fear and had so many expectations.

She spotted movement...a deer. He saw her, too. For a moment their gazes locked. Then it sprinted effortlessly away, over a fallen tree and up a rocky knoll. She marveled at how the thin, spindly legs could carry it with such grace through the many obstacles the wilderness engaged. But nature had compensated the deer, giving it legs of muscle and strength to meet the challenges it encountered.

*Grant us the same compensations, Lord.*

Chapter Nine

Josh glimpsed the recognition reflected upon Amanda's face as the wagon proceeded down the familiar farm's trail. He could only imagine the memories she envisioned, as his own came to mind. The many times he had traveled down this path in the years he pastored in town could hardly be counted. His first Thanksgiving meal, a holiday only Americans honor, was eaten at the Gregory's table. Amelia made him...a young clergyman so far from home...feel welcome and a part of the family. British born as well, Amelia took pride in adopting an American tradition and enjoyed every minute of introducing him to the festivities of such a memorable historical holiday.

After Amelia's death he was there for Ethan and a young Amanda, becoming the glue that held a family ripped apart by grief together. And again he came to Amanda's assistance when Ethan was murdered. All of it unfolded at this farm, the laughter, the sorrow, and the burials of those people he loved and respected. But nothing crippled him like the day he returned to find the place burnt to the ground and Amanda gone.

Even now, as the scene played over in his mind, it stung like a thousand angry bees.

"Acute misery paralyzed me when I came upon the ruins of this farm," he began.

"After the Chiricahua burned it down?"

"Aye. I actually felt physical pain as a maelstrom of grief assailed my heart while my gaze fixed on the burnt homestead and barn. All that remained standing was the stone fireplace, where only days ago we sat in front of, eating lunch."

"I'm so sorry you had to go through that," she said.

He swallowed hard. "Regrets ripped through my thoughts like a hurricane. Why hadn't I laced your tea with Grace's sleeping herbs and taken you back to town?" He frowned. "I knew the danger you were in if you stayed alone on the farm...why didn't I make you leave?"

"Because I was an extremely stubborn and willful girl, and probably would have threatened to never speak to you again if you did," she confessed.

"Even if that were so, you'd at least be still alive." He cleared his throat of the emotion building within. "Such a heaviness of guilt lodged in my heart, and I remember climbing down from the wagon with a numbing sorrow as I made my way to the scorched structure of the house."

"I had no idea," she choked out. "If I'd known..."

"I shuddered inwardly at the thought of finding your remains," he interrupted. "But I forced myself to search for your body, a dull ache of foreboding stabbing at my heart. And I remember wondering if I could even bear to look upon you, bloodied and blackened, when memories of your vibrancy were still so clear? But I knew you needed to be laid to rest. Far be it that my feelings should hinder a proper burial. So I swallowed the nauseating, sinking torment that rose to choke me, and continued to seek through the rubble."

"God forgive me for causing you so much pain,"

she whispered.

"I couldn't help thinking, when I dug your father's grave weeks before, that I had no idea you would soon lie beside him. And at that point a sudden sob escaped from me, at the thought of your voice forever silenced."

She took an audible breath. "What was it you always said to ease my heartache?"

"Don't grieve as those who had no hope; we can rely on the truth that we will all meet again," he supplied.

"Were those words no comfort for you?"

"Nay, they failed me completely, and the empty void inside me grew like an insurmountable gorge...too difficult to pass unscathed. I thought you too beautiful for death. And then, when I found no remains, I became even more terrified. The raw truth turned my torment into fear, then rage and repulsion...because I realized you'd been kidnapped by the murdering heathens."

Her voice trembled. "And you had heard of the tortures and indecencies the savages inflicted upon their victims before death...especially the women."

"Aye, and my stomach knotted. All I could do was pray...implore God that in His infinite mercy you did not linger in their hands, before I fell to my knees and wept for the loss of your life...the loss of your love."

"I am here with you now," she said softly.

He turned to look at her, thankful she sat beside him. "I am so very blessed for that. To be here with you, and be able to bring whatever peace and comfort I can to you, means everything to me."

She reached out to him again, placing a hand on his forearm. "I am also blessed to have you again in my life. Never...never will I take that for granted."

"Nay, never should we take anything in this life for granted. It is too fleeting," he added, knowing full well what life would feel like if he ever lost her again.

For the rest of the ride they kept to their own thoughts, until she broke the silence.

"We're almost there."

"Aye." He turned to look her way.

She sighed heavily, glancing down with sad eyes at the urn. "Have you remembered to bring a shovel, or do we need to meet with Mr. Washburn?"

"I've remembered," he admitted. "And if my mind further directs me, the family burial plot is just off the road here, to the left."

She nodded, not raising her gaze.

"Then it might be best if we lay Proud Eagle to rest first, just the two of us, and venture back to Washburn's cabin after."

"I was hoping you would say that," she said softly, looking to the sky. "Anyway, it seems like a storm approaches. Better to get the burying done while the earth is still dry."

He caught a glimpse of the dark clouds swirling above them and inhaled. The air was swollen with the promise of rain. "I agree." He yanked on the reins to hurry the horse along.

When they came upon the burial ground, Amanda's eyes widened. "There are head stones marking the graves." She walked first to where her mother lay, touching the marker. "The stone is of the finest quality." She traced the letters etched upon the marker with the tip of a finger and read aloud.

*"Here lies Amelia Bentley Gregory*
*Born - June 21, 1825-Died - December 13, 1858.*

*Beloved wife and mother. May she rest in peace*."
She glanced over to her father's grave and read.
"*Here lies Ethan Gregory*
*Born - May 20, 1818 - Died - October 10, 1864.*
*Beloved husband and father. May he rest in peace*."

She frowned. "I don't understand any of this. Who would take the liberty?" She turned to look at him.

He placed the shovel he held aside. "Amanda, perhaps I should have..."

Tears filled her eyes. "The only one who would know their names and the dates is you...you marked their graves."

"Aye, before I left for England I commissioned the work to be done. And Washburn saw to it my wishes were carried out." He took an audible breath. "I apologize if I've overstepped my boundaries here."

"No...no, you haven't," she corrected. "I'm just overwhelmed by your consideration."

"I just thought your parents deserved to have their resting place marked. We all deserve some sort of memorial or tribute after leaving our days on this earth." He pointed to a lone grave, twenty feet away beneath a tree. "There lies Mrs. Washburn. When I learned of her death, I sent word for the same stone cutter to mark her grave. I thought it was the least I could do for her...for Vernon after he's tended so respectfully to your deceased family all these years on my behalf." He neared her and took the urn from her chilled, trembling hands, placing it upon the ground. "And I will have a stone placed on Proud Eagle's grave as well. The stone cutter's son has taken over the business and his work, I hear, is as good as his father's."

She looked deep into his eyes. "You would do this for him as well?"

"Aye, I would...for him and for you, so you will have a place to come and pay your respects. And for his children and their children, to have a way to honor a good and decent man...a loving father and husband." He placed his hands upon her shoulders.

"And this place was made possible to us by another good and decent man, who has for as long as I've known him, been nothing but loving and caring, loyal and trustworthy." She wrapped her arms around his waist and laid her head upon his chest.

His blood heated and his heart raced, as he fought down the urge, the overwhelming desire to pull her tightly into his embrace. His body yearned for hers, but patience had to be his companion right now, otherwise he'd push her away. And the timing was not right...one does not try for a woman's affections at the burial of her husband.

Gently he planted a light kiss on the top of her head, feeling her heartbeat next to his. "Your assessment of me warms my heart and could surely be a eulogy fit for a king."

"But you must remain alive." She turned to look into his eyes. "I could not bear to lose you, too." She sighed and glanced at the urn. "As it is I don't know how I am still able to breathe without Proud Eagle." When she returned her gaze to him, her eyes were filled with tears. "I need you to help me through this time, beyond this sorrow."

"And I am here to do just that for you, Amanda."

The tears overflowed and slipped down her cheeks. "Where, oh where do we begin?"

With a gentle swipe of his thumb, he wiped the tears away, then glanced at the urn. "First we lay your husband to rest, then we take one day at a time...together."

It didn't take long to bury the urn, not like a body in a wooden coffin. He abided by Amanda's request, for Proud Eagle to lie beside her mother, as she thought Amelia Gregory would have liked him...admired his intelligence and wit. He agreed, and when the last shovel of dirt was cast, he blanketed the grave with large rocks until a headstone could be fashioned.

The eulogy he spoke came from deep within his heart, his own eyes welling as he bid a friend, a good and respected man, farewell. Her soft sobs wrenched his soul, as he concluded with prayer. And just as the last words were issued, cold droplets of rain fell, spattering the freshly turned earth and their clothes.

"There once was a lean-to not far from here. My father used it to gut and clean the fish he caught before bringing them into the house for my mother to cook," she said. "Perhaps, if it still stands, we could take cover there until the storm passes."

"Aye, that is best, since Washburn's cabin is quite a ways into the woods," he said. "By the time we'd make it there we'd be drenched, soaked to the flesh."

Both were relieved to find the three-sided dwelling, though overgrown with vines, still intact. And fortunately it had ample space for him to drive the horse and wagon right beneath its roof. He could smell the sweet rot of the wood as he brought the horse to a halt. Once situated, he rummaged around in the back of the small carriage for a couple of dry blankets. When only one was found, he draped it over her shoulders.

"And what about you?" She burrowed into the blanket's dry warmth.

He rubbed his hands together. "I will be fine."

"You're not fine," she disagreed. "You're just as chilled as I am." She commenced removing the blanket from her shoulders.

"Nay, Amanda, I prefer you stay warm."

"Then, we'll just have to share this one." She shimmied closer to him on the wagon's seat, offering him a piece of the blanket.

Their thighs touched, and he sucked in his breath as his body reacted to her on a primal level. The clean, lavender aroma of her flesh washed his senses, the very nearness of her awakening every cell in his body. And instantly a blistering heat intensified the seething desire to satisfy his yearning for this woman. His very breath crystallized in his throat, and he cleared it, swallowing past the lump forming there to choke him.

She looked deep into his eyes. "What is it?"

"Amanda." He closed his eyes briefly to calm the tongues of red hot passion licking through his veins, heating his blood. "Being this close to you is difficult." He opened his lids to glance into her sapphire orbs. "I just helped bury your husband, and I don't want to seem inappropriate, but there are certain feelings coming to the surface while we're sitting here so close that I am having a bloody time keeping at bay."

Her cheeks reddened. "I know what you mean."

He arched a brow. "You do?"

She gave a taut nod. "I am not immune, Josh. And I cannot be more...more," she stuttered.

"Surprised," he finished the sentence.

"That and embarrassed," she admitted. "I mean,

what sort of woman am I?" She sighed. "What you must think of me, widowed not even six months and already feeling...feeling..."

"Like you want to...need to go on with your own life," he supplied.

"Yes, yes exactly," she whispered.

"I believe it is what Proud Eagle hoped would happen when he asked for me to return." He took her left hand and brought it to his lips. Gently he bestowed upon the knuckle of her forefinger a tiny kiss.

"But is it right for me to like it so much?" She glanced at their hands intertwined. "To enjoy being so close to you, to feeling your touch...for looking forward to...to more?"

He felt his heart skip a beat. "Oh, my dear Amanda, aye...aye to all you ask. Never has anything ever felt as right as holding your hands this very moment and hearing it is what you want as well." He searched her beautiful face, high cheekbones, and almond-shaped eyes hooded by thick, long lashes and found his heart regenerated. In her very presence...with her unexpected and long awaited confession his spirit soared, his entire being alive again as though he were a younger man. "I have waited so long to hear these words from your lips."

"And all these years was there never any other woman for you to love?"

"Love, nay. Not with all my heart," he added. "There was only one woman I felt that way about, and she was everything to me but mine. And I had to run away from the only person in the world I knew could make me happy because she belonged to another man."

"But escaping to England didn't stop you from

loving her?"

"Nay, nothing could. Nowhere I went could remove her from my thoughts...from my heart. Loving you is the only way for my life."

"Oh, Joshua. Do you believe there a breath of hope this all could work, under such circumstances?"

"Aye, my love, I do, because hope can be found in the darkest corners, and during the most sorrowful times."

"And surely this is one of those times, with the earthly loss of such a good and caring man," she reflected.

"And yet his passing made way for some positive changes."

"But I could never erase Proud Eagle from my conscience, from my heart. Can you live with that? Can you accept my love knowing that?" A thin mist clung to the air, dampening her hair, causing havoc with her curls.

He pushed a stray lock from her forehead, draping it behind an ear. "Aye. As long as I know in time you will love me as well."

"In many ways I have always loved you. And now...now we..."

He hushed her with the tip of his finger, tracing her full lips, their softness beyond anything he imagined. "We will take each day as it comes. You will see I am a very patient man."

Oh how he wanted to lower his mouth to hers, capture the sweetness there with a kiss, but instead he pressed his lips to her forehead. With the feel of her flesh against his, he fought for control.

She had opened the door to him, but right now how

he proceeded would mean the difference between a sham of a life together or the real thing. And he wanted the real deal. He had waited this long for her, a little longer wouldn't hurt.

He pulled back to look at her, and for a moment, their gazes locked in a quiet exchange of emotions, non-verbal expressions, soft, hopeful, and beautiful admissions.

Did he dare rethink that kiss?

She decided for him. "It has stopped raining. And I believe now would be a good time to meet with Mr. Washburn."

He inhaled the air. It smelled fresh after the late winter rain. He surveyed the property's peaceful seclusion, once again the sun blazed in the afternoon sky.

"I couldn't agree more." He reached for the reins.

Chapter Ten

Amanda sat beside Josh in companionable silence as he drove the horse and wagon to Vernon Washburn's small cabin. The shower of emotions racing through her body set her on fire. Josh's touch, his declaration of love, and her acceptance of this admission brought to her senses an unexpected pleasure. And yet, how could this happen, how could she allow herself to hope for a life with him, to be happy again so soon after Proud Eagle's death? Wasn't she being selfish, fickle-hearted, or betraying her husband?

She reached up to pull the blanket Josh had draped over her shoulders, tighter. Uneasy thoughts bombarded her mind, as guilt scraped at her heart like the spines of a brush. But in truth she hadn't been deceitful in the least. You can't betray a dead spouse. Besides, Proud Eagle had sent for Josh, wanted the good reverend to love and protect her in his absence. She shifted in her seat and gripped the ends of the blanket close to her chest, where cold hands pressed against a racing heart.

"Is anything wrong?" Josh's concern for her escalated in the tone of his voice. When she glimpsed his way, he searched her face for a clue to her discomfort.

Her chest heaved in a great sigh. "I assume we will proceed slowly with this...this..."

"This attraction between us." His neck flexed as he

swallowed hard, the motion descending into muscle at his shoulders. A clear indication none of this was easy for him either.

Her pulse jumped, and she took another deep breath to regain her composure. "Yes," she said faintly, turning her gaze to the road ahead.

"The pace is for you to set," he answered, his tone now reassuring. "In no way do I want this to be an arrangement."

The words caught at the back of her throat. "But I believe that is exactly what Proud Eagle had in mind, if he really thought..."

He dropped his voice. "I'm not interested in what he thought, only what you think, what will please you. Is that how you want it to be, only an arrangement?"

"No...I don't know...no," she stammered. "Such unions can be so...so..." She hesitated to find the right word. "So unsatisfactory," she finally managed to say. "I can't...I won't live in a relationship that leaves me unfulfilled and lonely."

"Aye, I agree," he said simply.

She glanced over at him again and their gazes met. "I know, with a deep and unsettling certainty, living together in the wrong way will only rob us of our spirit and joy."

His mouth drew tight, forming a straight line. "And I don't want such a fate for either of us."

She bit her bottom lip. "And yet, I would think others will frown upon anything more between us. Knowing my love for Proud Eagle was genuine, anything real between us would muster some questions."

"I believe the good Lord gives us all a resilient

heart. Therefore the capacity to live on and love again is not so strange, not so wrong. Besides, what transpires between us is our business and ours alone," he added curtly. "Those who truly know and love us will be happy for our decision."

She cast him a withering look. "I'm not so sure my son would be happy to see me with anyone but his father."

His voice was acid. "Aye, I have already had this conversation with Gabriel in England. When I told him I was coming to your aid, he accused me of being glad Proud Eagle was dead. He claimed it to be a convenient chance to have you all to myself."

"I'm so sorry, Josh. He had no right to come at you so harshly, but I'm sure he was only trying to protect me."

His forehead creased slightly. "I don't doubt his motives. Gabriel had every right, Amanda. He's your son, and he is worried for you, coupled with hurting over the loss of his father. Then there's the case of pride, not wanting his father betrayed. But when I showed him Ben's letter, proof Proud Eagle requested my presence, Gabriel calmed down. I'm not saying he'll be an advocate for our decision," he added abruptly. "But I'm hopeful, with the help of his wife, he will learn to accept it."

"That's right; if he didn't have a resilient heart as well he would never have been able to wed again after his first wife's death."

"He came to me before he proposed to Riley, wrestling somewhat with his decision to take another as his wife," he admitted. "Obviously I must have put his mind at ease, or he would have never remarried. But

I'm sure he'll still hold some resentment for our situation. He doesn't want to believe anyone could take his father's place."

She squared her shoulders. "And he'd be right, no one could," she said tartly.

"Aye, I fully realize this fact. And I don't intend to ever try. That's exactly why I must make it clear to him...to anyone...and especially to you, I didn't return to Willow Creek to step into your late husband's shoes." A polite smile curved his lips. "I want my own time with you, a chance to win your heart by my own merits, not as a substitute or replacement for Proud Eagle, even though he requested my presence."

Nothing further was said on the matter as it seemed both needed time to think over their conversation and the impact moving ahead with various decisions and plans would make on their lives...on everyone's life.

Vernon Washburn sat on the porch, whittling, when Josh brought the horse to a halt in front of the small, two-story cabin. Setting his carving aside, Vernon squinted, before standing and making his way toward the wagon.

Josh jumped down from his seat and met the man halfway. She watched as the two conversed, their voices too low to hear. Then Vernon nodded, smiled, and shook Josh's hand. In that instant she felt a weight lifted from her shoulders, and a small tear formed in the corner of her eye. Quickly she wiped it away, slipped off the blanket wrapped about her shoulders, and readied herself for the introduction.

As Vernon approached her side of the wagon, he held out a polite hand. She smiled and set her own hand into the man's large, rough grip.

Vernon nodded in greeting. "It's a pleasure to meet ya, Mrs. Eagle."

She tried to keep her voice light. "Mine, as well, Mr. Washburn."

"Ah, just Vernon will do, ma'am," was his quick response.

"Only if you call me..." She hesitated, as she almost referred to herself as Golden Lady. But they were no longer on an Apache reservation. "Amanda," she finally said, suddenly a bit self-conscious as he watched her with great fascination.

Josh helped her down from the wagon seat, and the three of them stood for a moment in awkward silence. Many folks were uncomfortable around her, or acted rude, once they learned she married an Apache man. Would this be Vernon's case? And if so, how would they be able to build a new village on this land for the remaining tribe members? But her concerns were put to rest when she and Josh were ushered with a welcoming gesture inside the cabin.

Vernon Washburn was a large man with workman's arms—tendons tightly coiled and muscular. He was tall and stood straight, his broad shoulders held back, his flesh sun-brown and freckled. Bushy dark brows pushed ahead of his deep brown eyes, and slightly spaced, white teeth filled a wide smile. He wasn't handsome, but his looks were pleasing in a rugged way. And if she had to guess at his age, she'd say he was probably somewhere in his early fifties.

Amelia Gregory would have called Vernon a mountain man, burley, resourceful, doing what was needed to get a job done. Washburn was much like Casper Johnson, a man living a few miles south of the

Gregory land when Amanda was at the age of seven. He came down to the creek to fish with Ethan Gregory and brought along his daughter, Thea, who also happened to be seven. There wasn't a Mrs. Johnson, as the poor woman had died giving birth to Thea.

*She hadn't thought of Thea Johnson in years, but now she could almost see her smiling, freckled face. Or the way she stood, shyly with her hands behind her back, in a worn out dress, the hem frayed and swishing around her ankles. Thea's feet were bared and her back-side bloomer-free, as her papa was a man too proud to accept hand-outs, but too poor to buy the feminine amenities. His fishing and trapping work hardly brought in enough to feed them, let alone be able to purchase undergarments and shoes. Thus was the reason Thea only went to school in the warmer months, when not so many garments were needed. But what she did wear was always clean, her hair combed and braided, and her face washed.*

*Amelia Gregory thought that was a magnificent feat of character and parental concern on Casper Johnson's part, him being a mountain man and all, with little education himself. For a while the Johnsons were frequent visitors...Thea even spent the night while her father was away on hunting expeditions. She adored Amelia, following her everywhere, wanting to please her, loving the motherly attention. Amanda enjoyed pretending Thea was a sister, as they shared a bed at night complete with secrets and giggles. But then one night, on Casper's return from a hunt, he caught Thea, while she helped to serve dinner, pocket a blue hair ribbon Amanda had left on the sideboard table. Casper's face turned red from his forehead to his neck.*

*No one expected what happened next. They had all been seated to a delicious meal of chicken and potatoes, fresh corn-on-the-cob, and a medley of vegetables from Amelia's garden cooked in butter when Casper flew into a rage and shot out of his chair. In one fluid motion he grabbed Thea, bent her over his knee, whipped up her skirt, and punished her bared bottom with the worst spanking anyone could imagine.*

*"Stop, oh please stop," Amelia pleaded, rising from her chair.*

*"No child of mine is gonna take what don't belong to her, especially from folks who've been like family," he said through gritted teeth.*

*The blows turned Thea's lily-white bottom crimson, Casper's handprint making red-raised welts upon her flesh. She cried out in pain and humiliation, squirming, trying to cover herself, and begging him to stop as he administered another and another...and still another hard whack to her bottom.*

*"Here now, Casper, the child's had enough," Ethan Gregory interjected.*

*But Casper kept beating Thea, until her small body lay limp over his knee.*

*It was then Amelia pulled Thea off Casper's knee and covered her nakedness, holding the child close to her bosom. "Never...never are you to humiliate this child in such a way ever again," Amelia said, tears filling her eyes.*

*It was almost like Amelia had been the one beaten. She sobbed while she held Thea, soothing her as she carried her over to the rocker chair, whereby Amelia began to rock Thea as you would a newborn baby, muttering, "I can't allow this to happen...I can't...not again, not ever again...to you, to anyone...not again."*

*Casper stood, his face contorted with a mixture of anger and shame. "No daughter of mine is gonna steal from other folks, dishonor the family name, or sin in the eyes of our Maker."*

*Ethan made his way to Casper now and placed a calming hand upon the other man's arm. "I'm sure it was all a misunderstanding."*

*"It was," Amanda had choked out, her own tears streaming down her cheeks. If ever her parents punished her in such a way, she'd never be able to show her face in public again. "I gave those ribbons to Thea," she lied.*

*Casper's mouth curled in a snarl as he neared the rocker chair. "We Johnsons don't take charity."*

*"It was a gift." Amanda moved to stand beside her mother. Now her heart raced with fear...fear for Thea, and what her father would do if Casper tried using his rage on her or Amelia.*

*But Casper only reached for Thea, ripping the child from Amelia's embrace. With Thea thrown over his shoulder, like a sack of flour, Casper marched out the door.*

*A few days later Ethan Gregory rode out to the Johnson homestead, in the hopes of mending harsh feelings. Amelia had talked him into reaching out, beyond the anger and hurt, for Thea's sake. But the place was desolate, all signs of life absent. The small cabin was empty of the few crude furnishings the family owned...the cow and chickens gone, too. And no one ever saw the Johnsons again.*

"Would you care for a cup of tea, Amanda?" Vernon pulled her thoughts back to the present.

"Aye, Amanda, drinking a warm brew will stop your shivering." Josh glanced at her arms and frowned. "You are frozen to the bone."

She looked down at the goose bumps rising on her flesh.

Vernon gestured to a dark-wood rocker by the fireplace, its cushion covered in a soft peach colored material decorated with worn yellow flowers. "I would gladly bring the tea to ya there, so ya can get warm by the fire."

Josh took the liberty of answering for her. "That sounds like a capital idea, Vernon." Reaching for her hand, he escorted her to the chair.

While the men talked business at a small table in the corner of the room, she sipped tea from a chipped, blue and white china cup. Already the blazing fire had begun to take the edge off the late winter chill. Comfortable and warm, she surveyed her surroundings.

Surprisingly, Vernon Washburn was not a messy man. Though the cabin was void of a woman's expertise in cleaning, the place was neat enough. Touches of Mrs. Washburn still remained, however, as the curtains and sofa cover matched the rocker cushion, and braided rugs scattered here and there covered the scrubbed, wooden floor. The great room consisted of both a parlor and dining area. To the right was the kitchen, just big enough for the woman of the homestead to cook and bake in. She had a feeling Mrs. Washburn might have liked it that way.

With three men in the house, a husband and two sons, the small kitchen was probably her sanctuary, a place where the men wouldn't tread and were too large to comfortably fit. To the left of the parlor was a staircase, no doubt leading to the sleeping quarters of the house. Due to the size of the home, she estimated a count of two bedrooms, one for Vernon and his wife, and the other shared by their sons. Family pictures lined the mantel. There were a few of the sons, both at a young age and then in older years, as well as ancestors long gone.

One picture in particular caught her eye. It appeared to be Vernon and Emily's wedding photo. Light-haired and with a timid smile, Emily gazed up at her husband with an adoring gaze. The warmth of Vernon's return glance brought sudden tears to her eyes. They appeared so in love, happy, and hopeful. Why did death have to rob them of a long life together? Why had it robbed her and Proud Eagle from growing old with each other? She sighed and brushed a tear from her cheek.

"Is everything right with you, Amanda," Josh asked softly. His attentiveness made her feel so special and warmed her heart.

She glanced in his direction to find his light, blue eyes piercing hers. "I'm fine."

His tone sounded tentative. "Are you sure?"

"Yes, really." She forced a smile before bringing her attention to Vernon. "You have a lovely home."

"Thank ya, kindly, but my Emily's the one who fixed it up so nicely." His eyes quickly shot to the picture on the mantel. "She had a knack for makin' somethin' out of nothin', whether it be a meal or a home." He cleared his throat from his growing emotion. "Ain't a day that goes by I don't think of her, 'specially since my sons are grown and gone." He shrugged. "It can get mighty lonely around these parts at times."

"Then what's been proposed here today should be to your favor," Josh said.

"Yup, I'd welcome the company, the chance to have myself some neighbors."

"Even if those neighbors are Apaches," she said drily.

Vernon ignored her tone. "Don't make no difference to me what God made them, as long as they're decent folks."

"And they are decent folks," she replied. "I've lived amongst them for thirty years, and they've been nothing but good and kind. They're my family now, and I would do anything for them."

"This here's your land, ma'am, and I expect ya can do whatever it is ya like upon it. I won't quibble a tad. I just appreciate being able to squat here as long as I have in order to make a home for my own family."

"And this will continue to be your home, for it never was my intent to drive you from it. I'm also appreciative for the way you've looked after my father's land all these years, and the family plot."

Vernon sat forward. "If ya don't mind, Miss Amanda, I'll be takin' ya up on that offer 'til I take my last breath. Then I'd like to take my eternal rest beside my Emily. She's the only woman I ever loved, and I won't be leavin' her."

"I understand completely, Vernon."

"Yup, I suppose ya do, being ya lost a loved one as well." He relaxed again in his seat.

"I will tell you here and now," she added, "that I give you my word your request shall be honored." She smiled. "And I always keep my word."

By the time they decided to return to the

parsonage, the confidence built within her that their plan to construct a new village on her father's land would actually come to pass. Vernon's exuberance, even in the short time they talked further, grew to such an immense high; he looked quite forlorn when she and Josh stood to take their leave.

As they made their way to the wagon, Vernon pulled Josh aside. Figuring it was just more business the men needed to discuss, she kept her pace ahead, climbed into the wagon without assistance, and waited there for Josh. When he finally caught up with her, his face was flushed, registering anger.

Her initial sense of victory began to fade. "Is there anything wrong?"

"Not anymore." Josh yanked on the reins and set the wagon in motion.

The tone of his voice made her anxiety rise a notch. Did Vernon have second thoughts about the land deal...would he now give them a problem to proceed with their plans?

"Clearly something had transpired from the time I departed from the two of you, until this moment to make you so upset," she said.

"And what makes you think I'm upset?"

A few deer grazing on the path skittered away when they heard the wagon approaching, hiding behind the protective shadows of the trees lining the dirt roadway. "It isn't hard to see the huge change in attitude you've adopted." She pointed out, her own irritation mounting.

Suddenly he pulled the wagon to a halt, turning on the seat to face her. His eyes narrowed to slits. "Vernon pulled me aside to tell me he thought your flesh covered your bones beneath perfectly, which made you all the more appealing."

She gasped, giving him an incredulous glance. "Truly you joke with me."

He met her eyes without a trace of foolery. "I would never jest about such a thing."

She studied his creased brow and tense shoulders. "Could you have somehow misunderstood him?"

His tone was clipped. "Nay, I understood him completely, though his vocabulary was not as polished as mine in retelling it."

"Well, suppose you tell me exactly what was said. I believe I can handle it, after all I am not some innocent school girl." Her curiosity completely roused.

His expression was grim. "School girl or not, it would be unthinkable for me, as a gentleman, to let slip"—his face colored—"to reveal Vernon Washburn's crude rendition of how he felt about you, your beautifully perfect body, and how he would take his *jollies* if you were his woman."

Josh's last comment about Vernon's *jollies* brought into perspective the real conversation Josh had with the other man. Lewd scenes filled her imagination suddenly made her shy, the heat rising to burn her cheeks. "Well, I'd say this has become somewhat of a...of a..."

"Tawdry afternoon," he interjected.

She nodded. "In ways I care not to envision."

"Aye, well Vernon is visualizing them with baited breath." His lips tightened with displeasure. "The bloody gall of the man to speak to me of all people, a clergyman, about his tasteless desires, and to boast about them in regards to a lady, a newly widowed lady at that." Scowling, he ran his hand through his hair.

"Listen to me, what a hypocrite I've become."

"How are you a hypocrite?"

He arched a brow. "Am I not doing the same thing, stating my claim upon you so soon after your husband's death?"

"First of all, I am not a piece of property anyone can set a claim to," she snapped. "And secondly, you and I have a history together. You sought my hand in marriage before Proud Eagle, and if he hadn't come along..."

"You would have accepted my proposal," he interrupted.

She let out a soft sigh of fatigue and quickly changed the subject. "What on earth could have prompted Vernon to be so inappropriate?"

Josh became more flustered by the second. "To be precise, I believe his behavior can be contributed to a strong case of loneliness and the fact you reminded him of his wife."

Her eyes widened, perplexed. "He told you that?"

He cleared his throat nervously. "Aye."

"But I look nothing like Emily Washburn."

"The way you sat in her chair and sipped the tea by the fire was much the same way she would do...the light hair, blue eyes...he saw the resemblance. It brought back feelings he's, no doubt, had to repress. After all, the man's been alone for five years. For all anyone knows, perhaps even without the benefit of a woman all this time."

A sense of unease squeezed her heart. "What are you trying to say?"

In spite of his apparent agitation, he paused, took a calming breath and sat back in his seat. "Vernon

Washburn just asked my permission to court you."

"Your permission," she snapped. "Why did he think you had the right to speak for me?"

"Perhaps he thought it was the proper protocol," he said hastily.

"Oh, now he decides to act proper." Her stomach clenched as the cold, sharp wind cut through her clothes. She shivered and reached for the blanket. Quickly he lent a hand. "And what did you tell him?"

Josh arched a brow, his voice intense. "I told him that wasn't a possibility, because the lady was already spoken for by another chap."

She sighed with relief. "I assume you told him who the other chap was."

"Aye, I did at that, in very strong and certain terms," he grumbled beneath his breath, reaching over to secure the blanket draped over her shoulders. "Let's get you back in front of a fire." He sat forward.

Then he grabbed the reins and headed the wagon toward town.

Chapter Eleven

Josh remained quiet on the rest of the ride back to the parsonage, since Amanda seemed to retreat into a world all of her own. If he had to guess her thoughts, he'd say she was probably confused, a bit shocked, and strongly mortified at the concluding events of the day. At dinner she spoke only when spoken to, then after helping with the meal's clean-up, politely excused herself on the pretense of being totally exhausted. Sylvie offered to help draw her a bath, and once it was agreed, the two women went upstairs—Amanda to stay.

Alone and occupying his own quarters, he looked out the den window to the city that had grown up around the parsonage in the years he'd been gone. It had quieted somewhat, as the shadows of dusk elongated, but never again would it be as desolate as he first remembered. Willow Creek, a tiny and remote town, was now not either.

Standing in semi-solitude, he reflected upon the events of the day. Vernon Washburn's request to court Amanda had stuck in his craw, and he couldn't seem to shake the unsettled feeling nagging at his conscience. To pin-point the trouble, he'd have to admit he was jealous, and that perturbed him greatly. As a man of the cloth, there was no room for such an ugly emotion. Had he not preached to others about the dangers and decay a soul undertook when desirous? And yet, here he was

91

battling the green-eyed serpent himself.

"The only way I can stop being jealous is to stop caring, and that isn't about to happen," he whispered to himself. Running a hand through his hair, he sighed, disgusted with his behavior. Love wasn't supposed to feel this way...guarded, anxious, and troubled.

"I lost you once, Amanda, and I'm not about to let you slip through my fingers again," he softly vowed, as a wave of possessiveness flooded his senses, curling up inside of him. He needed to do something quickly, before it totally consumed him. So much for biding his time and taking things slowly. A Bible passage crossed his mind—Phillipians 4:6—*Be anxious for nothing, but in everything by prayer and supplication with thanksgiving let your requests be made known to God.*

"I've made my request known for years," he whispered to himself again. "Now it's a matter of keeping her safe from Vernon Washburn or any other man who sets his eyes upon her." Proud Eagle had summoned him to Amanda's side for that exact reason. But keeping her safe was no longer just about loving and caring for her. It had become second nature—instinctive. She was a part of him...his woman, and no one would take her away from him ever again.

He groaned, combing his fingers again through his hair. What if moving too quickly pushed her away...frightened her? Then all could be lost once more. How would he go about doing what had to be done without upsetting the woman's emotional balance, delicate as it was in a stage of grief?

He shook his head to clear it and made his way to the bookcase. Perhaps reading something would put him into a better mood. He scanned the shelves for a mystery, searching for his favorite author, Sir Arthur Conan Doyle. He'd become quite a fan of the Sherlock Holmes series. He smiled to himself. It appeared Benjamin Newcomb was also a fan of the same author, as a volume of *The Memoirs of Sherlock Holmes* sat on the top row. He reached for the book and was just about to sit with it by the fire, when he was interrupted by a knock at the door.

After placing the book on a nearby table, he opened the heavy oak portal. Amanda stood on the opposite side, wearing a pale blue nightgown, covered by a matching robe. Her feet were bared, and the long golden curls clinging around her shoulders were still damp from her bath.

"I'm sorry to bother you, Josh, but we need to talk." She nervously bit her bottom lip.

"I agree." He stepped aside to allow her access into the room. As she passed, a delightful aroma of fresh violets filled his senses. Immediately he pictured her reclining naked, soaking in a tub full of the sweet-smelling bath salts. The thought swept a surge of desire through him, forcing his eyes to briefly close while he gathered his composure.

She spotted the book on the table and went to pick it up. With the tip of her finger, she traced the gold-letters of the title etched upon the brown leather cover. "I haven't read a good book in so many years."

He closed the door behind them and neared her. "Didn't Ben bring books to the reservation?"

"A few, now and then. But they were mostly books for learning so I could teach the Apache children how to read and write." She caressed the book's cover with the palm of her hand before replacing it upon the table, and sighed wistfully. "But never something that would entertain or stimulate the imagination like this novel." She met his gaze. "I've come to realize, after living here at the parsonage for these last four months, while I upheld my husband's way of life, I missed out on so many of the pleasures enjoyed by my own."

"But you were fully aware this would be the case when you married him."

"Yes, I was, but somehow as time went on—and I got older, the loss of many things got stronger."

He watched her closely. "What other things do you refer to?"

She paused for a moment, seeming to gather her thoughts. "Well, for one, having an outside door, something to shut and lock against the night. Our wickiup only had a door flap, easily raised by both human and animal. I can't even count the times throughout the years I woke to find critters roaming about the place. Squirrels, a raccoon, even snakes invited themselves in." She shook her head. "When my children were small, I never allowed myself to fall into a deep sleep, for fear one of them would be bitten." Her face darkened. "And when the white agents took over the village, I feared one of them would just walk into the wickiup."

"Surely Proud Eagle wouldn't have allowed anyone to harm you."

She shot him a troubled glance. "We were all in harm's way by then."

He reached out to tuck a wayward strand of hair behind her ear. "I'm so sorry you lived in fear all these years."

"I want a home with doors and walls, windows,

furniture," she blurted out. "A fireplace to read beside, a stove to cook upon, an icebox to keep the food from spoiling. I want to bathe in a tub of warm water instead of a cold creek, and when I sit to do my business, I want privacy." She didn't wait for his response. "Women my age, married as long as I have been, with grown children and grandchildren have memories to look at...like the scratches on the doorframes showing their child's growth throughout the years. Or family pictures on a mantel. A favorite quilt handed down from generation to generation on the bed, a lace tablecloth on the dining room table. A vase with flowers, rugs, pillows, linens, and books on shelves...dishes, cups, forks, spoons...they have all these things."

He pulled her close and held her. "I know, I know. And I sympathize with your feelings."

She rested her head on his chest and wrapped her arms around his waist. "How could you, you've had all these things all your life."

"Aye, to some extent, but they weren't really mine."

She pulled back, angling her head to gaze up at him. "I don't understand."

"I've never had a home of my own. As a pastor," he explained, "I was sent to whatever congregation in need of shepherding, and I had to dwell in a home appointed to me while I was in service. Like this house." He made a sweeping gesture with a hand. "It was where I lived, but it was never mine. The only things I took with me when I left for England were my clothes and my Bible." He pointed to a chair by the fireplace. "I loved to be seated there after a long day, to sip my tea while I read or smoked a pipe. The cushions fit me just right, the material comforting, but even though that chair gave me pleasure for a time, I did not own it."

Her face softened. "Then we shall build a home together, whereby our collective memories and those we cherish will have a permanent place to gather."

His heart fluttered, this small declaration meaning the world to him. "Aye, I have often dreamed of such a home, filled with family, friends, and love."

Her voice was no more than a whisper. "It all sounds so normal."

"This isn't what you came to talk to me about, is it?"

A terrible distress washed over her face, and she quickly turned away. "No, there's something else on my mind."

He searched her face. "You know you can tell me anything."

She moved from his embrace to make her way over to a window—the bare floorboards creaking beneath her steps. For a moment she stood gazing out at the night, then in a soft, yet stern voice she said, "I am tired of looking over my shoulder, fearing for my safety. And I won't, I can't do it any longer."

"You will never have to feel threatened again. I am here to make sure of that."

She turned to face him and for a moment eyed him warily. "How can you assure me this?

He went to her, cupping her face in the palms of his hands. "This is about Vernon Washburn, isn't it?"

"Yes, after his remarks today I will be very uncomfortable around him."

He frowned. "It has always been a difficult task for anyone to leave me unsettled, but it seems Washburn has done the trick for me as well."

"What if his boldness becomes out of control?"

Her words proved to him all the more that Vernon's raging needs had to be clipped, and removing Amanda's availability on the single market had to be done quicker than either of them planned. "I believe I know of a way to keep him at bay."

"What possible way is there to keep him in line?"

"First off, I want you to realize Washburn isn't an evil man. A bit crude," he added, "but not mean or bad."

She nodded. "He's just very lonely, and I feel sorry for him. But don't you think at some point his loneliness could be dangerous?"

"Aye, I do. Desperation can sometimes alter the best intentions," he said. "But I do believe he respects the sanctity of marriage, and even in his desperate state will honor such a union."

She arched a brow. "Just exactly what are you proposing?"

He lowered his lips to her forehead, and after planting a tender kiss there, he whispered against her flesh, "Why, marriage, my dear lady...to me...and as soon as you will allow."

Chapter Twelve

Amanda rose from the bed she shared with Rising Sun and made her way to the window. She peered out onto the black and bottomless night. Not a star to be seen, only a quartered moon. She focused on its brightness, and inhaled sharply—her conversation with Josh circling in her thoughts.

She had said *yes* to his proposal. As soon as her son arrived from his Ireland trip, she would wed Reverend Joshua Holmes. Did her decision to wed only four months after the death of her husband make her callous? She was suddenly washed with anxiety, desperately heaving for more air. Her lungs felt overworked, like she was trying to catch her breath through lumpy gravy.

"Is anything wrong, Golden Lady?" Rising Sun inquired from the bed, turning up the lantern's wick.

She wrapped her arms around herself and took a calming breath. "No, I'm fine...sorry I woke you." She turned to face her sister-in-law. "It seems I'm always disturbing your sleep."

"My husband wakes me as well, with the noises his nose and mouth make when he breathes," Rising Sun said.

"Still and all, I'm sure you count the days until you can once again share a bed with Falling Star."

Rising Sun giggled. "True, he wakes me in other

ways now and then."

She sighed wistfully. "Ah, yes. I remember too those moments."

Rising Sun's face grew somber. "I know none of what has happened has been easy for you...for any of us. But we will get pass the sorrow, even if we never forget the hurt. And what else is there for us to do but live on, do the best we can, love and laugh until the Great Spirit calls us to join our ancestors."

She sighed. "The loving and laughing part seems like an act of betrayal."

"Proud Eagle would not have wanted you to be sad or alone." Rising Sun sat up to rest her back against the bed's headboard.

Amanda made her way to the bed and sat on the edge. "Well, he might just get what he asked for. Reverend Holmes proposed to me this evening."

Rising Sun gave her a sideways glance. "And what was your answer?"

"I agreed," she said softly. "We are to be married as soon as Gabriel arrives."

"I know he loves you deeply and will make a good and caring husband," Rising Sun said.

"I know he does too, and I share a love for him...not as I did with Proud Eagle," she added quickly. "But still in a good way, enough for it to be a real marriage between us."

"If this is true, then what troubles you?"

Amanda folded her hands in her lap. "Change, I suppose. And not knowing how change will affect those I love."

"Proud Eagle summoned the holy man to care for you, and his people understand and honor his wishes.

Gabriel will learn to do the same in time," Rising Sun reassured her.

She bit her bottom lip. "I pray you are right."

"And soon, we will all be settled in our new homes," Rising Sun reflected.

"Yes, it will be nice to have our own dwellings again." She looked deep into her sister-in-law's large, chocolate eyes. "And I know of a lovely and quiet patch of cleared land by the creek that would be a wonderful place for you and Falling Star to build your wickiup."

Rising Sun shook her head. "No more wickiup—I want a wood house, like this." She glanced around the room. "I do not like the white woman's clothes, but I do like the stove and cold box where food is kept. I want a bed like this one." She patted the mattress. "As well as windows and doors."

She arched a brow. "Does Falling Star agree?"

Rising Sun smiled. "He will if he ever wishes once more for those other moments now and then."

Both women giggled.

"Now, come...take your rest," Rising Sun demanded.

Amanda nodded and climbed into bed, then reached over to snuff out the light.

****

Josh, after numerous attempts to become engrossed within the pages of Sherlock Holmes, finally put the book aside. He reached for his jacket lying across the back of the desk chair and took himself out to the garden. To his surprise, he came upon Ben, standing beside a rose bush, eyes lifted to the sky as he puffed on a pipe.

"I see you're having a difficult time sleeping as

well." He approached the other man.

Ben turned slowly to look his way, the light of the moon the only illumination upon them. "I just needed a quiet moment to be by myself."

He nodded. It was understandable that after living with a household of people, time alone was well needed. "Sorry then, old chap, for the interruption." He turned to leave. "I bid you a goodnight, then."

"Stay, Josh." Ben made his way to a wooden bench. "It vould please me to have this quiet time vith you."

Again he nodded, joining Ben on the bench. For a while both sat without saying a word.

Josh broke the silence, keeping his eyes on the quarter moon. "I proposed to Amanda tonight."

Ben cleared his throat. "And did she accept?"

He smiled. "Aye, that she did."

Ben gave him an affectionate pat on the shoulder. "My congratulations, then."

He took an audible breath. "I've waited a long time for this moment. I just wish it was because of...under...under..."

"Happier circumstances," Ben supplied.

"Aye," he whispered.

Ben sighed. "Ja, this I understand."

"Proud Eagle was also my friend," he said.

"Ja, mine too. But this is vhat Proud Eagle vanted. It vas his dying request for you to return to Villow Creek, and take care of Amanda." Ben shifted in his seat to face him. "And that is vhat you're doing."

"True, but I feel a bit guilty to be so happy fulfilling that request," he confessed, meeting the other man's gaze.

Ben chuckled lightly. "And you think it vould be more honorable for you and Amanda to be totally miserable in the process?"

He frowned. "Nay, that's not what I meant."

"My friend, life is short—this much ve both know. Vhatever happiness ve receive, for vhatever reason, ve are to thank the Lord, count our blessings, and trust in Him for vhatever comes our vay. After all, He made the earth round so ve vould not see too far down the road."

He smiled. "Aye, you are so right." Glancing at the garden, his smile deepened. "All those many years ago, as soon as I realized Amanda had my heart, so many wonderful visions played in my mind. One was of me sitting on this very bench, reading my morning newspaper, while she tilled that garden, and our children played tag in this yard." He cleared the emotion rising to his throat. "I would have cherished a family fashioned from our love."

"I loved being a father, played ball and tag many times out here with my Sarah Joy. Now, she lives in Montana vith her husband, and a mother of five herself." Ben shook his head. "Time sure has a vay of getting avay from you...one minute I'm carrying Sarah Joy in my arms, the next I'm valking her down the aisle on her vedding day."

"You and Sylvie never wanted more children," he probed.

"Ja, ve vould have velcomed as many as the Good Lord decided to give us, but Sarah Joy vas all that came. But ve vere happy anyvay, vith just the one." Ben sighed. "She vas a handful all by herself." Shifting the focus from himself, he said. "I think you vould have been a vonderful father."

"Aye, I would have loved my children with every fiber of my being." He turned to look at Ben. "But I'm quite sure that chance has passed me by."

Ben chuckled again. "One vould think." Then he shrugged. "But then again, anything is possible vith the Lord. Have you forgotten vhat happened to Abraham and Sarah?"

"Nay." He joined in on his friend's mirth. "I haven't forgotten."

****

In the weeks that followed, the winter's chill gave birth to the soft breezes of spring. The land flourished with color, turning bare and brown trees lush and green. Singing birds harmonized as the vibrant shades of each flower came in bloom. The passing of time also encouraged her favor toward Josh. And soon his face became the object she best liked to view each morning, along with his wide smile and pale blue eyes. His presence warmed her through and through, like a hot cup of milk or a blazing fire on a cold night. And her anxiety slowly turned into anticipation of their wedding day and the new life they'd share together.

The others in the tribe also began taking the steps toward their future. Rising Sun managed to convince Falling Star to break with tribal tradition, but their son, Rising Star decided to stay with building an Apache dwelling and took the little patch of land Amanda offered his mother as their building site.

"It is Apache custom the wife, along with the help of the other women in the tribe, build the wickiup for her husband," she explained to Josh as she sat beside him in the wagon, the two of them on their way to her father's land to help with the construction.

Josh arched a brow, "The Dickens, you say...women building homes?"

She giggled. "It's true."

"And how did you do completing the task?"

She paused a moment, taking stock of the memory. "Well, I was as shocked as you to learn this was required of me. And as time went on and the courting process was complete, my heart raced whenever I thought of the next step I had to take. So, I began to survey the basics involved in erecting the modest dwelling."

He frowned. "Which is?"

"First, I noticed it was made of a framework of poles and limbs tied together, over which a thatch of bear grass, brush, and yucca leaves, are placed. Then a canvas material is stretched over the structure on the windward side, and open at the top to allow the smoke to escape from the fire pit, which sat in the center of the wickiup. Although I figured out these calculations, I couldn't imagine being able to build one, even with the help of the other women in the tribe."

"Obviously you managed," he concluded.

Memories flooded her thoughts, and she spoke as it all unfolded again in her mind. "For days we labored, everyone becoming quite pleased at how the dwelling took shape. At the end of the third day, I walked around the outside of the new wickiup to clear a pile of grasses left for thatch and heard a scream. I feared someone had gotten hurt, and so I ran blindly through the door opening, stumbling over a pile of broken wood. My foot slammed against a pole, causing it to come loose from the ropes holding it in place. The large post began to fall. I tried to move out of harm's way, but my ankle was badly bruised and wouldn't hold my weight."

Josh's eyes widened. "My God, Amanda."

"I remember screaming for help just as the huge dowel came down hard across my shoulders, pinning me to the ground. Intense pain shot through my body as I tried one more time to call out for help. Then the second beam came loose, hitting me hard in the back of the head. And then, my world blurred and darkened." She cleared her throat. "I woke up several days later, to find the other women had finished building the wickiup for me."

He frowned. "I smell foul play at hand."

"And you would be right. As you know, Running Doe, a young maiden who thought Proud Eagle would marry her, was out to vanquish me from the tribe. It was by her doing the building site was sabotaged."

"And you walked right into her trap," he said.

"Unfortunately it wouldn't be the only time I fell victim to her tricks. That girl's jealousy almost killed me three times." She bit her bottom lip. "Running Doe was the reason I decided to commission Proud Eagle to teach me how to fight like a warrior." She smiled victoriously. "And when we finally faced off, I beat her to a pulp, even knocked out one of her teeth."

He chuckled lightly. "I wouldn't have minded seeing that."

Her face grew serious. "Well, the last time she tried to do me in, it ended very badly for her."

"If I remember correctly Running Doe's envy finished her life in the long run," he reflected.

"Yes...yes it did." She took an audible breath, Running Doe's features suddenly coming to mind to haunt her...round dark eyes filled with hate and a mouth too large for her face. "That seems so long ago now. I haven't thought of Running Doe in ages."

"And there's nay a need for you to ever think of her again," he said.

With everyone chipping in to build Rising Star's home, the structure was completed quickly. Along with his wife, Water Lily and son, Bear Star, Rising Star left the parsonage to live in his new home within a matter of days. A week later Little Elk and his wife, Owl Woman followed the same Apache tradition when their wickiup was finished being built...as well as their son, Night Wolf, his wife, Earth and their baby Micah. The two families erected their dwellings side by side and near the creek, opposite Rising Star.

But Rising Sun's daughter Dawn decided she wanted a wood home, like her mother. So, she and her husband, Messai and their baby, Dear One stayed back at the parsonage along with Rising Sun, Falling Star, Josh, and Amanda. It would only be a matter of days now that Gabriel and his wife would arrive, and the location of the wood homes would then be decided. There would be four to build, as she was sure Gabriel's wife, Riley would prefer a house to a wickiup. However, Gabriel, as the new chief, would also want to stick with tradition. Land at the head of the creek remained free for him to build a wickiup, whereby tribal counsel and meetings would be held. It too waited for her son's arrival.

With fewer guests staying at the parsonage, Rising Sun was finally united with her husband, leaving Amanda to sleep alone. But she didn't mind. In a way she welcomed the privacy, as she had been under the watchful eyes of someone since Proud Eagle's death.

On the first night of her solitary sleeping arrangement, she sat up until dawn, gazing out the window until a fresh ray of sunlight shone through the open drapery, highlighting the cracked paint on the walls.

On the second night, she cried herself to sleep. And upon waking the next morning, lingered in bed to study the sunbeams spattering the room past a gap in the drawn curtain. The dust particles within its ray played off the walls, resembling an army of tiny little fairies.

On the third night, she removed all her clothes before she climbed into bed. The sheets felt cool against her flesh. She stretched out her arms and legs, and took a deep breath. A vision of Josh, shirtless as he worked on building a wickiup, came to mind.

His broad shoulders grew tan from working days in the afternoon sun, the bronze flesh looking healthier than the pale. As she neared him with a flask of water, she noticed the thin web of veins marking his muscular forearms, like an ancient tattoo, every time he tightened his grip on the axe. She reached out and traced the blue, raised lines with the tip of a finger.

When he felt her touch, his body stilled. Then he wiped the perspiration from his forehead with the back of his hand and met her gaze. The light blue of his eyes were tender and sincere as they searched her face. His attention, the yearning in his glance, warmed her through and through. And when she offered him a smile, he returned with a bit of a roguish one of his own, leaving her heart racing.

While she pictured him, she moved her hands over her breasts, down to her belly, and between her thighs. Placing a finger on the slippery nub of her passion, she allowed herself to dream of love again...to desire his touch upon her flesh, his lips consuming hers. She was embarking on a new beginning—encompassed within another true and beautiful love—a safe haven to grow old in.

And on the fourth night, she looked around the room, at the strong walls, the door with its lock and key that brought her privacy, the windows covered with glass that kept out the elements, and she slept like a baby.

On the fifth day after the wickiups had been built, she rested in a lounge on the back porch, partially warmed by the noonday sun. Her thoughts drifted to the time when she returned to the parsonage with Proud Eagle, to see if Josh would accept his gifts. Tradition was, after a period of time passed, whereby the bride cooked and kept house for the groom, her family was to receive and accept gifts from the groom before the marriage was consummated. The closest to a family Amanda had was Reverend Holmes. Therefore, she requested the gifts be brought to the parsonage. Now, closing her eyes, she thought back to the first encounter and how it didn't go so well.

*Josh stared at her, baffled, as she made her way from the brush to the porch where he sat. He appeared confused, a tumble of thoughts assailing his gaze as he tried to comprehend what he was seeing.*

*Now that he shared with her the day he found her farm burned, she understood his confusion. What followed only added to the inconsiderate way she'd acted toward him...professing her love for Proud Eagle, announcing her plans to wed him, then asking for Josh to accept the gifts and bestow his blessing. God, she might just as well have rubbed salt into his wounds. She never thought of herself as cruel or thoughtless toward others, but on that day, at that moment, she was almost heartless.*

She rubbed her hands over her shut lids. "You not only accepted the gifts, but in time helped to save Proud Eagle's life," she whispered to herself.

And in that instant, she knew her love for Josh was just as strong as it was for her husband. They were different men, but their hearts were grand, and both were dedicated to her.

"I can marry Josh now, without reservation," she mumbled.

"There is no need. I am here now to take care of you," came a familiar voice.

Lifting her hands, she opened her eyes. The sun blocked out his face, but there was no mistaking his form, the broad Apache shoulders, or the long, black hair gracing his lapel.

It made no difference if she moved ahead with her life and became another man's wife; Proud Eagle had left a profound imprint behind.

His essence would never be a soft resonance or a mere shadow, but rather a great element to remember with awe and respect. And his son was proof, evidence, standing in the flesh, so tall and strong before her.

She rose quickly to her feet and embraced her oldest child. "Gabriel, thank God you've finally returned."

His muscular arms gently encompassed her. "All will be well now, my mother," he said softly, the timbre of his voice so much like his father's it brought hot tears to her eyes. "At last I am home...and I will be here to stay."

## Chapter Thirteen

Respect...it was all about the line of respect. The Apache people were proud and honorable, and deserved respect. Josh knew their lives hadn't received reverence from the white man, but they would always have it from him. That was the main reason he hadn't swept Amanda away to the chapel for Reverend Newcomb to marry them, the day after she accepted his proposal.

Certain protocol had to be remembered, like her son's presence and the ceremony that would make him the new chief, before Josh could call Amanda his wife. His full awareness of such matters now found him seated beside Gabriel, hashing over the situation at hand and others set to come.

"So, my mother has accepted your proposal." Gabriel sat back in his seat.

"Aye, she has." He crossed a foot over his knee. Ben's den, which had been restored to him since the other guests had left and Josh was moved to occupy a bedroom, was now being used as a private chamber for their conversation.

"I would like to argue the fact her decision was made too soon after my father's death. But as she has already pointed out to me, when I spoke my thoughts on the matter to her, by Apache tradition...should my father have had an unwed brother, she would have been required to marry again without hesitation," he remarked.

"Aye, I have been made aware of this tradition." He cleared his throat. "You must also remember, Gabriel, it was your father who requested I return to Willow Creek and take care of your mother."

Gabriel frowned. "Which is something I am perfectly able to do."

He inclined his head respectfully. "I do not disagree with you, but obviously Proud Eagle believed my marriage to Amanda would be beneficial in other ways."

Gabriel chuckled sardonically. "Well, I know the benefits you would reap."

He took an audible breath. "I am sorry to hear you think so little of me, that you would believe my main aim in all of this was only to have the right to bed your mother."

Gabriel arched a brow. "Do not tell me that right has not crossed your mind with great pleasure."

His voice came out harsh with his frustration. "Then I won't tell you, because as a man you must fully understand how such a thought would pleasingly cross my mind. But it was not the main objective here." He placed both feet upon the floor and leaned forward. "Your mother means—has always meant—much more to me then a roll between the sheets. And I refuse to listen to such rot, because this sort of rubbish not only insults me, but tarnishes Amanda's worth as well." He shook his head in disgust. "I'm grateful your mother cannot hear your words right now, because she'd be so disappointed of your insinuations, in your translation of the truth and what really matters, which has nothing to do with me being a cheeky chap."

Gabriel's face flushed. "You speak the truth, and I apologize." He combed his fingers through his hair and stood, making his way to stand before the fireplace. He placed an arm upon the mantel and turned to face Josh. "It just feels like everything is happening so fast with too many changes so quickly. This world is made up of so many uncertainties."

"Then I would say that fact never changes," he countered.

"No, we can always count on the indefinite," Gabriel agreed.

"Perhaps it might help if you tried to focus on the unchanging presence of the Lord. Hebrews 13:8 tells us *Jesus Christ is the same yesterday, today, and tomorrow*."

Gabriel reluctantly nodded. "And to turn weakness into strength."

"Aye, and to do that you might begin to put aside your resentment toward me. I am not your enemy. Nor do I plan on doing anything to harm your mother." He stood, nearing the other man. His tone was sympathetic. "I know it is not easy for you to hear this, but I love your mother with all my heart. I have loved her for as long as I can remember."

"I know this," Gabriel said, eyes meeting Josh's. "And you speak the truth—it is not easy for a son to hear these words toward his mother from a man who is not his father."

"Then perhaps it might help for you to understand and remember I cared for and respected your father as well. In spite of the fact we loved the same women, Proud Eagle was my friend."

"I know this to be true as well," Gabriel said, his

tone softening. "My father often recounted your part in his rescue from Lieutenant Ryan Duffy's murderous hands. He would tell me of the jealous Running Doe, and how she tried to kill my mother on three occasions, because she wanted my father's love for herself. And yet your love for my mother only wanted to see her happy. Your love for my mother was not selfish, as was Running Doe's for my father...yours was the truer love."

"It still is," he whispered. "And I swear to you on my mother's grave, I will love and care for Amanda until I take my last breath. I would give my own life to save hers, if need be. Her wellbeing is of the utmost importance, and the first and foremost consideration in any actions I take."

Gabriel sighed heavily and nodded. "Then, in view of this, other measures must be taken in regards to my grandfather's land."

He frowned. "What measures do you speak of?"

"The matter of adding three names to the property's deed," Gabriel said. "You signed it over to me, but it would be best if your name, as well as my mother's and my wife's names, also appeared on the document. In this way, should anything happen to me or my right to own land is disputed, the property cannot be confiscated or taken away."

"I will have Ben Newcomb send for a barrister in the morning so these additions can be made legal."

"Strange, is it not, that we now take stock in a piece of paper and the correct words upon it to protect us?" Gabriel's forced smile did nothing to alleviate the sorrow in his eyes. "And money—how much or how little one possesses—has become our honor and courage. Soon, how well a man can hunt or fish, build a fire, or construct a home will not matter. Only how much he can pay for others to do the job for him."

He placed a hand on Gabriel's shoulder. "All will be well, in spite of the sorrow we've all endured, the changes, and the new ways of doing things. You have good wits about you. And there's no doubt in my mind you'll be a strong and brave leader. I know your father would be extremely proud of you. But you must always remember nothing can really be accomplished unless we all are united, in trust and respect." He affectionately squeezed the younger man's shoulder. "That's the key to winning, Gabriel. We must all stand strong...together."

\*\*\*\*

Amanda took great favor in her new daughter-in-law. The moment her sapphire orbs met Riley Eagle's emerald gaze, the bonding began. Auburn hair framed a sweet, freckled face...pale with delicate features and a full mouth. Yet her son's new wife was not born a privileged child, pampered, or as gentle as her beautiful visage insinuated. What Riley endured at an early age, growing up in London's poor district, served to make her flexible, give her a hearty soul. And Amanda was all too aware of the fact tenacity and courage were two important things a prairie woman needed to survive.

There were six women who sat around the dining room table to take afternoon tea. Sylvie was to Amanda's left, Riley to her right, and opposite sat Rising Sun and her daughter, Dawn. And to Riley's right sat Margaret Mulligan...or Maggie, as she liked to be called...a long lost cousin of Riley's from Ireland. Maggie's fire-red hair and hazel green eyes made her stand out in a crowd, but her loveliness was of an acquired taste. The more you grew to know her, and the cheery disposition she maintained, the more she blossomed in beauty. Maggie had a matronly build, thick around the waist and hips, and an ample bosom. At thirty she had been widowed and childless, and forlorn as well...thus the reason, when invited by Riley and Gabriel to accompany them to America, Maggie quickly accepted.

"I thank you again, Sylvie for opening your home to us while we wait for our own to be built." Riley reached for her cup to take a sip of tea.

"Aye, and I thank ye as well, lass," Maggie chimed in.

"I'm just glad the others left for their own places in time to give ya all room," Sylvie responded.

"I bet you can't wait until we're all out of your hair." Amanda gave her friend an affectionate pat on the hand.

"Truth is, Amanda, I kinda enjoyed ya all," Sylvie confessed. She gestured to Rising Sun and Dawn. "I'm gonna miss these two makin' dinner every night."

"And I am going to miss cooking on your stove," Rising Sun commented. "That is why I have told my husband I want a kitchen like you have, Sylvie. As well as walls, windows, and doors that lock."

"As do I," Dawn added. "With a pump that brings water into the house to fill the sink and a tub with warm water to bathe in."

"And let us not forget the ice box or the feather mattresses on the beds," Rising Sun concluded.

Riley frowned. "Gabriel and I never really discussed what we'd build. I just naturally assumed it would be a house." She bit her bottom lip. "Now I'm somewhat worried, and I hope he favors a house. One with all the amenities mentioned, along with several bedrooms for a growing family. And a cousin." She glanced in Maggie's direction.

Amanda reassured her daughter-in-law with a pat on the hand. "Do not worry yourself, my dear. As chief, my son will have both, a large wickiup at the head of the creek for tribal meetings and a house beside mine for the family living."

Riley sighed and took another sip of tea.

"At least you won't have to build either of them." Rising Sun stifled a smile.

Riley's eyes widened in horror. "Me build? I don't understand."

Rising Sun and Dawn began to giggle, and Amanda stifled her own smile while she explained the Apache tradition and her experience with Running Doe. Rising Sun chimed in now and then, adding her perspective.

While Amanda spoke she thought of her mother-in-law, White Dove, and how at one time this kind woman took it upon herself to guide and school a new daughter-in-law in the ways of the Apache, as well as teaching Amanda the role of the chief's wife. It was her turn to do the same for Riley.

Squeezing Riley's hand she concluded with, "Though I will teach you many Apache ways, Riley, this time building a wickiup will not be amongst them. Some traditions only need to be honored by their remembrance, and otherwise remain in the past, I'd say."

"Amen to that," both Rising Sun and Dawn said

simultaneously.

And then they all broke out in laughter.

## Chapter Fourteen

"Ya might call upon a fella by the name of Edmund Dodd," Sylvie suggested to Josh. "He's the young attorney in town who just hung out his shingle. 'Course, he's the only attorney in town, so I'd say ya ain't got much of a choice." She kept knitting while she talked, her experienced fingers never dropping a stitch. "I know this 'cause I met his wife, Muriel, at the general store just last week. She was buyin' apples...Mr. Dodd's fond of 'em." She clicked her tongue in reproach. "Poor souls, business ain't all that good, it seems, 'cause the two of 'em are livin' in the three rooms behind the office." She dropped her voice. "Not enough funds to rent themselves a proper place." She shook her head. "And Muriel's just a wisp of a woman, pale hair, from Boston society I reckon and looks like a fish outta water in such a harsh place as this."

Josh arched a brow. "I'm amazed you got all that just from meeting the women in the general store." But as he thought twice about it, Sylvie Newcomb could probably get a confession from the devil.

"Yup, that and a lot more, but the rest's just women's talk—nothin' ya need to know," Sylvie added. "Ya be surprised at the rattlin' on of a lonely person, far from their own kin, feelin' out of place in a new town. I've been meanin' to have the two over for dinner, but with such a house full of guests, it just plumb slipped my mind." She cast him a sideways glance. "Not too many here now, though. And I reckon, since yer needin' to talk to the Mister, maybe it's the right time for that invite."

He inclined his head politely. "I'd be extremely grateful for whatever you could do, Sylvie."

She gave him a taut nod. "Then come mornin' I'll make a peach cobbler and take it over to 'em—see if we can set this all rollin' along."

Rolling along, indeed...the following day the women in the house were cleaning and preparing food for the guests that would arrive on the next evening for dinner. The men knew enough to get out of their way, and since Gabriel had yet to see the new village, it seemed like an opportune time to take him there.

Josh climbed into the wagon with Gabriel, who by all purposes was extremely anxious to view the property. Falling Star, and his son-in-law, Messai joined them as well, but on horseback since the wagon only seated two. They sat proud on the mares they rode, which belonged to Ben Newcomb. It was another generous loan and means of support from the reverend. What any of the tribe's people and Amanda would have done without Ben and Sylvie, Josh didn't even want to imagine.

Gabriel eyed the riders waiting to pull out with the wagon. "We're going to need horses of our own, and a wagon or two." He frowned. "There's so much to do."

"First, the ceremony to make you chief," Falling Star advised. "We must start this new beginning in the right way."

"You speak wisely, my friend," Gabriel said. "It is

most important to the tribe to feel strong and united once again." Then he turned his attention to Josh. "And I imagine thereafter you wish to marry my mother."

"Aye, that is the plan." He searched the other man's tired face. How hard it had to be for Gabriel to return home to find nothing the same, all he knew gone, and grieve the loss of a father. There was so much resting on his shoulders. Josh softened his expression and his tone. "I believe it would be another wise move for Amanda to be legally wed to me before we sign the deed papers."

Gabriel nodded. "We will speak with Edmund Dodd tomorrow on that matter after dinner."

They rode the rest of the way in silence. Falling Star and Messai followed the wagon close behind, their mumbled conversation carried on the wind in bits and pieces.

When the wagon rounded the bend onto the property's path, Gabriel broke the silence. "My mother said she buried my father in her family's plot."

"Aye, I helped her lay him to rest a few weeks ago, or I should say, a small urn containing those ashes remaining from his Apache burial. And I have commissioned a stone cutter to make a marker for the grave."

"Then he was sent to his ancestors by both of my parents' traditions," Gabriel said, relief sounding in his voice.

"Aye, a final farewell that appeased each of them," he said.

"Compromise...it was what they did best. But then again, with each of them coming from a different way of life, if they did not cooperate with one another, they would have never survived as they did—especially my mother. What white women, during such times, would have stood by my father against her own people, as she did?"

"She is a remarkable person," he admitted, feeling the love for her rising within his very core. "I don't believe I have ever met such a brave woman."

"Courageous, you mean," Gabriel corrected. "Men are brave, but women are courageous."

"Aye, courageous, but with or without courage I plan to protect her," he said, his tone resolute on the matter.

Gabriel arched a brow. "To the death, if need be, as my father once swore?"

"Aye, I swear the same oath." He squared his shoulders, realizing this was the second time he gave his word thusly to such a matter. "As your father knew I would."

"Then, I welcome you to my family," Gabriel conceded.

His heart warmed at Gabriel's declaration. If things had been different and Amanda accepted his proposal instead of Proud Eagle's, the strong, intelligent young man sitting beside him might have been his own son. What things would they have shared...would he have gone to school in England, took up the clergy, followed in Josh's footsteps?

"I would like to stop at my father's resting place before seeing the others." Gabriel broke through Josh's thoughts.

He nodded and when the destination came into view, he brought the wagon to a halt in front of the family burial plot. Falling Star and Messai slowed the horses, bowed their heads in reference, then rode on ahead to the wickiups...leaving Josh and Gabriel to pay their respects.

He lingered in the wagon, giving Gabriel time to mourn in private. The younger man made his way to Proud Eagle's grave, bowed his head, then got down on one knee. Josh's emotions swelled with grief as he watched Gabriel mourn his father. The lump in his throat grew so large he had trouble swallowing. He took a deep breath to compose himself and glanced over his surroundings.

The soft breeze carried the promise of spring, as it gently rustled the treetops. Bees buzzed, butterflies fluttered about, the birds sang. Life was all around him, and yet the dead lay only a few feet away. This was how it always was...life and death simultaneously co-existing in the world...each co-companion to the other. If you lived you would die—if you died then you once lived. It was an inevitable fact.

He climbed down from his seat in the wagon and made his way to Proud Eagle's grave. As he neared Gabriel, Josh could hear his low, soft chanting. Placing a hand on Gabriel's shoulder, he bowed his own head and began to mutter a prayer. To his surprise, Gabriel covered Josh's hand with his own, and together the two stayed in such a stance until their prayers were completed.

Then Gabriel stood and surveyed his surroundings—a mixture of pride and hope flickering in his eyes. "This is all my land?"

"Aye, and much more," he said.

Gabriel squared his shoulders. "Then perhaps it is time you showed me."

Washburn's cabin was the first dwelling they came to. As always, Vernon sat on his small porch, whittling. Josh felt a bit apprehensive while making the introductions, even though Vernon was pleasant to the other tribe's people and even helped in building the three wickiups standing along the creek. He hoped Gabriel's strong character didn't make Washburn feel his stance on the land was threatened.

But then Gabriel extended his hand in a greeting to the older man, and Josh breathed a quiet sigh of relief. His gesture of peace and friendship was just enough to win Washburn's confidence. Amanda's son had inherited his father's looks, but his heart was that of his mother. And although he was every inch the proud and strong warrior his people needed, he also had a tender side to his demeanor.

"I am thankful for the care you have taken of the plot where my ancestors are laid to rest, and of my grandfather's land." Gabriel waved his hand in the air, indicating the property surrounding him.

"I'm the one who should be doin' the thankin," Vernon countered. "If it weren't for the years I spent on this here soil, I can't say what kinda life or home I'd been able to give my family."

"Then, from this day on, we will work together to make it all of our homes," Gabriel said.

Washburn's sun-bronzed face crinkled into a smile. "Sounds about right to me."

The three of them made their way on foot to the creek, Gabriel taking in each bush and tree, listening to Vernon's account of the foliage he had planted and of those he had taken down in the years he lived there.

When they arrived at the small cluster of wickiups,

Gabriel stopped short, pausing to admire the scene before him. His face brightened, eyes moistened, as he noticed the first traces of his new home. Not more than fifty feet away from where they stood, an eagle landed on a large rock. Cocking its head sideways, it just stared at the three of them for a moment before taking flight again. "And there before us lies Eagle's Landing," Gabriel whispered.

"Aye." Josh glanced at Ben Newcomb's horses tied beneath the shade of a large tree, munching happily on grass, while Falling Star and Massai helped Night Wolf to tan deer hide not far away.

"We all went huntin' last night—caught a good sized buck." Vernon made reference to the men at work with a nod. "I 'spect that's the hide they're tannin'."

"I would say you speak the truth." Gabriel looked the situation over; as though it were a dream...and one blink would make it all disappear.

Every bit of that buck would be made useful, as his time with the Apache taught him they weren't wasteful hunters. The deer's veins, or sinew as it was called, would be used to line their bows, string beadwork upon, and used as sewing thread. The animal's hide would be the fur pelt that would line the floor of a dwelling or a sleeping cot, and supply clothing. And the meat would be smoked for preservation or cooked in several different ways for serving in many meals to come.

"A few nights ago, I had dinner with my new neighbor folks," Vernon beamed. "Great story tellers. Dang if we didn't sit all night by the campfire and weave a yarn or two."

"Aye, they are famous for their stories and their hospitality." Josh realized with great joy this new beginning he would also share.

Vernon chuckled. "I made Water Lily and the one they call Earth a bed. It seems these two ladies got used to sleeping off the ground at the parsonage, so I built a frame to hold their bedding and a crib for each of their youngin's. A few cabinets for their dishes, too." He shook his head. "I enjoy workin' with wood, and it sure feels good to have somethin' to make someone—to have the company."

Walking closer to the little cluster of wickiups brought the aroma of the deer being cooked over an open fire. Owl Woman and her daughter-in-law, Earth were turning the skewer. Gabriel approached them, using their Apache names in greeting. "Nascha...Ela...it is so good to see you both."

"Golden Eagle." Owl Woman returned the greeting with the same respect. "How glad I am to see you as well."

Earth just smiled, a shy slow curve of her full lips, and nodded in agreement.

Cupping a hand around her mouth, Owl Women called out to her husband. "Little Elk, come...see who has finally arrived home."

From a nearby wickiup Little Elk emerged, his tall form filling the door frame. He was the only one dressed in traditional garb, buckskin tunic, breeches, and moccasins. The others had taken to wearing a combination of the white man's clothing—shirts and boots, along with the buckskin breeches and vests. The Apache women wore their traditional tunics and footwear, coupled with the white woman's skirt.

With a large grin upon his sun-tanned face, Little Elk came forward and embraced Gabriel. "Golden

Eagle, my friend, how happy my eyes are, to rest upon your face. And happier still to know our tribe will once more have a chief."

Gabriel stepped back to meet the other man's gaze. "I only pray I can be the man my father was."

"You have his blood and you know his ways, so all will be fine," Little Elk reassured him. "Besides, Falling Star and I are here to help you."

Night Wolf and Falling Star joined them, giving Gabriel an encouraging smile or pat on the shoulders.

Gabriel inclined his head respectfully. "Many years, Little Elk, you and Falling Star were my father's counsel men. I would ask you both now to be mine."

Little Elk's chin rose. "I am honored and will stand by you as I did Proud Eagle."

"And I," Falling Star agreed.

"We all will," came a voice from behind.

Gabriel turned to find Rising Star making his way from another nearby wickiup. The two embraced. "Ah, cousin, I have missed you so much."

"Then say you will never leave us again," Rising Star said.

"You have my word." Gabriel broke the hold and surveyed the young man before him. "You look well."

Rising Star chuckled. "I have a wife that feeds me good meals and loves me in spite of my stubborn ways."

"How is Water Lily?" Gabriel probed.

"Come, see for yourself. She is in our wickiup with my son, Bear." Rising Star gestured to his wickiup. "All of you come, we will sit by the fire pit and eat nuts and berries the women gathered this morning while we wait for the meat to cook."

Josh followed Gabriel and Vernon into the large wickiup, divided into two units. On one side the sitting, socializing, and eating area of the dwelling sat. A few wood cabinets were placed about, holding cooking pots, dishes, and other kitchen items. Cushions surrounded the fire pit, which was in the center of this section, and straw-woven mats were placed about to cover the earth floor. Only a small blaze burned now, with the weather being warmer and the meal being prepared outside.

The sleeping quarters were situated to the right and behind a large hanging blanket. The blanket hung slightly ajar, whereby Josh could see the wood-framed bed and a baby's cot, or crib as Vernon called it, were placed side by side. As he made a quick assessment of the modest living quarters, he couldn't help but think of Amanda, living all these years in such a primitive fashion. Not being born to such a tradition, how did she learn so well to cope with her new-found conditions? Obviously there had to be nights of despair. She had shared some of her discomfort. He wondered if she'd ever, in time, bring herself to speak in detail of them.

Water Lily's soft, even features broke into a warm smile when Gabriel entered the wickiup. Sitting on a cushion beside the cabinet with her three year old son upon her lap, the young women greeted them all. "Welcome to our home." Placing the child gently aside, she rose and made her way to Gabriel, embracing him. "So good to have you back where you belong."

Gabriel returned the affection. "It is good to be back, if only it were under better circumstances."

Water Lily pulled back to search Gabriel's face. "I am so sorry for the loss of your father. He was a good and honest man, and he will be greatly missed."

Gabriel cleared the emotion from his throat. "I thank you for those kind words."

"Come...sit." Rising Star led the way to the fire pit.

As they all took a seat around the fire, Josh was flooded with the memory of the first time he was a guest at the Apache village. It was for Thanksgiving dinner—a holiday Amanda had brought to the tribe and by her request he was invited. They were all seated in Cunning Eagle's wickiup, Proud Eagle glaring at him from across the flames. They were rivals of a sort then, even though Amanda was considered to be Proud Eagle's wife. It would take many times of trust and trial before the two men would call a truce.

"He has grown since I last saw him," Gabriel glanced at the child, now making his way to his father.

Rising Star gathered the boy into his arms and kissed the top of his head. "Soon he will be one of your warriors."

"He has many years yet to go." Water Lily brought to the circle dishes of berries and nuts.

"Not long, *she'aad*, my wife," Rising Star countered. "See how broad his shoulders are already." He caressed his son's arms. "And how tall he has become." He ran a hand down the length of the child. Then he stopped at the boy's backside...making a face.

Water Lily giggled. "And how wet his bottom is," she finished for him.

Rising Star only nodded.

The other men laughed.

"Perhaps your mama is right," Gabriel ruffled the toddler's thick crop of dark hair.

"Come, my little warrior." Water Lily took Bear from his father's grasp. "Time for me to clean you up, and then help the women with our meal." She then turned to Gabriel. "I look forward to meeting your wife."

Gabriel nodded. "I will bring her tomorrow, as she is very anxious to meet all of you as well."

Water Lily nodded, and then smiled. "Again, it is good to have you home." With that said, she left the wickiup.

Vernon stood. "I think I'll lend a hand with that meal, too."

"Would you ask the other men to join us," Gabriel said.

"Will do," Vernon agreed.

Rising Star arched a brow. "Our first tribal meeting."

"Something like that." Gabriel reached for the bowl of nuts and scooped some into his hand.

It wasn't long before Falling Star, Messai, Night Wolf, and Little Elk joined them. Once the other men were seated, Gabriel proceeded. "I have heard my father died in a hunting accident." He looked around at those sitting in the circle. "We all know my father was an excellent hunter—completely focused, extremely cautious, and highly skilled."

"All you speak is true, Golden Eagle," Little Elk agreed.

Gabriel frowned. "Then how is it he could be brought down this way?"

"I asked the same question when Proud Eagle returned to the reservation wounded," Falling Star admitted. "But he would only say it was an unwise move on his part."

Gabriel's frown deepened. "And you believed

him?"

"No, but I would not disrespect him by questioning him further," Falling Star responded sharply.

"It is not hard to understand the reason your father would keep his silence. Proud Eagle tried to keep peace between the white agents and the Apache people. It meant our safety...our lives. If Proud Eagle admitted what we all suspected, he knew we would be forced to make a stand," Little Elk explained.

"He wanted none of his people's blood on his hands, or anywhere else," Falling Star added.

"Did my mother suspect foul play?"

"Golden Lady is a wise woman. Not much ever got past her," Falling Star said. "But she knew the trouble the tribe would see if the situation was not kept under control."

Gabriel's lips thinned. "I had dreams—visions something was not right with my family. The spirits of our ancestors were trying to tell me of the trouble ahead, but I did not heed their warnings. I should have been here, by my mother's side. She must have been so scared—felt so alone without her children nearby."

Josh's heart ached for Amanda's sorrow as he also sympathized with the desperation and fear she must have experienced...knowing the truth, sworn to silence for the sake of others, and having to watch her husband die as well. Again he wondered of the despair and anguish she suffered throughout the years. A white woman's life as an Apache chief's wife could not have been easy. Only a woman with a strong and loyal love for her husband could endure such circumstances. Would she love him just as truly and fiercely after they wed?

"We were with Golden Lady," Little Elk said. "My wife did not leave her or Proud Eagle's side."

"You were where your mother and father wished you to be," Falling Star consoled.

Gabriel combed his fingers through his hair. "And did no one try to go for a doctor—some sort of medical help?"

"Owl Women did her best, but the wound became infected. When her efforts failed, I sent word to the holy man Ben," Little Elk said.

"We knew a medicine man would not come to the reservation at our request," Falling Star added. "Ben was our only hope."

"By the time a white medicine man finally arrived..." Little Elk didn't need to finish his sentence.

The muscles at Gabriel's jaw throbbed. "Though it will not bring my father back, I need to know what happened to him, my friends. It is the only way he can rest in peace—the only way his family can move on. And now that we are no longer under the white agent's rule, it will not be as dangerous for us to discover the truth."

"We are small in number, cousin. Dangerous or not, how can we do this?" Rising Star said.

"I agree," Night Wolf chimed in. "All know us in these parts and will become suspicious if we start asking questions. Besides, the Apache still is not welcomed by the white man, and we are unable to go into those places that might tell us what we seek."

"I understand what you say, Night Wolf. And since I received news of my father's death, I have thought of nothing else but to hatch some sort of plan to help us find out the truth and keep us safe as well." Gabriel paused long enough to take a fist full of berries from a bowl and pop them into his mouth.

"While in Ireland, I shared my thoughts with my sister, Raven, and her husband, Lord Braiton Shannon. He is a good man, honest, loyal, and has done right by my sister, so I respect him greatly. What interested me was he owns much land he allows tenants to rent. For a fee, or tax as it is called, the tenants are free to live on his private estate...under his protection. His people live quite well and are content.

"As they tend to his land and make it flourish, they are also carving out a prosperous life for themselves. They are honored to stand with him through good and bad times. Not all landlords are as fair as my brother-in-law, but as I said, he is a good man and his people are treated like one big family. As I walked around the grounds, talked with the tenants, I could see where such a system might benefit our new village. There is strength in numbers, and all these tenants united keep the land safe from intruders, making the whole situation a success."

"Who could you trust to rent land with us?" Messai said. "We are hated for just having a different color skin."

"I thought the same, Messai," Gabriel agreed. "But then it was not long after my conversation with Braiton, that he introduced me to two men. One was a doctor. The other is a blacksmith who trains and breeds horses. He is also an investigator. My brother-in-law said this man was very successful in completing every job placed before him, finding the truth for others, as well as being a champion horseman."

"How will we find such men as these?" Little Elk

probed.

"It happens I was able to strike a deal with them both, as they wished to bring their families to America. When they learned of the new village I was going to build my people, they asked to be a part of it. In place of their passage to our land, they promised to help build our homes. And when I agreed to build them each a home as well, they in turn pledged their loyalty, offered to share their skills...the investigator promising to help me look into my father's death."

Josh suddenly realized Gabriel wasn't building a village, but instead a town. He repeated what he heard the younger man whisper earlier. "And there before us lies Eagle's Landing."

"Yes." Gabriel turned a hopeful glance at Josh. "The beginnings of it, anyway."

"Brilliant idea," he said.

"When do these men from Ireland arrive?" Little Elk said.

Gabriel took an audible breath. "In about two weeks."

"And when will you commence the investigation to begin," he inquired.

"Not until we are all settled in our homes," Gabriel said. "I want to go about this in a wise way. My father taught me the importance of keeping a calm spirit and controlled head. A man who is careful with the moves he makes—finds what he seeks. First I will become chief." He motioned to Josh with a wave of a hand. "And my mother will wed the holy man, here—as my father wished."

"Is it what Golden Lady wishes?" Little Elk said.

"We both have happily agreed." Josh's heart

skipped a beat with joy at the thought of finally wedding the woman he loved.

The rest of the men nodded and smiled with approval.

"Then we will build our village," Gabriel continued. "With stables whereby horses can be shod, trained, and bred. We will build barns to house chickens, cows, and pigs. We will plant gardens, both the vegetable and herbal kind—and even those with flowers. Now that I have the means to do all of these things, we will be able to grow strong and independent—be once again united as a tribe, as well as a town."

"And you will be a lord," he said.

"As well as a chief," Rising Star added.

"Though such titles are honorable, I would much rather be a wise and efficient business man, as that will be the way to truly lead my people."

Messai arched a brow. "How so, Golden Eagle?

"Just think, Messai, how much better, quicker it will be for the country folk to go for a doctor? It could mean, for them, the difference between life and death if they do not have to travel all the way into Willow Creek for medical help. The convenience alone will please them greatly, especially on a brutal winter night. Imagine how suitable a nearby blacksmith would be for a rider in trouble who has already made his way out of town? Or the opportunity to purchase farm goods— eggs, milk, only a stone's throw away. And what use could other objects our people make be to the community, like pottery, baskets, beadwork, and blankets? We could have a general store of our own and sell these items."

"The profits gained will constantly supply all of our needs...keep the town thriving," he said.

"It is exactly what I planned," Gabriel said. "But I ask all of you to keep the part about the investigation into my father's death only between us. I do not want to worry the women."

Again all the men nodded.

"Then when no one expects it, we will unleash the investigator, quietly, privately, to seek the truth," Gabriel said.

"What then, my cousin, after we find the truth?" Rising Star said.

"Then," Gabriel said, raising his chin. "We will seek justice."

Chapter Fifteen

As Amanda watched her daughter-in-law set the dining room table, it wasn't hard to see why her son had fallen in love. Riley spoke softly, listened with close consideration, and chose her words with care. She also performed the most meager of tasks with great respect and definition. As she placed a dish upon the table, Riley took the time to admire the pattern, little yellow butterflies lilting along a border of blue. While folding the napkins, she creased the cloth to line up evenly. As she added the silverware, she hummed. And while arranging a center piece of pink roses and baby's breath, she inhaled the scent of the blooms with appreciation.

"You've done a lovely job, Riley," she praised. "But then again I would expect nothing less from such a lovely young woman."

Riley's fair complexion blushed. "I can't wait to have my own home, whereby I shall set a beautiful table every night for my husband." Just the thought of Gabriel had her daughter-in-law beaming, and in that simple moment, she knew her son was completely and unconditionally loved by his young wife.

She smiled and touched Riley's arm with motherly affection. "My son is a lucky man." And she meant every word, as she was so pleased Gabriel had finally found happiness.

He had been so despondent, so troubled after his first wife and son's deaths, that she almost gave up hope at him ever finding another woman to love. But her prayers were answered, as it seems so were those for her daughters. What a mother's joy to hear both Raven and Sunny had also found happiness. Riley gave her a woman's account of her new sons-in-law, and Amanda was pleased to learn her daughters had also married well. Proud Eagle would have been relieved to know his children were safe, happy, and loved.

When the men returned from viewing the new village property, Gabriel took his bride by the hand and led her upstairs. "I have much to tell you about our land."

Amanda smiled as she watched them make their way to the second floor of the parsonage. She had no doubt in her mind there would not be much talking done. Sighing, she said softly, "Ah, young love."

"I am finding love at any age is bloody grand," a deep voice came from behind.

She turned to find Josh smiling, his light blue eyes twinkling with a hint of mischief. "Yes, I suppose it is." Warmth colored her cheeks like a schoolgirl.

Taking her hand, he brought it to his lips and placed a gentle kiss across her knuckles. "Can I have a moment with you, my dear lady?"

She raised her gaze to meet his. And in that moment, she suddenly felt much desired, loved, cared for, and cherished. "I would like that," she found herself breathlessly responding.

He led her out to the garden, the sky pink with the promise of sunset. A light breeze cooled her hot cheeks, and she inhaled the fragrances of Sylvie's various blooms swaying gently in the garden. "Did all go well at the village site?"

"Aye, exceptionally so." He looked like a child ready to burst with the announcement of good news.

She giggled. "Do tell, then."

As they sat together on a wooden bench, Josh told her what Gabriel planned...the building of a town—Eagle's Landing. "He's bringing two men, a doctor and a blacksmith who trains and breeds horses, plus their families from Ireland to America, to round out the town."

Her son's cleverness, his sense of business swelled her heart with pride. Gasping, she reached for Josh's hand. "Pray tell, can such an idea really work?"

A smile spread across Josh's handsome face. "Aye, I believe it can—it will." He paused, looking deep into her eyes. "As I sat around the fire pit in Rising Star's dwelling, I took a long look at my surroundings, and I couldn't help but imagine you living in such a fashion all those many years."

"It wasn't all bad." She shrugged. "It took some doing to get used to, but I managed."

"I didn't mean to imply..." He cleared his throat nervously. "What I meant to say is the harsh conditions would have undone the best of us, and you survived with so little—not a shred of convenience whatsoever." He studied her face closer. "You won't have to manage or just get by any longer."

"I don't need...don't want you to think..."

He interrupted her. "I am not without means, Amanda. I have saved a considerable amount in these past years—living sparingly, not having to support a wife and children. Plus an inheritance of my own that

I've stashed away."

"You don't have to explain yourself."

"Aye, I do, because I want you to know I can build you a home fitting for the times we live in, with glass windows and strong walls—woodworking and a fireplace—a well-stocked kitchen, fine wood floors. No expense would be spared to build a home for the genteel and fine woman you are, that you always have been. I can give this all to you and it..."

"Josh, I am not after your money," she interrupted.

He silenced her words with the tip of a finger. "I know this, Amanda. But it would please me to provide such a home for you. It's important to me you feel secure, so you're able to close your eyes at night and sleep with contentment." He kissed her forehead. "My dear, sweet Amanda, outside of loving you with all my heart and soul, nothing more would bring me such happiness."

Joy burst throughout her entire being. "Nor I, Josh."

He beamed. "Then you are pleased with my plans for us...with the new town we will live in?"

"Yes, I am overjoyed to finally be able to believe we really are on our way to a better, safer life."

"Aye, we are." He brought her hand up to his lips for another tender kiss. "It will take some doing, and much time, but I feel we're moving ahead nicely...all of us together, in the right direction."

For the first time in many years, she felt encouraged, a real and strong sense of hope growing deep within her. "All of this could mean so many extraordinary possibilities and..." She paused, actually feeling giddy with joy. "I can honestly see a wonderful future for us all."

"I do as well," he said, searching her face, reflecting her happiness within his light blue orbs. "However, for just a moment"—he slid closer to her on the bench so their thighs touched—"I'd like to talk a bit about our future together."

Her heart raced. "I'm listening."

He slowly and gently caressed the side of her face with the tip of a finger. "It's obviously not news to you I've loved you for what seems like an eternity."

"Or that I've also held you dear," she whispered.

"Aye, but for the sake of your marriage, I've held myself in check and you..." He cleared his throat before continuing. "And you were otherwise occupied."

She bit her bottom lip. "But now..."

He arched a seductive brow. "But now there is nothing to keep us at bay. And so, my love, I shall actually claim your heart, as I was only able to dream of doing." He knelt on one knee in front of her and pulled from his vest pocket a ring. "Amanda Gregory Eagle, will you do me the honor of becoming my wife?"

And there it was—the gentleman's proposal. The moment every girl dreams of from the time she could speak. Looking down at his earnest and loving face melted her heart. With tears welling in her eyes, she smiled. "Yes, Joshua Holmes, I will."

The gold ring he slipped on her finger was etched on the sides with hearts and vines, and inlaid with three diamonds across the top. "It was my mother's. There is a matching wedding band as well. And I've also inherited my father's gold band, which I will wear after we've wed."

She took an audible breath. "It's beautiful."

"Nay, you are what's beautiful." He stood and pulled her to her feet.

Once within his embrace, she responded by bringing trembling hands to rest upon his chest. She could feel the rapid beating of his heart, which kept pace with her own.

Then he lowered his mouth, gently pressing his full, warm lips against hers.

Slowly she moved her hands up and over his shoulder, to rest along his neck, winding fingers in the thick, dark curls at his nape.

Her touch ignited his desire, and he possessively pulled her closer, his hands locking against her spine. Hungrily his mouth captured hers completely, deepening the kiss.

Elated, and with pulse-pounding certainty, her feelings for him intensified. His eagerness excited her. And as his tongue explored the recesses of her mouth, a delicious shudder heated her body from head to toes. She gave herself fully to the passion of the kiss, and her reaction brought from him a deep groan of pleasure.

His lips became more demanding, and she found herself succumbing to the domination. Her thoughts spun, emotions swirled and skidded—her limbs trembled to near collapse.

But his strong arms supported her quite sufficiently, as she somehow knew they would. Never was there a time when he let her down, even when it caused him great emotional pain. Steadfast and loyal, righteous and caring, all the qualities a woman hoped for in a husband, this man possessed. And as a young girl she could not appreciate him, the life he offered and the security he stood for.

But now...now things were different. She was given another chance to make a life with such an incredible human being. In all the sadness of losing Proud Eagle, something beautiful had arisen. And she no longer would feel guilty about taking the opportunity that presented itself to her.

She leaned against him, allowing herself to be completely dependent upon him to keep her from falling to the ground. He broke the connection of their fused lips to whisper in her ear, "I've got you, love, forever and ever."

She savored his words, burying her face beneath his chin. "Can I hold you to that?"

"Aye." He raised a hand to caress her hair. "I shall make sure of it."

And she would have kissed him again, become lost in the feel, smell, and taste of him if the back door hadn't opened and Sylvie popped her head out to announce, "Edmond Dodd and his missus have arrived. 'Spect it would be nice if ya two came to make their acquaintance."

Her cheeks heated. How long had Sylvie been watching them?

He chuckled lightly and called back, "Aye, I expect it would."

The back door slammed shut, and they both laughed. "Poor Sylvie, what would we have all done without her?" When he didn't make a move to release her from his grasp, she whispered, "I think she meant now, Josh."

He sighed. "I was hoping I misunderstood." As she moved to step away, he held her in place. "I need a moment, Amanda."

She stifled a giggle. Being held so close to him as she was, she could feel the reason he needed that moment poking her thigh. Looking up at him, she smiled. "Suppose you keep that thought for after we're married?"

His silky voice held a challenge. "My dear lady, you've got yourself a deal."

## Chapter Sixteen

Josh forced himself to taste and swallow the food he ate and remain focused on the conversation going around the dinner table. But in truth all he could think about was the way Amanda felt in his arms. The warmth of her soft lips upon his, the way she responded to his touch, the smell of her hair. It was better than anything he ever imagined. Finally she was pledged to him. In a short time she'd be his wife, and he'd never take her for granted...expect her to live under perilous conditions or with a fearful heart.

His gaze met hers from across the table, and she bit her bottom lip in a most seductive way. She knew exactly the effect she had on him, and she was teasing him now with the knowledge. It thrilled him to the core...her playfulness heating the blood coursing through his veins. Arching a brow he inclined his head slightly in response, accepting the challenge. She smiled, a warm and glowing expression of pure joy brightening her features. Such happiness made her appear younger, more beautiful than he ever thought she could look. And the transformation pleased him...to think he brought such a pleasant change into her life.

"Is that not right, Josh?" Gabriel said.

He cleared his throat and turned his attention to the younger man at his left. "I'm afraid I was otherwise preoccupied." He could feel his face heat with the thought of his distraction being discovered. "Could you reiterate yourself, please?"

Gabriel glanced quickly in his mother's direction, and stifled a smile. Casting his gaze back to Josh, he repeated his sentence. "I was telling Mr. Dodd that soon you and my mother plan to marry."

He glanced over at Edmond Dodd. "Aye, as soon as possible, actually."

The young barrister was fair-haired, lean, and tall with chiseled features and dressed professionally in a gray suit. He nodded. "Good, very good. It would be preferable for you to be legally bound before signing the deed to the property in question."

"I always find it so unfair that women must be protected by their husband's name when dealing with owning property," Muriel Dodd interjected. "I always tell Edmond he needs to change the law, stand up for women's rights." She giggled nervously, her pale complexion blushing with her declaration. She cast large, appreciative brown eyes at her husband while pushing a flaxen curl from her forehead. "I just know he is capable of doing great things one day, as he does not hold bias when representing a client."

"I am glad to hear this about you," Amanda said. "Am I to assume then, you would have no problem doing business with the Apache people?"

"None whatsoever, ma'am," Edmond said.

"See, did I not say he is the best at what he does." Muriel beamed.

Edmond, a bit embarrassed by his wife's admiration, placed a hand affectionately over hers. "She has such faith in me." He smiled lovingly at Muriel. "And I in her."

"I would say that is a wonderful way to feel and the only way to be married." Amanda reached for her tea cup. After taking a sip, she addressed Mrs. Dodd, "And what do you like to do?"

"Weave—I am a weaver, and I have my own loom," Muriel said.

"The loom takes up most of our living space...which isn't much as it is," Edmond said with a chuckle.

"And I am also a teacher," the younger woman added.

"And an excellent one, at that," Edmond boasted.

Gabriel's features brightened. "Our village could use a weaver—and a teacher. Not only for the tribe's children, but also for those of the two Irish families that will be arriving. I am told there is a total of eight children in all. And as our town grows, so will that number."

"It would probably be only fittin' then if ya built a schoolhouse on yer land as well, Gabriel," Sylvie suggested. "Then the missus here can teach the children, if she's inclined to agree, that is." Sylvie's face brightened with a further idea. "It might be right nice for ya to build them a house too, since they're livin' now all cramped in the back of an office with that there loom."

"Oh no, please...I wasn't implying...we wouldn't expect you to..." Edmond stuttered.

"I think that's a splendid idea, Gabriel," Amanda chimed in. "My mother was a school teacher—came to America from England to start a school here in Willow Creek," she explained briefly to the Dodds. "So, I'd be very pleased for our children to have the opportunity to learn from a professional." She turned to smile at her son. "Perhaps the building could serve as a schoolhouse during the week and a gathering hall on Sunday mornings, until we can build a chapel, as we will need a place to worship." She glanced over at Josh. "We already have the clergyman."

The sweet, tender look she held on Gabriel left him at her mercy. The expression of love and respect flashing across his face was so completely genuine, you knew before he said, "I think you speak wisely, my mother," that he would agree with her on the matter— probably on just about any matter.

Josh immediately realized he'd also be defenseless in her wake...surrender himself completely. If she turned such feminine wiles on him, he'd probably agree to hang the moon for her. And there was no doubt she would make him a victim as well. Hadn't he heard from her own children Amanda had a way of getting what she wanted?

*Aye, I will be next for sure.*

Strangely enough, he couldn't wait for such a circumstance to arrive. He wanted to give her everything, keep that enchanting smile he now longed to kiss, burning bright.

Casting a glance in Riley's direction, he caught the younger woman watching closely—absorbing fully— the way Amanda handled her son. He stifled a smile. Poor Gabriel, his young bride was taking mental notes from the dealings of a pro, and it wouldn't be long before she followed suit. Gabriel didn't stand a chance. Then again...what man, who was totally taken with his woman, ever did?

After dessert he joined Amanda, Gabriel, Riley,

and the Dodds, in Ben's den to talk business. As Edmond pulled from his vest pocket a pair of specs to read over the deed, the others chatted softly, sharing and adding further ideas to make Eagle's Landing a wonderful place to live. The room was charged with excitement, and he found himself chiming in with a few suggestions of his own.

However, the voices were immediately silenced when Edmond looked up from the document and cleared his throat. "Everything appears to be in order." He removed his glasses and returned them to their prior place. "I will draw up a legal appendage to accompany the original deed, whereby all of your signatures will be recorded." He glanced specifically at Josh. "Reverend, it would be to Amanda's benefit, that by the time I am in need of those signatures, you two were wed."

Amanda moved nearer to him and took his hand. "We plan on taking our vows on Saturday, at noon." Glancing up at him, she added. "Isn't that right, Josh?"

She caught him somewhat off guard with her remark, as Saturday was only five days away. But the sooner the better to make her his wife, so he smiled and nodded, then said. "We'd love for you to be present as well."

"Oh, I just love weddings," Muriel squealed with delight.

"It would be an honor to join you, sir," Edmond said.

Gabriel moved to place a kiss upon his mother's cheek, and Riley hugged them both.

After the congratulations were said, Gabriel turned his attention to Edmond. "Will you also join our town?"

Edmond cast a quick glance at his wife, who

looked as though she was ready to jump up and down like an overjoyed child. Stifling a smile, he returned his attention to Gabriel. "That would also be an honor."

Gabriel extended his hand to the other man. "Welcome, my friend."

As the other two men shook hands on the matter, Josh moved forward to do the same.

And the women began to chatter about wedding plans.

When they moved out into the dining room, the others were still around the table, enjoying tea. He announced their upcoming nuptials, and another round of congratulations ensued. Amanda showed off her engagement ring to the other women, and more wedding plans were discussed. Ben brought out a bottle of wine he had saved for just such an occasion, and everyone toasted them. It was a night he'd never forget.

Later that evening, after the guests had left and the other members in the household made their way upstairs to bed, he joined Amanda, Gabriel, and Riley in the parlor.

Amanda took from her pocket two gold wedding bands, holding the larger one up for Gabriel to see. "This belonged to your grandfather, Ethan Gregory, and your father. Now, it belongs to you." But instead of giving the ring to Gabriel, she handed it to Riley. "It is for you to place on his finger."

Riley moved closer, taking the ring. Then she slowly slid it on the ring finger of Gabriel's left hand. It went on smoothly...fit perfectly. "It is like it was made for him."

Amanda smiled. "I had no doubt it would be a perfect fit." She paused to clear the emotion from her voice. "And this ring"—she held up the smaller band—"belonged to my mother." She slipped it on the ring finger of her right hand. "I will keep it for now. But perhaps one day I will have the opportunity to pass it on to another heir."

Gabriel hugged his mother. "I fit in my father's ring, but can I fill his shoes?"

"I have no doubt you'll be just as great a man, Gabriel." She tightened her embrace. "What's more, I know your father would approve and be proud of all you're doing."

After Gabriel and Riley went to bed, Josh lingered with Amanda in the parlor. Sitting on the sofa, she laid her head upon his shoulder. "It has been an incredible day."

He kissed her forehead, inhaling the scent of her hair. "Aye, I was just thinking the same thing." He put his arm around her shoulder and drew her closer.

"I'm sorry I didn't talk over with you first about our wedding date." She buried her head beneath his chin. "I just thought there was no real reason to wait, and the signatures needed to be on the deed sooner than later."

"I agree," he said, his whole body heating with her nearness.

"I know I can be stubborn and willful at certain times," she said.

"Only at certain times?" he teased.

"Well...fine...often times," she conceded. "Even still, rest assured, I am not the sort of wife who does not consult her husband on serious matters."

"I'm not concerned about that, my love."

She pulled back to meet his gaze. "What does

concern you, then?"

He felt a lump form in his throat. "That as a husband I will fall short. I fear I will never be able to fill his...his..."

"No, you will never be able to fill Proud Eagle's shoes," she interrupted.

He swallowed hard, his heart sinking.

"No more than his own son could, or anyone else for that matter," she continued. "We are all unique onto ourselves." She placed both hands on each side of his face and looked deep into his eyes. "I never expected you to be like him, nor do I want such a thing. But I do expect you to fill your own shoes, be the sort of husband who will love his wife true and often, hold her tight and dear. Respect and care for her with all your heart."

His heart soared. "I can be that sort of husband, every day until I die," he promised. Then he sealed that promise with the longest, deepest kiss any man could bestow upon a woman.

And long after they parted to enter their separate sleeping quarters, he lay in bed thinking of that kiss, her sigh of contentment still echoing in his ears.

Chapter Seventeen

The next few days passed in a blur. So much needed to be done. The men headed off to the property site to construct Gabriel's meeting wickiup. This dwelling, larger than the other wickiups, would be placed at the head of the creek. Generally it would serve as the place where the chief and his family lived. However, since Riley preferred a wood-framed home, and Gabriel agreed, the chief's wickiup would be used as a gathering place for tribal council meetings and vision quests.

Also, a holy place was to be erected from piles of stones. This small alter-like construction would be where passersby added twigs and shingle rock, then sprinkled cattail flag pollen as they spoke to the Gods of the Zenith and Nadir, and those of the four winds. It would be where Gabriel would take his vow as chief in two days' time, and where the tribe's people would go for their spiritual comfort.

The deer hunted a few nights ago served many purposes. Its hide, for one, would now be used to make Gabriel a traditional buckskin tunic, breeches, and moccasins to wear for the ceremony. Owl Woman, her daughter and daughter-in-law, as well as Rising Sun's daughter-in-law all worked diligently on that task. The outfit would be topped off with Gabriel wearing the full Apache chief headdress.

Amanda, Rising Sun, and the other women stayed at the parsonage to bake and cook for the wedding. It was to be a small gathering of about twenty people. The ceremony would be held in the church, Reverend Newcomb officiating, and afterwards a small luncheon would be served in the garden. A menu of roast duck, corn on the cob, minced beets, boiled potatoes in garlic-butter sauce, a three bean and a garden salad, chock full of tomatoes, cucumbers, radishes, and green peppers was planned—along with Sylvie's famous apple cobbler, coconut-vanilla cream cake, and homemade brownies for dessert.

Congregational tables and chairs, used for the church's annual strawberry festival, were taken from the storage shed located in back of the barn and washed. The morning of the wedding, the tables would be covered with white linen tablecloths and set up amongst the rose bushes and other beautiful blooms.

The matter of what to wear became her concern, now. One specific marriage ceremony whereby the reciting of vows was said was not performed when she wed Proud Eagle, as it wasn't an Apache tradition. But later, when she had a Christian ceremony, to appease Josh's insistence that it was the only way he saw her and Proud Eagle as legally married, she wore her mother's wedding gown. That heirloom would do her no good now, as it had been sent to England with her daughters. Besides, there was just something inappropriate about dressing in the same gown used at the first wedding, also for the second wedding. There really wasn't enough time to sew an outfit or order one from a catalogue, so Sylvie generously offered her the gown she wore when she married Ben.

The problem with this solution—Sylvie was a tall women, well over five feet, six inches, with a larger frame. Even in her youth Sylvie was well endowed, and the gown accommodated her size. Whereby Amanda had a tiny build at five foot, two inches. The gown would have had to be taken in drastically and cut down considerably with most of the beautiful lace trim removed. Amanda didn't want to subject the wedding dress to such a change. It was a memory Sylvie held dear and worn also by her daughter, Sarah Joy when she wed. It would be selfish of Amanda to rob Sylvie of passing the gown down to one of her two granddaughters, or onto future generations. So, there was nothing left to do but purchase a gown from Flora's, the only women's dress shop in Willow Creek.

Flora Remington, widowed for many years, was a pleasant woman in her fifties. She wore her light brown hair pulled high atop her head in a thick bun and had large, round hazel-green eyes. She smiled a lot, agreed a lot, giggled often, and had nothing but nice things to say about everyone. Short, plump, and fair-skinned, she didn't particularly stand out in a crowd, but once you got to know her, she shined.

Flora's dress shop was a small establishment located on the corner of Main Street and Danvers Avenue. The front half of the building served as the store, and the back part and upper floors were Flora's living quarters. Here, she raised a son, who was grown, married and worked as a bank teller in New York City. Employed in the fashion industry, Flora's daughter-in-law kept the little Willow Creek shop well informed and amply stocked with the latest styles.

Early Wednesday morning, Amanda walked into

Flora's. Never had she ever bought a dress off the rack, or even been in a position to shop in such a way. For the last thirty years, she'd worn buckskin dresses, tunics, and skirts handmade by the tribe's women. Nothing went on beneath, as it was not the Apache way. Free from frills and fuss made for easier living in a wickiup, while hunting with a bow and arrows, or spear, and doing laundry beside a creek.

Upon entering the shop, she was struck with the displays of handbags, gloves, hats, shoes, jewelry, and hosiery. It all became very intimidating, as she hadn't exactly lived a conventional pioneer woman's life. If not for Flora's warm welcome, she probably would have turned tail and immediately walked out the door.

"How can I help you on this beautiful day, miss?" Flora offered. Her soft tone was a true comfort to the tangled mass of nerves jumping beneath Amanda's flesh.

"My name is Amanda Eagle, and I'm getting married on Saturday, a second marriage as I am widowed, and I need a dress. Not a white dress, as that wouldn't really be appropriate. But something still as nice—you know—romantic, or should I say pleasing to the eye...to my new husband's eye, that is—as I want him to think I am beautiful." She took an audible breath. "Oh, listen to me...I'm making no sense at all," she said, clipping her tongue, embarrassed at the way she was rattling on.

Flora giggled. "You've made complete sense to me, Amanda Eagle. And whether it is your first marriage or the fifth, all brides are nervous and anxious to look their best for their man. So, if you'd take a seat over here." She led her to a rose-colored arm chair. "I think I have the perfect gown."

She watched Flora's round form waddle down a hallway and disappear into a back room. While waiting for the shopkeeper to return, she glanced around again, this time leisurely, at all the merchandise elegantly exhibited. Pearl-beaded handbags of all shapes and sizes hung from hooks. Chains of gold and silver supported stone pendants and lockets. Gloves of white, black, made of cotton and lace, complemented monogramed handkerchiefs, hosiery, and shoes.

When Flora returned she carried a light blue gown, so pale was the color that at first glance it appeared to be a dusty-white. But then, up close the bluish hue became more obvious with its satiny shine swirling in the material. The scooped neckline and wrist cuffs were lined in a cream-colored lace, so delicate and fine it looked like a web spun by a spider.

"Was this what you had in mind?" Flora handed the gown to Amanda.

She gasped. "Yes—exactly."

"And this little headband with the blue and white flowers accompanies the gown nicely to be worn around a bun...the wisp of veiling flowing only to the back of your ears. A nice touch, I would say. Distinguishes you as the bride, yet not overpowering," Flora said.

"It's all so perfect." She ran her fingers over the tiny artificial buds.

Flora smiled. "Then, shall I show you to a dressing room for a fit?"

"Yes—yes, please," she said, her heart racing with anticipation. "And I will need undergarments, and gloves, shoes and a handbag...and...and..."

Flora giggled again. "One step at a time, Amanda." She placed an affectionate hand on her arm. "I assure you, by the time you leave my shop today, you will have everything you need, and be the most beautiful of brides."

She bit her bottom lip. "I hope so, Flora—I truly hope so." She followed the other woman into the dressing room.

When she exited Flora's shop, she had not only purchased her complete nuptial attire, including the wedding night sleepwear, but also a nice frock to wear to Gabriel's ceremony. Added to the lot was a few simple yet comfortable day dresses, skirts, and blouses as everyday apparel, a couple of Sunday suits to wear to church, the appropriate undergarments worn beneath each outfit, and accessories to match.

She made up for the many years she didn't shop, in this one excursion. And truthfully, she didn't know when she had as much fun. Flora, of course, was also extremely pleased. After the shopping spree, the other woman invited her to partake in afternoon tea and finger sandwiches. The thought of such an invite thrilled her, and immediately she accepted. Since the afternoon business was slow, she was able to learn much about Flora, and vice versa, as the two women chatted well into the afternoon.

"My word, Amanda, you've lived such an adventurous and interesting life." Flora poured her the third cup of tea.

"Hard at times, and tedious as well." She sipped the brew.

"But was it all worth it?" Flora's large, round eyes searched Amanda's face.

She smiled. "Extremely, I wouldn't change a thing." She relaxed in her seat. "Although, now that my sad circumstances have plucked me from those times and plopped me into different terms, I am anxious to make the very best of it all. I've known my husband-to-be since I was a little girl and love him for the good man he is...has always been to me and my family. I am confident we can have a wonderful life together."

Flora sighed. "And an empty bed, with no loving arms to hold you at night, can be so cold and lonely."

"Yes, it can at that." She tilted her head sideways and contemplated the lovely woman sitting across the table from her. "Have you never thought of marrying again?"

Flora's creamy complexion crimsoned. "Oh, my word, no. I mean, who would want...who would I..."

"Many men would be honored to claim your hand in marriage, and if you don't seek you will not find," she said.

Flora giggled like a school girl. "I wouldn't even know where to begin."

She joined in on the mirth, as the other woman's bubbly laugh brought a joyous lilt to her own heart. "How about being a guest at my wedding on Saturday, for starters?"

Flora's blush deepened. "Oh, I couldn't possibly be so bold."

"Oh, but I wish you would. Outside of the few women in the tribe and Sylvie, I haven't any other female friends." She arched a brow. "Besides, perhaps it's time for you to have an adventure of your own. And I just happen to know someone just as lonely as you who is in need of being sought—should you suddenly decide to do some seeking while you join us."

Flora bit her bottom lip, thinking over the idea. "And does this lonely someone have a name?"

She could see the hopeful gleam in Flora's eyes. "He does indeed."

"Do tell," Flora said, a small spark of interest flavoring her tone.

She leaned forward in her chair. "He goes by the name of Vernon Washburn."

## Chapter Eighteen

Josh sat around the outdoor fire pit, legs crossed like the others. The flames illuminated the beauty of Amanda's angelic features while the lanterns lit and hung in various locations cast eerie shadows about the place. She sat close beside him, her chin raised in pride for her son, who now took the vow of chief.

Amanda wasn't dressed in traditional Apache garb. Instead, she chose a green-checked cotton dress, trimmed with white lace. It hugged her tiny waist, the neckline dipping just enough to accentuate the full bosom concealed beneath. Around her shoulders was a plain green shawl. She sat in a cross-legged fashion, her full skirt covering her knees, beautiful knees that were once in full view when she wore the deerskin dress.

He remembered well the night he saw her dance in that dress for Proud Eagle's father, Chief Cunning Eagle. The whole, flesh-thrilling scene came back to him in full volume, as the drums began to beat all around him. The way she swayed her hips, lost in the rhythm of the drums, and wearing nothing beneath the deerskin so skimpily covering her beautiful body.

"This is the first time I am seeing this ceremony," Amanda whispered. "I was in Willow Creek, with you and Grace, at the parsonage when Proud Eagle became the tribe's chief, remember?"

He nodded, fighting with his thoughts to focus on

the present.

"I was waiting for my Aunt Kaylena Bentley to arrive from England when Cunning Eagle died, and Proud Eagle was made chief," she reminded him further.

"Aye, that's true," Josh whispered. "Truth be told, only Little Elk, Owl Woman, Falling Star, and Rising Sun have seen this ceremony. All the others are too young and would only remember Proud Eagle as their chief."

"You're right, Josh. This ceremony is a new experience for many here. We are witnessing a historic moment," she said with a smile. Then added somewhat awed, "And to think, my son is a huge part of it all." She waved a hand, gesturing to the land surrounding them. "All of this—Eagle's Landing, those coming from Ireland, the wickiups and wood-framed homes dwelling in peace on the same land—I know one day will be in the history books children read in school. And they will see how different cultures can come together, live in harmony, become a village...a town...a place where everyone helps their neighbor and the strong sense of family."

He arched a skeptical brow. "We must take one step at a time."

Her smile faded, and instantly he regretted his words. "I am not a fool, Josh. There is much yet to do, a journey we must all make before we come to such a wonderful place. But it is beginning, and a mere five years ago all this wouldn't have ever been something the Apache people could even dream of happening. So, in retrospect of what was and what is now planning to be, I'd say much progress has been made and hope abounds."

"I was only trying to remain..." he began.

"Negative," she interrupted.

He frowned. "Nay, practical."

"Which is one thing I admire about you, the practical and steadfast way you are there to smooth over every situation, get us through the hard times, and keep a level head while doing so." She leaned closer...so close, their knees touched, sending currents of desire through his body. "But sometimes you have to let the practical go and give dreams a chance." She placed a hand over his. At her touch his flesh burned with passion. "Perhaps I can show you how that's done—now and then—when practical isn't always necessary or the only answer."

He looked deep into her sultry sapphire eyes. "Aye, I'd like that."

Her smile returned. "So would I."

*Oh, my beautiful wife-to-be, if you should ever discover how easily I would yield all to you...that with a bat of your eyes or a small caress you could keep me spellbound. You enchant every facet of my being. Like a sorceress casting magic, you have captured me to do all you bid, give to you anything you ask...and I do it willingly.*

Very slowly she brought her lips to his cheek and planted a tender kiss there, which warmed his heart and heated his loins even more so. "I want to always make you happy, please you, give you a loving home." She sighed, her warm breath upon his chin exciting his senses further. "Will you let me be that kind of wife to you?"

He swallowed hard, forcing his voice to respond.

"Aye, you must know I welcome such care." Taking her hand, he entwined his fingers with hers. "And will you accept the same measures from me?"

"I will." She turned her attention to the ceremony, leaving him riddled with a yearning so strong, he was ready to scoop her into his embrace and carry her away. He would show her how much he could comply with the promises he spoke.

"Amanda, I..." he began.

She arched a brow and relayed to him his own words. "One step at a time, Josh."

"Aye, my love," he agreed reluctantly. Then he added. "But after you are mine, I..."

She giggled like a school girl, interrupting him again. "Say no more, just surprise me."

Her playfulness, boldness, willingness to be his, thrilled him. "My dear woman, you are a bloody tease."

She flashed him a seductive look. "And you love it."

He chuckled, comfortable with how well she knew him, how easy they could banter. "Aye, I do...I love you."

Her eyes softened. "As I do you, Josh."

And at that moment, it happened—his heart soared.

But her face froze at the sight of Falling Star placing the chief's headdress upon Gabriel's head.

He had a strong idea what was going through her mind. "Amanda..." He hoped to comfort her, but his attempt was interrupted by Gabriel's acceptance speech.

"I promise to listen with a wise and caring heart, and to stand by my people. To keep alive the Apache traditions. To be fair, to be loyal, to be responsible for my actions at all times. To walk the steps of my elders and remember the path of wisdom bestowed upon me by my ancestors. And I will always know I am born of proud blood," Gabriel announced. "This village, which will one day be a town called Eagle's Landing, is my father's legacy—his hope of freedom for his people. Out of the sorrow and grief of his death, we will change our lives, blazing a new trail and leaving a better place to live for generations to come. I vow Proud Eagle's passing will not be in vain."

The tribe's peopled cheered.

Then Gabriel held out his hand to his wife, and she came forth from the circle to stand beside him. "And my wife, Riley Redbird, will also be available for any that might need her council, as she is also a part of this tribe. I wish for her to be just as welcomed as I have been." He met his mother's gaze. "Just as welcomed and trusted as you made Golden Lady when she married my father."

She remained unmoving, her eyes focused on her son, tears glistening in her gaze. Josh squeezed her hand, and his affection provoked a small, thankful smile from her full lips.

After the ceremony, roasted chicken and rabbit were served, along with cornbread, dumplings, and a variety of nuts and berries. She ate little, speaking only when spoken to, forcing a smile here and there. Her sadness tormented him, broke his heart. And as the evening wore on, he grew more and more concerned over her behavior.

He grabbed a lantern and tried to chivvy her from her seat. "Please, come with me to a quieter place so we might talk."

Reluctantly she agreed, and they walked to the other side of the creek. He led the way, stopping behind a tree. Leaning against the trunk, she placed her feet apart, like the roots of the giant oak shielding her.

"Please, love, talk to me."

She swallowed hard and took an audible breath. "I don't know if it would be appropriate, this being the night before we are to wed."

"Because it has to do with Proud Eagle," he guessed.

She nodded. "I don't want you to start believing you're living in his shadow because such a notion would be far from the truth. I see you for who you are."

"I realize this, my love," he reassured her. "Please, tell me what troubles you."

"It was a bit of a shock, seeing Gabriel in the headdress." She cleared the emotion from her throat. "He looked so much like his father, or as his father once was."

Gently he caressed the side of her face with the tip of his finger. "I had an idea such emotions were the culprit for your change of heart."

She searched his face. "You have witnessed many deaths, I'm sure."

"Aye, it is a fact that comes with my clerical calling."

"And do you not agree death is a mysterious thing?"

He hooked the lantern on a nearby limb. "Aye, it is much like a veil suddenly brought down between the one dying and those left living."

Her eyes widened. "Yes...yes, exactly. As Proud Eagle lay dying, he appeared to look the same, but in all actuality he wasn't. He was no longer the robust man I once knew—that my son is now. His skin color changed with each passing day, his breathing was labored, the clarity in his eyes faded, his muscular form dwindled. And he talked less and less as the infection spread and ravaged his body. Nearer and nearer death approached, and he became weaker and weaker to resist it." She shivered. "I felt so alone sitting by his side, watching—waiting for him to take his last breath, even though there was an entire tribe there to mourn with me."

"But you weren't alone, my love. God was also there at that deathbed, ready to take Proud Eagle's soul. And He was there for you as well, for the sorrow of all those left behind. And in His divine peace, He left you all a calm reverence...a holiness, so to speak, that is the aura of death...and the noble way it brings us to heaven."

"I felt so helpless," she whispered. "There was absolutely nothing I could do for him."

"You were with him, my love, beside him at the most pertinent time of his life. I'm positive your presence meant everything to Proud Eagle, brought him comfort in those last moments." He tightened her shawl around her shoulders.

"Is that ever enough, Josh?"

"Aye, I believe so," he said softly. "Not to die alone is so important." Pulling her close, he placed a tender kiss upon her lips. Even in her saddened state, she returned the affection. "Come with me back to the fire, before you catch a chill." Again he adjusted her shawl for better warmth.

She nodded, and together they walked hand in hand

to where the others made merry on Gabriel's important night.

**\*\*\*\***

Amanda was met by her daughter-in-law.

"There you two are." Riley stifled a smile when she glanced down at their joined hands.

Her cheeks heated at the notions her sweet, romantic daughter-in-law was having. "We just needed some time to chat."

"No need to explain," Riley said. "I just wanted to tell you Gabriel and I will be staying in his lodge tonight, so we won't be traveling back to the parsonage. And my cousin Maggie has been invited to stay with Little Elk and Owl Woman. The two ladies share an interest in herbal healing."

She frowned. "You do not mind sleeping in the wickiup?"

Riley shrugged. "I would not want to live full time in such a dwelling, although before Auntie Lucinda took me in, my accommodations in London were much worse. But until our home is built, I think it is important the tribe's people see I am committed to their chief— and them. It appears to be quite comfortable and clean, and everyone has gone out of their way to make it presentable for my presence. Besides," she blushed, "I've never slept a night apart from my husband since taking my wedding vows, and it is important for him to remain in the village."

"I understand fully," she said. "And you are wise for making such a sound decision."

"And don't fret; we will all be on time for your nuptials tomorrow. After all, Gabriel and I are your witnesses," Riley added. "Gabriel has already set things up with Mr. Washburn, who has been kind enough to agree to hitch his two horses to the two wagons he owns, making it possible for us all to secure a ride into Willow Creek."

"That is extremely thoughtful of him," Josh said. "I must remember to thank him for his consideration before we leave."

"Then, you will be gathering your belongings after the wedding and staying here at Eagle's Landing?"

"Aye, that's the plan. It will enable Gabriel to have a bird's eye view of the village's construction, which should happen as soon as the folks from Ireland arrive. Plus, with us gone, it will free up some space at the parsonage and give Sylvie and Reverend Ben a little more privacy," Riley said.

She sighed. "Ah, yes, those two have been overly generous with their home. I, myself, am anxious to leave."

Riley frowned. "I was wondering, is there anything you can advise me on...I mean, you were the chief's wife for three decades, and a white woman."

She placed a reassuring hand on her daughter-in-law's arm. "I am here for you in every way you need, although you seem to have it together all on your own." She looked around at those surrounding her, laughing and chatting, enjoying the evening and eating the food. "These people are good hearted, forgiving, helpful, and friendly. If you show them loyalty and respect, they will welcome you as one of their own. They will comfort you in times of sorrow, and stand with you through times of trial. And they will always be your family."

Riley moved to embrace Amanda, placing a gentle

kiss upon her cheek. "Thank you, Mother Amanda. Having you in my corner makes the uncertainties easier to control."

Her heart swelled at the tender affection the younger woman displayed. "I trust you will take over the position I once held with love and grace, and you will make my son a very proud man." She smiled pushing aside a wayward lock of auburn hair from Riley's forehead, a motherly gesture she was moved to express. "So, trouble yourself no longer, my daughter."

On the way to the parsonage she remained silent. Thankfully Josh didn't question her mood, allowing her to continue in deep thought. His care this evening, and the consideration shown her while they rode to Willow Creek, proved his support and understanding. She had some matters to sort out, and the nature of those issues didn't offend him. Quite the contrary, in fact. He saw her point fully, only wanting to help her through the healing process. His patient and loving attitude reinforced her decision to become his wife, as she had no doubts he would be a devoted husband.

That night, alone in her room and snuggled beneath the patchwork quilt, she said her final goodbyes to Proud Eagle. He would definitely remain a part of her. After all, a man one loved for over thirty years and shared three children with wasn't going to go completely away. Proud Eagle would always be with her in a son's eyes or a daughter's smile, but he must now be placed in a part of her heart where he belonged, making room for Josh.

"This moving on is hard to do," she whispered. But it was what Proud Eagle wanted, what Josh hoped for, and what she needed to do. Priorities shift, times change, and a resilient heart can find true love a second time around.

Chapter Nineteen

The sun shone brightly on Josh's wedding day, to his profound relief since the festivities would take place out-of-doors. He looked over at the overnight bag packed and standing in the corner. His surprise for Amanda heightened his anticipation. He made his way to the kitchen early, swallowed down a cup of tea, and then hurried to the garden, where he found Ben and Sylvie setting up the tables and chairs for the reception.

As he lent a hand to the task, Vernon's wagons arrived carrying Gabriel, Riley, Maggie, and the other tribespeople. And then the household erupted into one chaotic clamor, with the last minute food preparations and other outstanding details that could only be accomplished that day.

Amanda stayed in her room, and her breakfast was brought to her, as was a tub for bathing. He had hoped to speak to her, but the women made it clear it was bad luck for the groom to see the bride before the wedding. He had no chance of even catching a glimpse of his love, with all the female activity coming and going in and out of Amanda's bedroom.

But he did catch a whiff of the jasmine bath oil being used, and pictured her smoothing it over her soft flesh. The thought of them being skin to skin come nightfall, the aroma enticing his senses along with every other part of her being, brought a thrilling bolt of

171

heat to his loins. He would have every right, as her husband, to caress and make love to her, an act he dreamed of doing many evenings before falling asleep. He prayed she would be as willing to love him as fully as he planned on loving her. And with all these feelings, thoughts, and emotions circling within his mind and body, he made his way to his own quarters, to rest and get himself ready for the vows he had waited to take for most of his adult life.

****

Amanda's time to leave her room arrived. Garbed in the beautiful day-gown, tinted with only a whisper of blue, she watched in the mirror as Riley put the finishing touches to her hair, which was swept up in a bun atop her head and adorned with the veiled headpiece of white and blue flowers.

Flora removed the tissue paper from around the matching shoes and helped Amanda slip her feet into each one.

"Mother Amanda, you look exquisite." Riley stood back to admire her handiwork.

"She's right, Amanda." Flora straightened the lace at the collar. "And the blue of your eyes complements the dress's shade perfectly."

"The Reverend will be so taken with your beauty; he will have a hard time swallowing his meal." Riley giggled.

"I'm not so sure I will have much of an appetite myself." Her stomach felt as if butterflies danced within.

"Aye, I know what you mean," Riley agreed. "I can't even remember eating on my wedding day."

She turned to face her daughter-in-law and placed a

hand upon her arm. "I wish I could have been there to see how beautiful you looked and how happy you made my son."

Riley squeezed her hand. "Well, we are all together now, to share *your* special day."

She smiled. "Yes—yes we are."

"We should be making our way downstairs." Flora walked to the door, then glanced again at Amanda before turning the knob. "Are you ready?"

She took a breath to settle her nerves. "As ready as I'll ever be."

Gabriel waited for her at the foot of the staircase. When she approached the bottom step, he smiled and extended his arm.

She had to look up to meet his gaze. "I remember when you stood no higher than my knees." She looped her arm through his and gently caressed the material of his jacket. "How did so much time pass?"

"It is the way of life, my mother. We are born, we grow, we learn, and we die," he said, his smile fading. "And if we are fortunate, in between we love, laugh, and cry."

"I miss him too, Gabriel," she whispered. "My heart will never forget your father, even though I've found love again."

"Of all people, my mother, this I understand."

"No sad thoughts, today." Riley picked up on her husband's sullen mood. "Today is about love and laughter and maybe crying only happy tears."

Gabriel chuckled as he watched his wife walk on ahead to open the front door. "My beautiful Redbird is a spirit-lifter."

She sighed. "To know your heart as well as she

does is a true showing of love. I hope you realize how blessed you are, my son."

"Every day, my mother, every single day."

"Then we both have resilient hearts."

Upon entering the church, her buoyant heart leapt with joy. Candles lit the room, some in lanterns and others in ornate candle holders. Vases of flowers were placed about, their aroma filling the church. As her son escorted her down the aisle, her friends' smiles added to her joy. Josh stood at the altar, proud and handsome, wearing a light gray suit perfectly tailored to fit his muscular frame.

The outfit was set off by a shirt with only a hint of blue...like her day-gown, and a charcoal gray tie. His ensemble complemented her own so well, she knew Flora coordinated it all, but when and how? She would have to thank her new friend for all she'd done to make both bride and groom look so nice.

She smiled at him as she approached, catching his scent of musk and spice...a soft, manly aroma that sent her yearnings into a tail-spin. His first glance was so loving, so warm her eyes pooled with tears...happy tears...which glistened in his gaze as well.

And when Gabriel took her hand and placed it in Josh's, her future husband whispered, "You are the most beautiful vision I have ever seen."

As they spoke their vows, her heart was filled with love and hope for the years ahead they would share as husband and wife. His soft touch as he placed the wedding band upon her finger melted her heart. The ring she in turn slid on his brought her the realization he was truly hers. And his kiss stirred her desire to the point where she happily anticipated their wedding night.

When they made their way to the garden, her head was buzzing with bliss. She gasped as she took in the sight before her. Transformed into an elegant dining veranda, the garden patio was dressed in garlands of flowers matching the ones garnishing her hair.

Several tables were placed about, covered in white tablecloths and adorned with crystal vases filled with the same blooms decorating the church. Off to the left, a long buffet table was spread with all sorts of hot and cold dishes. And to the right, another table housed the wedding cake, frosted in a blue and white combination.

"Everything is perfect."

"A perfect wedding for a more than perfect bride." Josh escorted her to their table.

After Ben said a prayer blessing the newly married couple, wine was served for Gabriel to propose the toast. Her son stood, pausing a moment to collect his thoughts. "To my mother, and my stepfather, may they live long and love true for all the days of their lives."

Though his salute was brief, it warmed her within. As she raised her glass to click against Josh's, everyone shouted, "Here, here."

Looking around for Flora, she spotted her sitting alone at a table. On a further survey she found Vernon, also sitting alone. Excusing herself from the table, she shared with Josh, she made her way over to where Flora sat.

"Thank you for all you've done to make us a handsome couple."

Flora's round face broke into a cheery smile. "It was my pleasure."

"Now, come with me." She grasped her friend's

hand and led her to where Vernon sat. "Vernon Washburn, I'd be right proud to introduce you to my dear friend, Flora Remington."

Flora's plump cheeks turned crimson, and Vernon just blinked—like an owl.

Amanda bit her bottom lip, suddenly worried she made too bold of a move. But then she thought of how lonely these two were, and it encouraged her to speak further.

"On this joyous occasion...mine and Josh's special day...I wanted two of my friends to become friends as well. I hope you won't mind indulging the bride."

"I don't mind in the least." Vernon stood and bowed to Flora.

"Nor I." Flora tilted her head slightly.

"Splendid, then I shall return to my husband." She left the pair to work things out for themselves.

When she reclaimed her seat beside Josh, he merely arched a brow.

She shrugged. "What can I say...I believe in second chances."

He smiled. "As do I."

"Besides," she added, "love is in the air."

He inhaled sharply, his smile deepening. "Aye, that it is. And I intend to bathe in it tonight, with my dear wife, in privacy." His eyes twinkled. "I have a surprise for you."

She smiled. "I love surprises."

"I've rented, for the next three days, a honeymoon suite at the Willow Creek Hotel."

Her eyes widened. "Surely you jest?"

He chuckled. "Oh, love, I assure you I speak the truth." He leaned in to whisper in her ear. "I want no interruptions as I am making you mine for the very first time."

Her entire body flushed. "Why, Reverend Holmes, you are intolerable."

He cast a roguish smile. "Aye, Mrs. Holmes, and it would serve you well to get used to it."

She pretended to pout. "Well, I suppose if I haven't any other choice..."

"You haven't."

"Very well then, Reverend Holmes, I am all yours to do with as you wish."

He swallowed hard and cleared his throat.

She giggled. "Have I left you speechless?"

He cleared his throat a second time. "Aye, love, that you have. But no harm done because I hadn't planned on us doing much talking."

Leaning in, she planted a gentle kiss upon his lips, then whispered against his mouth. "I'm extremely glad to hear that."

Soon, the food was served. Then Little Elk played the drums, and Vernon played his guitar. Everyone danced, laughed, and enjoyed themselves.

When it was time for them to cut the cake, she noticed Josh had barely touched his meal.

"You were not hungry?"

He pulled her close and whispered in her ear. "Nay, love...not for food."

\*\*\*\*

Though his wife was dressed in a gown much the color of the large ice block beneath the food chest, she was anything but a cool presence. Truth be told, heat radiated from her being, and it set him on fire. Jasmine from her silky flesh heightened his senses—desire for her burning within him.

So when she turned to him, with those large, almond shaped, sapphire orbs, and softly said, "I'm going upstairs to change and pack a few essentials for our get-away," he quickly agreed, but was interrupted by Edmond Dodd.

"I know this isn't exactly the best time to bring up business, but if the two of you could sign the deed papers, I can get to work the first thing on Monday to file the claim."

Reluctantly Josh agreed. "We can use Ben's den.

Gabriel and Riley joined them, along with Ben and Sylvie, as they needed to be witnesses to the signatures.

"I think it would be best, Amanda, if you sign with your maiden name, as well as your previous and present married names. In this way there is no misunderstanding you are related to all past and present people listed on the deed, and fully entitled to inherit the property should any deaths occur," Edmond advised.

She nodded, smiling over at Josh before she signed. "It will be the first time I am writing my new name."

He felt a surge of pride wash over him and returned the smile.

After the others left the room, Riley turned to Amanda. "How exciting for you two to have some time alone."

"I was truly surprised and very pleased." Amanda glanced at him.

"We really should be on our way, my love," he said, anxious to get her to himself.

"I'll help you change and pack a few things for

your honeymoon," Riley said.

"And I'll ready the wagon," Gabriel offered.

Once in his own quarters, he shed his wedding clothes. Looking around the small, quiet room he smiled. Never again would he sleep alone, wake alone, go through life alone. He was wed—he had a wife—he was a husband. The impact of this truth suddenly hit him in volumes.

He sat upon the bed, wearing only his underwear, and contemplated his new status with awe. This had to be the happiest day of his life, and tonight, tonight he would live what he'd only dreamed. With his passion mounting, he dressed in a light-weight black pair of trousers and a white shirt, then made his way downstairs to wait for his bride.

Amanda had changed into a coral dress trimmed with a white collar and cuffs. She wore her hair plaited in a braid that hung down her back and to her waist. The garden party played on; laughter and music could be heard.

"Should we say our good-byes to the rest of the guests?"

"Nay. Let's just slip away quietly." Josh led her to the wagon at the side of the parsonage, deposited their bags in the back, and helped her into the seat. He took the reins. "I think it is best only Gabriel and Riley know where we are going, just in case someone decided to continue the party beneath our window."

She giggled. "You are a wise man."

The twenty minute ride to the Willow Creek Hotel felt much longer to Josh. Anticipation for this night grew, as did his hope of fulfilling her with his love. But then a rush of doubt crossed his mind. Would she submit to his yearnings, and if so, could he please her?

His misgivings must have reflected on his face, because she gently placed a hand upon his thigh and sighed. "All will be fine, Josh."

And like a soothing balm to an open wound, her words and actions calmed him—reassured him, and once more complete and utter contentment filled him. He imagined this was how it would always be when he became anxious, just an encouraging word from her or a tender show of affection, and he'd be at peace once again. He'd seen such closeness between his sister and her husband, as well as the devotion his parents showed for each other. He always hoped he'd have a marriage much the same.

Before now, he'd given up ever achieving such status. And although they were not a young couple, her forty-nine and him sixty-one, they were relatively in good shape. There was nothing to say they wouldn't have many more years ahead of them to enjoy and cultivate a relationship like he admired between the folks he loved.

He had spared no expense. The large, exquisite honeymoon suite he rented was done in red and gold. An oriental carpet blanketed the floor and several rich tapestries hung on the walls, all proving what money could buy.

She gasped upon entering the doubled-oak doors. "My heavens, such elegance."

He beamed. "You are pleased, then?"

She tore her gaze from the marble columns separating the sitting room from the bedroom area to glance in his direction. "Pleased hardly explains it."

He made his way to the bottle of champagne and

glasses sitting on a nearby table. As he opened the bottle, she meandered over to the large, marble fireplace. In admiration she ran the tip of her finger over the polished mantel. He poured them each a glass of the pink bubbly and made his way over to where she stood.

"Can you fathom such beauty?" She took the glass he handed her.

He searched her face. "Aye, for it stands right here in front of me."

She giggled. "You are way too kind."

"I only speak the truth, my love."

She raised her glass. "To always speaking the truth."

He saluted her in turn and added, "And to true love."

"Yes, always to love." She took a sip of the champagne.

After downing his drink, he took her empty glass and placed them on the table. She remained by the fireplace, watching the flames. Spring nights in Arizona were always cold, even if the day was warm.

He made his way to the window and closed the heavy, gold drapes. For a moment an awkward silence filled the room.

Then, very softly she said, "Would you help to unbutton my dress?"

"Aye," was all he could manage to say, knowing this would be the prelude for wonderful things to come. And for an instant his stomach fluttered, his heart raced, as he turned to face her. But she still gazed at the flames, her back to him, the long braid cascading down the path of buttons he'd soon be unfastening. He wiped his sweaty palms along the sides of his trousers, and reached her within a few steps. As he began working the tiny, pearled fasteners, his hands trembled, his fingers suddenly feeling foreign and clumsy.

She remained staring at the fire until the last button was released, then she turned to face him. "All will be fine." She placed a hand upon his cheek.

With that small but intimate gesture, his body reacted. He turned to kiss her palm, and then pulled her close. While his lips kissed her neck, his hands slipped the dress off her shoulders, down her arms, and then to her waist. She threw her head back, allowing him to explore her cleavage with his mouth...her warm flesh burning his lips. He released the straps of her chemise and pulled it down to her waist, freeing her full breasts. The erect nipples beckoned him, and he suckled each one, drawing the hard peaks into his mouth—caressing them with a swirling tongue. She groaned with pleasure, encouraging him to go further.

With his loins on fire, he swept her up into his arms and carried her to the large canopy bed, covered with a gold satin bedspread and heaped with red pillows. He removed her dress like he was unwrapping a priceless gift, slowly, savoring every moment, until she stood naked before him. When she sat, he removed her stockings and shoes, thrilling over the shapely legs he was privileged to touch.

When she was free from all her garments, she stood and did the same to him. Her dainty hands stroked his arms, caressed his chest as she peeled away his shirt. And then she hesitated, her sapphire eyes gazing deep into his. Within them his heart and soul reflected in their core. She was his, he was hers—the way it always should have been. And in that second, standing naked before him, she said everything he needed to hear without uttering a word. Her eyes did all the talking for her, and they spoke volumes. Her bold desire fueled his. In one fluid motion, he picked her up and placed her upon the bed, then stripped himself of his trousers, shoes, and socks.

"Oh Josh...my Josh." Her eyes focused on the swollen member throbbing between his thighs.

As he joined her upon the bed, all things were enveloped by her in this room...her voice, her body, the flow of her hair. And nothing else outside of these walls mattered at that moment. He covered her mouth with his, the feel of her soft lips against his broke his resolve. He deepened the kiss, tasting fully her sweetness, and drank in the welcoming sensations of desire and want rippling through him. Already his body was addicted to needing more of her, and he would never again be able to settle for less than everything she had to give.

Kissing her had altered him...weak with fervor and strong with passion, he set about learning every inch of her body.

First with his touch...she groaned with pleasure as his finger teased her wet crevasse. Gently he entered her willing tunnel, probing its moist, hot walls. Her surrender brought a longing, an unyielding desire to his loins as his finger circled within her juices.

Then he pleased her with his tongue. She gasped when he brought his mouth down to meet her womanhood. Opening her thighs wider, she arched her back, pressing herself against the feather-like flicks. He increased the motion, and soon she shattered with passion, trembling with ecstasy.

His body craved a blissful release, and he moved to enter her with his engorged staff. But to his shock and excitement, she moved to straddle him, shifting to position herself over his erection. Her long, thick braid floated down one breast, as she sank onto him. Her moist heat slid over his length, enveloping him in feverish desire.

Their gazes locked as her hips moved up and down, teasing him to explode. His hands grasped her waist, slowing the tempo and gliding her along to prolong his pleasure. After dreaming of this very moment for decades, he wanted to savor the sensational feeling of an earthquake building inside of him. And then he felt the muscles in her thighs tense as her body again trembled with the waves of pleasure that washed through her.

As she pulsed around him, his orgasm overtook him—rocking the foundation of his very existence. He filled her with his hot juices, finally becoming one with the woman he loved—had always loved—would never stop loving. And with this intimate act of affection, new life breathed into his spirit, set his heart afire, and he saw nothing...wanted nothing but her in his world.

When she collapsed onto his chest, he embraced her, their heartbeats mingling as they raced. She nuzzled her face beneath his chin, and he caressed her back. Then he moved his hands down to her soft, round bum and caressed her there...the tip of a finger probing the entry. She was his now, and he was free to touch her wherever he wanted. But what thrilled him the most was that she wanted him as well. She did not protest his boldness but instead parted her thighs, protruded her bum, and remained in his arms to accept his explorations. She was relaxed, sighing contently as he stroked her in such a personal way, the slickness of their sweat coating the flesh between them.

"You are amazing." He kissed the top of her head.

"Then you are pleased with me?" Her hands moved to his shoulders.

He took an audible breath, his body still tingling. "Pleased hardly explains it."

She lifted her face to meet his gaze. "I love you, Josh...truly I do."

"And I love you, Amanda, forever and for always." He captured her mouth once again.

## Chapter Twenty

A lot can happen in three days' time. Amanda, feeling at ease with her new role as Josh's wife and accustomed to sleeping in the raw, had no problems continuing this practice. "Nightclothes are way too confining, and besides I've slept in such a fashion for decades, I don't plan on changing now."

Her husband arched a brow. "You'll get no argument from me, my love."

And so it went, the two of them barely clothed, eating in bed, taking the time to explore each other's bodies. There was no blood on the bed sheets, for her maidenhood had been long gone. She didn't quiver with innocence or blush with shyness, for she knew what her body craved and what satisfied her. In return, she knew how to please her spouse. Without coaxing or instruction, she complied—bringing Josh to complete ecstasy.

She thought memories of her time loving Proud Eagle, who taught her how to express her desires, would come between her and Josh while in their bed. After all, he was the only man up to that point to be intimate with her. But Proud Eagle's spirit remained quiet, allowing her to focus on sharing familiarities with her new husband. And Josh bathed in her experience, was thrilled by her boldness, and hungrily wanted more. She fulfilled his hunger, as well as her own, and as a result they did not emerge from the honeymoon suite until they were ready to check out and return to the parsonage.

Much had happened at the vicarage as well. The two Irish families had arrived and were camped on the property, ready to begin the house-building, and just in time since the paperwork was properly signed and the property legally claimed.

A man from Australia, by the name of Eli Granger, a sheep farmer coming to America to start his business, had heard of Gabriel's village and showed up at the door. Beaten by the thieves who robbed him of his money, Eli came to the parsonage in quite a pitiful state—dehydrated, half-starved, and feeling ill from a fever. Maggie Mulligan, taking a fancy to the man, immediately put herself in charge of his care, bringing food and water to the barn where he bunked.

And lastly, Riley announced she was with child the night of the wedding, giving more cause for celebration. She kept it hushed as not to steal the bride's attention but broke the news after the newlyweds departed. Gabriel nearly fell off his chair with joy. Thus the reason the two remained at the parsonage, near to Willow Creek's physician, Jonas Campbell...who confirmed the prognosis Owl Woman made days ago. Until Sean O'Clarity, the Irish doctor was settled and his practice open for business, Gabriel preferred he and Riley stay in town.

"Gabriel is being so overprotective," Riley said, exasperated. "The last three days he's acting as though I am made of glass, follows me everywhere, makes sure I eat everything on my plate, and insists I nap during the day." She sighed heavily. "I've loved Gabriel from the moment I knew he existed, but his smothering is going to drive me insane. It's not as though I'm ready to give birth at any given time. I still have another seven months to go."

"He wants nothing to go wrong this time," she explained to her daughter-in-law. "Losing a wife and child is devastating."

Riley sighed again. "I know about Fire Star and the baby, and I understand Gabriel's concerns. But if I'm made to heed his worries, by the time this baby is born, I will either be bored out of my mind or frightened to death."

She lovingly pushed an auburn curl aside from the younger woman's forehead. "Would you like me to have a talk with him?"

Riley's face brightened. "Could you...would you mind terribly?"

"Not at all," she said. "Now, it's a lovely day and a little exercise never hurt any expecting mother. So, how about a stroll in the garden?"

That evening after the late meal, Amanda searched for her son. She found him in the barn, chatting with Eli Granger, an interesting looking man with wide-set blue eyes and slicked-back, honey-brown hair grazing his shirt collar. His manners were in order, as he struggled to stand upon Gabriel's introductions, tipping his head in polite respect.

And she courteously inquired about his health. "I hope you are feeling better, Mr. Granger."

"Much better, thank you, ma'am." He winced as he sat back down upon a bale of hay, crossing a long, lean leg over the other.

"Eli will be joining us at Eagle's Landing," Gabriel

explained. "I have decided to set him up with a couple dozen sheep. Maggie is experienced in spinning, so come shearing time she can turn the sheep's wool into yarn. Muriel Dodd can weave it on her loom. Blankets, rugs, sweaters, all sorts of wool items can then be sold in Eagle Landing's general store to make a profit for the town."

"Yer son's a good business man, ma'am," Eli said. "I think we'll be able to work well together."

She smiled at the Aussie, her heart beaming with pride. "I'm sure you will, Mr. Granger."

"Eli, ma'am...just call me Eli."

"Well, Eli," she said. "If you don't mind, I'd like to borrow my son for just a few moments."

"Sure, sure, ma'am. We're done for now anyway; besides, Maggie's due to bring me my last cup of coffee for the day." He shook his head. "Never had a *sheila* make so much fuss over me." Then he smiled. "Kinda think I can get used to it."

Gabriel frowned. "Her name is Maggie, not Sheila....best get it right. No woman likes a man calling her another woman's name when she's fawning all over him."

Eli chuckled lightly. "In Australia, *sheila* is a word we use when referrin' to a female."

"Well, explain that to Maggie, would you? No sense getting her all riled up for nothing," Gabriel warned.

Once out into the garden, Amanda inhaled the night air. Pulling her shawl tighter around her shoulders, she glanced up at the pink sky as it bled into the red sunset. "You are awfully worried for Maggie."

The two of them approached a bench and sat.

"Truth be told, I am hoping Maggie and Eli hitch up with one another," he said.

She giggled. "I thought I was the only matchmaker in the family."

He combed a hand through his hair. "It is not so much I care in the way you do, as it is to keep Maggie from driving me insane."

She arched a brow. "Oh?"

"The woman follows me and Riley everywhere, asks tons of questions that are not any of her business, chimes in on our private time, and thinks she is a part of us as a couple. I do not even want to imagine how horrible this whole arrangement is going to become when she moves into our new house with us. And now, with a baby coming..." His voice trailed off.

She frowned. "What did you expect would happen, Gabriel, when you brought her to Willow Creek? You promised her a place with you and your wife, and that plan happens to be the single source the poor woman has for a home life. After all, Riley is her only family here, and you two are the only people she knows."

He stood and paced, booted feet crunching pebbles and twigs as he stepped. "I understand, but it does not make the circumstances any less annoying."

She took stock of the situation. "And so, you're hoping Eli Granger fills the void, and Maggie will then turn her attention to him?"

He nodded. "I am hoping as time passes, she will encourage his favor more and more." Then he added. "Everybody deserves to be with somebody, why cannot Eli and Maggie be somebody to each other?"

"Well, they can, if they elect to by their own accord. But shoving them together for your purpose is hardly proper," she explained.

"If it means keeping my wife from becoming annoyed during her expecting time, then proper or not, I will do my best to promote and cultivate this courtship."

She folded her arms across her chest. "Well, I wonder which one of you will drive poor Riley insane first, you or Maggie."

He frowned. "Why would you think I am part of the problem?"

"Because your wife told me so."

His mouth dropped open.

"Close your mouth and sit." She patted the seat beside her.

"Not until you tell me what my wife said."

"Sit, now, Gabriel."

He complied with a huff and a scowl, like he was eight years old *again*. She had to stifle a smile. As old and as large as he was, he still realized he had to obey his mother.

"Do you remember, when you were about ten years old, the baby wolf you saved after its mother was killed?" she began.

"Yes, but what does this have to do with..."

"You fed and nurtured that pup day and night for months," she interrupted. "You even brought it into the wickiup at night to keep it warm, until your father explained that smothering the critter would harm it greatly. By nature, it needed to be in the wilds to thrive. And coddling it would only stifle the pup's natural instincts so it could never...would never be able to take care of itself. You were so worried for the pup, so scared it would get hurt when left on its own, that you failed to see you were actually doing it more harm than good."

Gabrial frowned. "What are you trying to say, my mother?"

"You are doing it again, Gabriel. Because you are scared Riley will get hurt and lose the baby, you're coddling and smothering the poor woman."

"I am not." He sounded like the little boy she once knew.

She held up a finger for silence, and again he obeyed, though the scowl upon his face worsened. "A woman, during the time she is carrying a child, should be relaxed—content, and happy."

"How have I not made her happy?"

"By worrying extensively over her condition," she said.

"But I am worried extensively over her condition. And I have every right to feel the way I do."

"No, Gabriel, you don't," she snapped.

He frowned. "How can you say that, my mother?"

"Riley is not Fire Star," she began. "Fire Star was always frail and fragile. I believe part of the reason why you fell in love with her was because you could be the big, strong warrior to her delicate maidenhood. You were always there to whisk her off her feet, carry her over puddles, keep her warm, and all of that sort of protecting."

"And what is so wrong about that?"

"Nothing, if the women is in need of such pampering," she explained. "Which Fire Star was...her time expecting was troubled from the start. She was constantly ill, became very weak, needed constant bed rest, and gave birth almost three weeks before her time.

But Riley is of different stock. She is strong, robust, has fended for herself since she was a little girl. Growing up poor and destitute in the slums of England is not for the faint of heart. She learned to be independent, and you watching...commenting...and trying to control every aspect of her life, will only upset and annoy her."

His shoulders slumped, and he glanced down at his boots. "Then what can I do to protect her from...from..." He briefly closed his eyes. "How is it, while life is soon to be brought into the world, I can only think of death?"

"Riley isn't going to die in childbirth, my son," she reassured him.

"How do you know—how does anyone know what woman will make it and what woman will not?"

"Well, it is true; no one knows the outcome of any situation. But if I had to guess, I'd say Riley has a better than great chance of delivering this baby unharmed. She is a healthy woman and is quite able to carry this baby to full term. She's also very capable of going about a normal day without becoming ill...that is, if her husband stops badgering her."

Gabriel raised his eyes to meet her gaze. "What should I do?"

"Find common ground," she advised. "Do you think it was easy for me to adjust to living the Apache way when I was brought up so differently?"

"No, I am sure it was not."

"I can tell you it wasn't," she confirmed. "But what helped me was the loving way your father went about solving those differences. He gave in a little here—I gave in a little there—and together we met somewhere in the middle, able to work everything out." She smiled. "I believe I was in my seventh month carrying you

193

when I brought down a huge buck with a single arrow shot. Then I helped your father drag the carcass back to the village, clean and quarter it, and cook it for about ten tribespeople."

His eyes widened. "Well, I do not expect Riley to go hunting while she carries my baby."

She gave her son an affectionate pat on the arm. "I don't believe she would want to, either. But she would like a little privacy and control of her own body." She tilted her head sideways. "Perhaps you could treat her with respect, and not like a child who doesn't know any better...or an orphaned wolf pup," she added.

He nodded reluctantly.

Just then Maggie made her way to the barn, with Eli's coffee in her hands and a lilt to her walk. "You might be fortunate in that area as well." She gestured to Maggie.

"Why so?" He glanced in Maggie's direction.

"I can spot a woman in love when I see one," she said. "Look how happy and eager she is to serve Eli."

"Now all we have to hope for is Eli feeling the same toward her," Gabriel said.

As the week progressed, Amanda saw her son make a better than honest effort to heed her words, and Riley looked happier for the change and a chance at some privacy.

Then one morning she went to the barn to fetch the butter churn for Sylvie. Upon opening the door, she spotted Maggie bent over a bale of hay. Her skirt was thrown up over her head, and her bloomers were scrunched down around her ankles. She stood with thighs spread apart and her bared bottom was raised. And Eli was right behind her, his own trousers hanging well below his knees. Amongst their grunts and groans of pleasure, the two were going at it like dogs in heat.

Startled and red-faced for intruding upon such a private moment, Amanda closed the door quietly and ran back to the parsonage. Before entering the kitchen, she took a deep, composing breath.

She knew Maggie's feelings for Eli, but now it certainly appeared as though Eli was just as besotted with Maggie. Clearly the two of them had gained extreme favor with one another, and in her opinion gone way beyond the courting stage.

Then suddenly she broke into a fit of laughter, covering her mouth with a hand as not to be heard. It seemed Riley was not the only one to have gained a measure of privacy.

"Gabriel," she whispered, "you will be very pleased...very pleased indeed."

## Chapter Twenty-One

There was a crystalline acuteness to the air that morning, as there often is after a night of rain. But it would soon change. Arizona spring afternoons turned dry with an absorbing heat that seemed to cook a body from the inside out. Thus the reason for getting on the road early, headed for Eagle's Landing, whereby Amanda and her husband were finally going to meet the folks from Ireland, as well as view whatever building process they'd accomplished since their arrival.

Amanda waited for Josh to bring Ben's larger wagon with the double seats around to the front of the parsonage. Smartly dressed in a white shirt, brown trousers, and a camel-colored suede vest, her husband helped her onto the seat beside him. Gabriel assisted Riley, and Eli Granger—completely recovered from his ordeal, offered a hand to Maggie. The other two women occupied the bench behind her, leaving Gabriel and Eli to ride on horseback beside the wagon.

"Do not expect too much," Gabriel cautioned. "It has only been about ten days, and all that has been accomplished is clearing trees, planning the sites for the other buildings, and breaking ground for three homes."

"Ground has already been broken for our home, since it was where my parent's house once stood." She looked at her son as he sat tall in the saddle. He reminded her so much of Proud Eagle, except her late-husband always rode bareback.

He nodded. "That will be the first dwelling built. Since it still has the fireplace intact, we will not have to erect a new one. And our home," he began, glancing lovingly at Riley, "will be next, sitting right beside it."

Amanda shifted the picnic basket of food she held on her lap. "I am so excited for all of this to be done."

"As I am, Mother Amanda." Riley placed a hand on her shoulder. "And so very pleased we will be neighbors."

As they came upon the entrance to the property, the wagon halted so Gabriel could point out the certain areas marked with rope and sticks. "Here, at the roadside, will be the town's business district. This will consist of Doctor Sean O'Clarity's office and beside that his family's home. The General Store will be next. I've asked Maggie to be the shop's keeper, and she has agreed. So for her convenience, an apartment will be attached to the back of the store and will serve as her living quarters. And ample ground will be left in case Maggie needs more room in the future. Also a spinning wheel will be purchased so she can work the wool, sheared from Eli's sheep, into thread."

Amanda stifled a smile. Gabriel found a perfect way to give Maggie her own home and was preparing adequately in case she and Eli decided to make their arrangement permanent and honorable.

Gabriel continued. "The next lot will be the law office of Edmond Dodd. Like the General Store, the business will be up-front of the building and living quarters in the back, which will have ample room for Muriel's loom and a growing family. And since she is the town's school teacher, the next building will be a small schoolhouse."

She could picture everything Gabriel was saying. How she wished her parents were alive so see what good use all their land was going to serve.

"Beside the schoolhouse," Gabriel went on, "I have plans to build the chapel." He turned briefly to meet Josh's gaze. "I hoped you would come out of retirement to lead our tiny flock, or any other country folk who wish to be a part of our congregation."

Josh inclined his head politely. "It shall be an honor."

"A town hall or community building to serve as a meeting place will be attached to the worship house, whereby church socials, town events, and perhaps even a wedding reception now and then can be held," Gabriel explained further. "Farther back will exist a larger building, which will be the stables and blacksmith shop. This will be run under the experienced eye of Mickey McCrea, who is a professional horse breeder, trainer, and blacksmith. Beside the stables a home will be built for the McCrea family."

"So, the O'Clarity and McCrea families are those who have arrived from Ireland?" Amanda wanted to get their names straight for when she was introduced.

Gabriel nodded, then added, "Mickey's wife's name is Katie, and Sean's wife is Sadie. Each family has four children, but do not ask me to name them."

"I am anxious to meet them all," she said.

"Then I plan on building a large barn farther back, by the free running creek, so Eli can work his flock and be in access to water."

She glanced over at Eli, and he seemed to be beaming atop the horse he rode. He glanced quickly at

Maggie, sitting in the back of the wagon, and cast a huge smile. Though Amanda couldn't see Maggie's face, she had no doubts the other woman was returning Eli's grin with a large one of her own.

"The horse stables and sheep barns will also house rooms upstairs. These apartments will be the living space for Eli and any other hired hands he or Mickey employ. There will be enough space for sleeping quarters, a small parlor to rest in when off duty, and a kitchen for them to cook a meal," Gabriel explained.

"To the left of the property is the family burial plots, and a small walk from there is the exact site where your parents once lived." Gabriel captured her attention. "Of course, you and Josh will make your home there. Next to that site will be mine and Riley's dwelling, then Falling Star and Rising Sun's house will stand beside us, and lastly the home of Messai and Dawn. Further into the woods are Vernon Washburn's home, barn, and stables, as well as land to grow crops. And of course, going back to the creek, we have the tribe's wickiups—Little Elk and Owl Woman's dwelling, as well as the dwellings occupied by Night Wolf and his family, and Rising Star and his family. Amongst their wickiups is the one I will use for tribal council meetings and my vision quest meditation. And still, there is much more land for future generations to build homes on," he concluded.

Her heart burst with pride for her son. "Well, it looks like Eagle's Landing is off to a magnificent start, and it is all your doings."

Gabriel glanced out over the land. "I have dreamed of this moment since I was a small boy." Everyone fell silent, as they followed his gaze and envisioned the same dream. Then, turning her way again, Gabriel smiled. "Come, my mother. It is time you met the others."

Amanda liked Sadie O'Clarity and Katie McCrea instantly and admired them for traveling overseas, to a new land, with small children. Both women were friendly and warm, wholesome and motherly.

In Sadie's arms was little Tucker, just a year old. Snuggled into his mother's protective embrace, the child beamed with a beautiful freshness only the innocence of youth can capture. The rest of Dr. Sean and Sadie's brew consisted of Betsy, eight; Shailyn, seven; and Brodie, who just turned five.

Katie McCrea held six-month-old Mary on her shoulder, an affectionate pat to the baby's bottom kept the infant comforted and quiet during the visit. Katie, like Sadie, was outgoing but in more of a reserved way. Perhaps it was because Katie was older. She and Mickey were parents to three others: Michael, twelve; Patrick, nine; and Trina, six. All the children were carrot-tops with large green eyes.

However, Dr. Sean O'Clarity, his wife, Sadie, Brodie, and Katie McCrea's hair was more of a deep auburn or russet shade.

But Mickey McCrea and his oldest son Michael were dark, both their hair and eyes.

When she commented good-naturedly about the difference, his answer was, "My father was a Scotsman."

"And he's got the temper to prove it," Katie McCrea teased, then went on to talk about the schoolhouse and teacher. Both women were anxious to make Muriel Dodd's acquaintance.

Still and all, there was something, other than his coloring, that set Mickey McCrea apart from the others. It wasn't his burly demeanor or solid frame, as Amanda supposed a man who shod, trained, and bred horses needed to be. But more the way he listened when she spoke, almost as though he was storing away the words for future reference. He looked her straight in the eyes when he spoke in return, waiting for a reaction. He also seemed extremely aware of everything going on around him.

Once alone with Gabriel, Amanda confided her concerns. "There's something more about Mickey McCrea, but I can't quite put my finger on what." She frowned. "Do you feel you can trust him?"

"Him, above all," her son said.

Her frown deepened. "Why is that?"

"I did not want to worry you, but I hired an investigator to look into Father's death."

"And Mickey McCrea is the investigator you hired?"

Gabriel nodded. "He does it along with his other work which is a good cover-up as well."

She moved closer to her son, placing a hand on his cheek. "Oh, Gabriel, why are you stirring things up?"

His lips thinned. "Because I want to bring to justice the man—or men who killed my father."

It was her turn to heave a sigh. "Then you don't believe it was a hunting accident either."

"No. Father was too cautious, too good at what he did." They locked gazes. "And since you obviously feel the same way, why have you not come to me on the matter?"

"I didn't want you to do just what you are doing,

calling attention to yourself by looking for justice." She bit her bottom lip. "I knew you wouldn't let it be."

Gabriel arched a brow. "You would want Father's killer to get away with murder?"

"I want my son to stay alive so he can lead his people. Is it not enough that Eagle's Landing will open up opposition by others? Why give anyone more of an excuse to bother us?"

"I cannot let Father's death quietly pass, my mother. Whoever did this must pay."

"And do you really believe that will happen, Gabriel? In a time, where there is hatred for the Apache, do you honestly think you will get your justice?"

His voice broke. "I have to try, my mother."

"And in the middle of you trying, you put yourself, me, Riley, the tribe—everyone in danger. Have you thought about that?"

"Yes, I have thought of nothing else." His tone was defensive.

"And yet you will continue with this investigation?"

"I have to. I cannot let Father's death be in vain." He ran a hand through his hair.

"But it wasn't in vain. From this tragedy Eagle's Landing has been born, and the rest of the tribe can live on land without fear. Can't you see this, Gabriel?"

"I promise I will be extremely careful. That is why I hired an investigator instead of doing the job myself. No one will suspect me or any other member of the tribe."

"What happens then, Gabriel?" Before he could answer, she went on. "What happens after you find this culprit—how will he be dealt with—how will he be brought to justice when no one in town will condemn him for killing an Apache?"

"Then I will just have to make sure the townspeople stand with me," he said.

"How do you propose to do this?" she dared further, not quite sure she wanted to hear his answer.

"With money, my mother. I have lots of it now, and money speaks to everyone...makes a man do things he would not ordinarily agree to."

She arched a brow. "Then you would buy justice?"

He frowned. "No, I would buy people's favor. And then hope in time I would earn their respect."

"And how would you do this?" she probed, sounding like she did when she questioned his actions as a child. Only now the child was six feet, three inches and way more stubborn.

"With jobs. I will hire them to build Eagle's Landing." He made a waving gesture with his hand. "Look around you...do you think all that needs done can be accomplished with only the few men here? It would take us years. The more men, the faster the job is completed. I have asked around, and many men are out of work...have not the money to feed their families, buy seed to plant their crops. Reverend Newcomb sends boxes of food and clothing to poor families all over the county. While I watched him pack these boxes, I got the idea to broaden my resources, offer work to these men, gain their trust and respect. And hopefully, when the time comes for justice to be served in sentencing whoever killed my father, these men I've helped...given a job, too...will stand by me and with me."

"How are you getting the word out to these men?"

She was proud of the sound and sensible decision he made.

"Reverend Newcomb is announcing the jobs at Sunday's church service. Many men in his congregation are in dire need of a wage. And Ben is sure they will spread the word to their kin in other counties who are experiencing the same problem," Gabriel explained. "Those traveling far to work can set up camp on the property, as the Irish folks are doing. I will pay each man weekly and give him Saturday and Sunday off so he can attend church and go home to be with his family. If my plan goes well, I expect Eagle's Landing to be livable by late fall. And when Mickey McCrea finds who killed my father, hopefully those I employed will want to see justice served as well."

"Oh Gabriel—Gabriel. And if they don't?"

He sighed. "One thing at a time, my mother."

"Just promise me you will not compromise your honor." She laid a hand upon his arm. "Or do anything against the law so the authorities are coming after you as well. It will serve no good purpose for you to be arrested, taken away, and hanged. Your father would not want you to suffer such a demise. It was for just such a consequence he hid what really happened to him. Riley could not bear it, and I don't want to even fathom it, as the grief would be so acute it would take over every fiber of my being. And life as I know it would totally cease for me."

His hesitation with a response struck fear in her heart.

"Promise me, Gabriel," she repeated in a forceful tone. "Give me your word this very moment, as an Apache warrior and chief; you will refrain from doing anything dishonest or against the law to accomplish your means."

Finally he nodded, conceding to her request. "You have my word."

Amanda finished her conversation with Gabriel, although the discussion was hardly at rest and wouldn't be until the whole incident was over, because young Michael McCrea came running up to them, out of breath and excited.

"Mama asked me to fetch ye." He glanced from her to Gabriel. Then resting his gaze fully on Amanda, he continued, "Me mama will be layin' out the food ye brought, Mrs. Amanda. And the other women made food, too, so ye all better be comin' along to take yer fill before 'tis all gone." And with that said, the youngster ran back to the camping grounds, no doubt to make sure he missed out on nothing himself.

"The holy man knows my plans," Gabriel whispered. "But I will spare my wife."

She nodded. "Generally I don't like secrets between husband and wife, Gabriel. But in this case why worry Riley while in her present condition."

"I feel the same," he said.

"Obviously, so does Josh, or he would have told me about Mickey McCrea," she observed with a crease of her brow.

"Do not judge him harshly for his silence, my mother. He was sparing you out of love, not deceit," Gabriel said in Josh's defense.

Michael McCrea returned, hands on hips and totally disturbed he had to make a second run to fetch them. "Are ye two comin'?"

"Yes," Gabriel called. "We are right behind you,

my friend." Extending an arm to his mother, he smiled. "Shall we?"

She linked a hand over his forearm and returned the smile. Then she gave a quick glance in Michael's direction. "Might as well, before this poor boy makes himself sick."

They both laughed as they followed behind the hungry youngster down the path.

Chapter Twenty-Two

The tribeswomen and the Irish women worked beautifully together, adding to the picnic basket Amanda contributed. All the efforts combined made for a small feast. They sat around a large wooden table Vernon found in his barn, out in the open spring afternoon, much as she pictured the first Thanksgiving looked. And in some ways, the spirit was the same, as Apache and white folk, some from Ireland, England, and one from Australia, sat down to break bread and become each other's neighbor. Together they would all work for a common cause, and in their unity, a town would be established.

After the meal Amanda took a walk around the grounds. At one time she knew every nook and cranny of the property. While she walked about, many of those memories returned. The trees she climbed, the skinned knees she suffered, the dresses she dirtied with mud, and the painful tangles combed from her hair. She was an active youngster, loving the outdoors. She enjoyed playing tag and hide-and-seek with her best friend, Thea Johnson. She could see the bedraggled waif of a girl in her mind's eye, running with bare feet together in the woods, and the two falling down in fits of laughter when caught.

"Oh, dear Thea," she whispered. "What ever became of you?"

207

As she came upon the burned out ruins of her childhood home, she realized life hadn't taken her far. She was away for a time, but circumstances had led her back to her roots, to the land where she was born and raised. She hadn't set eyes on the place since she fled in the night with Proud Eagle, escaping from the Chiricahua as they attacked all she owned—burnt it to the ground. She had saved Proud Eagle's life, and he returned the favor. Then he took her back to his village and married her. For three decades she lived like an Apache, worked side by side with the tribespeople, and suffered their indignities by the white agents who infiltrated the village. Though she loved Proud Eagle, she never felt safe...not really...not like she did as a child, sleeping on these very grounds.

"When I came upon this burned-out mess I nearly died," a voice came from behind.

She turned to find Josh watching her.

"As I've told you before, I fell to the ground and wept," he said. "I thought you were dead, and all I could feel was a vast emptiness, a deep darkness so bleak..." He cleared his throat and swallowed hard before he could finish his sentence. "...so bleak it ravaged my entire being with grief."

She went to him, throwing her arms around his neck and burying her head beneath his chin. "I am so sorry for any pain I caused you. For the loneliness and sorrow—for the years you spent living without love."

He engulfed her in his tight embrace. "All that matters to me is that you are mine, and I will never let you go."

"No, never let me go," she echoed. "And I plan on holding on to you as well."

"I don't believe I've heard such wonderful news in all my life."

As she raised her gaze to his, he lowered his face and covered her mouth with a warm, sweet kiss. For a moment they were lost in each other—the kiss deepening, their bodies melding.

"If there weren't so many people milling about, I'd take you right here, strip you naked, and love you to complete and utter exhaustion," he whispered against her lips.

"And I'd welcome every bit of it and more," she whispered back, feeling his erection against her thigh.

He pulled back to look at her, a roguish grin curling his full, inviting lips. "You are a vixen, woman."

She arched a seductive brow. "Does that bother you?"

He chuckled lightly. "Aye, it bothers every facet of my being, and I'd not want it any other way."

"I am fully aware of one part of your being this very moment."

"Aye, my body once more betrays me. I shall definitely have to give it what for," he playfully responded.

"Well, you'd better do it quickly because I see Riley in the distance, and she's making her way right to us."

"We will pick up where we left off later." He released her from his embrace.

She flashed him a demure smile. "I won't hesitate to remind you."

He turned and walked a few feet away to compose himself, and she forced a welcoming smile in her daughter-in-law's direction.

"So, there you two are," Riley called, nearing where they stood. Standing with hands on hips, she surveyed the ruins. "So, this was your childhood home."

"Yes, here it once stood, just a modest, two bedroom cottage." Memories of the house's layout circled her mind. "My bedroom window faced west. The kitchen was in the center of the house. In fact, the dining table sat right here." She moved closer to the fireplace.

"Which looks almost all intact, as Gabriel said," Riley commented.

"Don't let looks deceive you," Josh chimed in, fully recovered from their quick romantic romp. "I'm sure after this many years some damage has been done. Although the stones might still be useful, the chimney will need to be rebuilt."

Amanda studied the stones. The way they were weathered and worn added a rich and unique patina to their surface. Reaching out, she fingered the brick-work along the opening. "There once was such a lovely oak mantel here. I remember hanging a stocking on a nail embedded in its center each Christmas Eve."

Riley joined her. "And what did you find come the morning?"

"A handful of gum drops, a few licorice sticks, and an orange." She smiled.

"We will rebuild it again, mantel and all." Riley caressed the small swell of her stomach. "So your grandchild can hang a stocking there one day as well."

That thought thrilled her down to her toes. "Oh, how wonderful that sounds."

Riley noticed the condition of the hearth. "You're right, Josh. Upon a closer look there is much to repair." She gave the brick a small nudge with the tip of a boot. "This whole area is overgrown with foliage and will have to be ripped out and replaced."

"The stones here, above where the mantel once sat, are loose as well." Amanda wiggled one free.

"Careful, ladies," Josh warned. "Lest the whole thing come tumbling down, trapping you both beneath it."

"Now it won't go back into place." She tried to maneuver the stone into its original resting space. "It seems something prevents it from sliding in the groove." She stuck her hand inside the open crevice. "I feel something in here."

"Careful, my love." Josh moved closer to protect her. "You could be disturbing a hornets' nest."

She stretched her fingers until she was able to grip the object. "I have it." She pulled the item from the slot. In her hand she held a journal—small, black, and leather bound.

Riley frowned. "What a strange place to hide a book."

Amanda opened the cover and read the inscription. "This belonged to my mother, and it is dated way back to 1842." She frowned, trying to recall the stories her mother told her. "If my memory serves me right, that would be right around the time she left England to come to America." Her frown deepened. "But how did her journal find its way stuffed behind a fireplace stone?"

"Perhaps, when the town was plagued by the Chiricahua attacks, your father placed it there for safe keeping," Josh commented.

"Perhaps," she echoed softly.

"Is it readable?" Riley looked over her shoulder.

Amanda thumbed through a few pages, recognizing the familiar script of her mother's hand. "Yes, to some degree. Many pages are missing, and the tops of some look chewed away. But there is still much I will be able to read."

"How positively exciting," Riley chirped. "You've just discovered a glimpse of your mother's life by way of her most inner thoughts. What a rare and marvelous treasure."

She closed the book and held it against her heart. "How very true, what a treasure indeed."

The rest of the day seemed to pass as slow as molasses in January. All Amanda wanted to do was return to the parsonage, brew herself a cup of tea, kick off her muddy boots, and sit by the fire to read a few entries of her mother's diary. However, it was late when they reached Willow Creek, and the long ride in cold, windy weather had her craving nothing more than to climb beneath the bedclothes and be warmed by her husband's body.

He complied most generously, bringing back to her frigid flesh a glorious heat, taking her to the height of passion, and leaving her exhausted in its aftermath. His even breathing lulled her to sleep, her eyelids heavy, and all her bones content. Rolling onto her side to turn down the bedside lantern brought her in full view of her mother's diary, resting upon the dresser. And in an instant she was wide away, her curiosity growing too large to avoid.

Slowly she pulled aside the quilt and climbed out

of the bed. As quietly as she could muster, she reached for her robe and donned it, then took the lantern and a pillow with her to the dresser. After retrieving the diary, she went to a far corner of the room, threw the pillow on the floor, sat upon it in a cross-legged fashion, and placed the lantern beside her.

With trembling hands she held the journal, as though it were a sacred and priceless relic. And in truth, it was—to her. She was only twelve years old when her mother died from a fever. As all these long years fled by, it had become harder and harder to recall the sound of Amelia's voice, the color of her hair, the way she smiled. But now, now Amanda held the pages of her mother's thoughts, written in the beautiful and unique script only Amelia owned.

"I've got you back, mother," she whispered, and opened the journal to the first page.

*Friday, April 1, 1842*
*Glenshire Sussex, England*
*We have finally arrived at Collins Stead.*
*The journey from Brighton with my parents,*
*younger sister, Kaylena, mother's handmaid,*
*Opel, and our handmaid, Aggie, was long and*
*tiresome. Most of the way the wind blew gusts*
*of cold air through the cracks of our old, out-*
*of-date carriage and rain pelted the windows.*
*But now all that is behind me (at least until the*
*return trip) as I sit beside a most inviting fire,*
*wrapped in a goose-down quilt, and sipping a*
*cup of lavender tea. Sleep eludes me, as I*
*contemplate the festivities of this weekend to*
*come, especially the party tomorrow night.*
*Tomorrow my dear friend, Lucinda Collins*

*turns eighteen, and a gala dinner, dancing, and the entertainment of an accomplished magician is planned for the evening. I hope father will let me have such a celebration when I am eighteen.*

\*\*\*\*

*Saturday, April 2, 1842*

*It is the first time I am wearing a full-length gown. Mother even allowed Aggie to arrange my hair atop my head, with curls cascading down my back.*

*If looking and feeling like a lady wasn't grand enough, the surprise delivery of a most wonderful letter from America arrived in time to be read at dinner. Lord Sherman's twin brother, Lord Silas, is a fur trapper living out west of the American colonies and has been for about twenty years. No one has heard hide nor hair of the man, until tonight. The Collins family thought Silas was dead, but he has been living with the Western Apache tribe in the Spanish territory of Arizona. He is married to an Apache maiden, has a daughter named White Dove. She is with child, and in six months' time Silas will be a grandfather.*

Amanda gasped. Silas's grandchild would one day be her husband, Proud Eagle. If only Amelia were alive to know how everything came to a full circle. Anxiously, she read on.

*Lord Silas Collins' letter conjured all sorts of pictures in my mind. So much so, that later on in the evening I asked Lord Collins if I might read the letter for myself. I was*

*overjoyed when he agreed.*
\*\*\*\*

*Tuesday, April 5, 1842*
*Brighton*
*We are all back home at Bentley Manor.*
*I'm supposed to be doing my lessons, but*
*instead I am thinking about America. How I*
*would relish an adventure there, but it appears*
*my fate has already been planned. My father*
*secured an arranged marriage for me when I*
*was born. As soon as I come of age, I am to*
*wed Howard Rawlings, the son of my father's*
*old friend. When I protested, Father called for*
*Ida, the nanny, to take me upstairs to my room*
*to be thrashed.*

*I knew what to expect. This wasn't the*
*first time father ordered Ida to discipline me.*
*She had been given the authority the year I*
*began my monthly courses, which was two*
*weeks after my twelfth birthday.*

*The walk to my room was one of shame,*
*but if it had to be, I'd rather it be Ida who*
*punished me instead of experiencing the rush*
*of humiliation when father performed the*
*deed.*

*Once in my room, Ida ordered me to stand*
*at the foot of the bed and bend over. Her*
*hands trembled as she raised my skirt and*
*petticoat, then lowered my bloomers to my*
*ankles before removing them completely. The*
*room's temperature cooled my nakedness, and*
*I   shivered,   making   it   all   the   more*
*uncomfortable   to   be   standing   in   such   a*

*position. I closed my eyes, willing myself to be somewhere else, away from my father's strict and tyrant hand...free from the contract he signed on my behalf.*

*I heard Ida taking the paddle from a bedside-table drawer, where it was kept...where it had always been kept since as early as I can recall. This was so I would remember the consequences I'd endure for not knowing my place. I once thought about burning the bloody thing, but to what good would that serve me in the long run? Father would only purchase another, perhaps thicker and bigger paddle. Or use a whipping strap or a birching rod, as he often threatened he'd do. I wasn't the only one he beat. Mother, Kaylena, and even some of the servants fall prey to Father's wrath.*

*The flat heels of Ida's high-angled shoes clicked on the floorboards as she made her way to stand behind me.*

*She doled out ten, sharp whacks to my bared bum. For a moment I thought I might lose my dinner, as my stomach slammed against the bed's footboard with each blow.*

*But I held my breath...and I wouldn't let her see me cry. I might have been stripped of my modesty, but there was still something prideful in maintaining my composure. However, as soon as Ida left the room, I sobbed. When Aggie arrived with a cup of chamomile tea, she got a fire going, stripped me naked, washed me, rubbed a poultice into my burning flesh, dressed me in a clean, cotton nightgown, brushed out my hair, and put me to bed, gently covering me with a linen sheet. All this was done without a word spoken by either of us.*

*I now lie in bed...exhausted but in too much pain to sleep. My abused bum is throbbing, my spirits are low, my pride is shattered, and my heart aches. I do not want to marry Howard Rawlings. I want to go to America.*

*I will go to America!*

*In spite of what my father thinks.*

She closed the journal abruptly, wanting to hide her mother's shame. Now she understood why Amelia never struck her in such a way or allowed her father to be so cruel. For the second time today, Thea Jackson came to mind. Amanda fully realized why Amelia was so upset when Thea's father beat the youngster in such a humiliating way. And it became clear as to why Kaylena acted as she did. The poor woman had been abused from childhood to adulthood. No wonder, upon their first meeting, Kaylena asked her if Amelia's husband was a good man and did he treat her well. And when Amanda vouched for Ethan Gregory's love and tenderness toward her and her mother, Kaylena was greatly pleased and strongly relieved.

"Amanda, love, why are you in the corner, sitting on the floor?"

She opened her eyes to find Josh sitting up in bed. "I'm sorry if the light woke you."

"Nay, it was the cold, empty bed." A concerned look creased his brow. "What are you doing?"

"Reading my mother's journal." She stood, placed the diary on the dresser, then bent to retrieve the lantern and pillow. "I thought I'd disturb you less on the other side of the room." She made her way to the bed, returned the lantern to the night table, and plopped the pillow down beside him. Removing her robe, she climbed naked into bed and his waiting arms.

"Did you know my grandfather was an abusive man to his wife, children, and the servants?" She cuddled against his warm, muscular body.

"Aye, I've heard stories to that manner from Kaylena and Lucinda Collins."

"Did your father beat you?"

"Beat me—nay. But there was a time or two when he reddened my bum. Nothing as severe or as humiliating as what your grandfather did, but a child cannot be allowed to run amok," he said.

"Did he spank your sister, too?"

"Nay, he never laid a hand on Marietta. My mother or the nanny would discipline her, but only as a last resort. My parents were passive people, believed in explaining and teaching us through consequences more than striking us."

She frowned. "What sort of consequences?"

"One night I was made to wash the entire entry hall, which was a good twenty feet long, as well as the kitchen, and solarium floors for misbehaving. It had to be perfect, with not a spot seen and shined to a high gloss. It took me nine hours to complete the bloody task. When I was finished, my knees and back were in so much pain, I couldn't walk properly for days afterward. Marietta, if I remember correctly, had to press all the linen from the huge closet stocked with several shelves. It took her three days, by the time she heated and reheated the iron, and she was allowed to stop only long enough to sleep, eat, and use the privy." He chuckled lightly. "A spanking in both instances would have probably been easier to endure, definitely quicker."

"My parents didn't believe in beatings," she said.

He chuckled again. "And many times it showed."

She pulled back to look at him. "I was punished for misbehaving, just not beaten."

"Yet you were—still are—a very stubborn woman," he said, stifling a smile.

She narrowed her eyes. "So you would be one of those horrible men who would beat his wife?"

"Nay, my love. I don't believe a man is much of a man if he can strike a woman." He then cast a roguish smile. "I assure you, my hands upon your naked bum would never be out of malice."

She smiled, satisfied and snuggled again beside him. "In that case I give you my full consent."

He ran a hand down her back, caressed her rounded cheeks, then gently inserted the tip of his finger into the entrance there. She opened her thighs, bringing one leg to rest across him. Upon feeling his growing excitement, she smiled and arched her spine.

"Why does my attention upon your beautiful bum not repulse you?"

"Why should it?" she whispered, enjoying the sensations his touch provoked.

"Most wives would feel degraded if a husband were to be so familiar."

"Isn't a husband supposed to be familiar to his wife, and her to him?"

"Well...aye...you would think so, but that is not always the case."

"Not for the white woman, you mean," she said.

"You are a white woman, my love."

"Yes, but I have not lived like one in three decades. Because of this fact, I was not subjected to other women's prudish chatter and advice. When I gave my maidenhood to an Apache husband, he cast a different light on things some thought repulsive. He was open and honest with me, not ashamed to teach me what pleased him or show me how to enjoy my body," she said. "Nothing I experienced at his hands made me believe I was wanton or feel degraded." She again lifted her gaze to his. "Such affections also serve a very good purpose, other than pleasure."

He arched a brow. "Such as?"

"The Apache believe they should never bring into the world more mouths than they can feed," she explained. "Yet, the love a husband and wife share is so strong, so great, that abstinence from one another is not something they wish to practice in order to keep their family numbers down. Or to keep their wives healthy, as delivering a child every year can take a toll on the body."

"Aye, so true. In England couples have seven, ten, even fifteen offspring with hardly enough food for two. In lower caste households, the woman becomes worn, sick, often dies young leaving all these motherless children to fend for themselves. And those forgotten souls become the beggars, the misfortunates who roam the London streets in poverty...hungry, dirty, and die young as well," he said. "And in the richer households, the men, after they've achieved the number of heirs desired, take leave of their wife's bed and house a mistress in town."

She frowned. "I would never want my husband to step away from my bed, touch another woman the way he touched me."

"You've nay a reason for concern," he reassured her. "I've been waiting my whole life to be with you...just you."

"All such behavior is so unnecessary, when there is an alternative to the problem," she said.

He arched a brow. "And, I imagine, quite painful."

"Yes, it could be, if not done right. But I was fortunate. Proud Eagle was considerate. He knew my body needed time to become conditioned to such ways, or the pain would be great. He prepared me slowly, in stages, using oral approaches as well as lots of bear grease. He gave me ample time to adjust to the Apache method. Because of his respect and thoughtfulness, I was able to crave and enjoy the different way to be intimate instead of being fearful or feeling repulsed by it."

He arched a brow. "Bear grease?"

She giggled. "Well, now petroleum jelly works quite well and isn't as messy."

He smiled. "Are we in possession of petroleum jelly?"

She nodded and moved to retrieve a jar from the bedside table drawer. "I bought this before we were wed, just in case." She turned back to look at him and held up the container for him to see.

"And what now do you propose to do with it," he said.

"Well, if you will permit me, I will coat you

thoroughly, my love."

His smile deepened. "Aye, permission granted."

## Chapter Twenty-Three

The way his wife loved him and the way she allowed him to love her were more than Josh ever imagined or believed could be his good fortune. Her warmth, the smell, taste, and feel of her flesh, drove him wild with passion. He was able to explore every inch of her, and in turn she grew familiar with each part of him. His body flourished with their lovemaking, rejuvenating him...whether it be during the act of foreplay, in the throes of ecstasy, or basking in the aftermath's satisfaction. He cherished every stage, becoming addicted to the way she arched her back, became moist with his probing, or tightened around his phallus as she climaxed. And upon the completion of each blissful encounter, though thoroughly spent, he thought for sure he'd recaptured the stamina of his youth.

He had to force himself to concentrate on building their home each day. And when he drifted off in his thoughts to their desire-filled nights, he'd be quickly brought back to the situation at hand, by hammering a thumb or tripping over a plank of wood.

"How is it you are so accident prone," she probed, while bandaging one of his cuts or applying salve to a bruise.

"I am constantly thinking of you naked in my bed, pressed against my loins, and joining me to the peak of

my passion," he whispered in her ear. Her boldness—
the straightforward way she viewed making love, fueled
his courage to speak his most secret desires.

She'd giggle, kiss him, and say, "Tonight, my
darling, I shall be right beside you to scale your
summit, but for now...build me a home."

After Ben Newcomb announced at Sunday's
service three weeks ago the need for help, thirty-seven
men showed up for a job. The call had been heard far
and wide. Gabriel put them all to work, building the
houses first, thus the families living in makeshift
dwellings would be able to move into a home by the
fall.

Curly Blackwell, Ernie Grant, and Oscar Hunt—all
made their way from Baker's Corners, a town twenty
miles downriver. These men were assigned to assist
him. Each day he mustered on, learning from his
helpers, taking their advice, and watching with
satisfaction his efforts taking shape. And he thanked the
Lord daily for the three skilled, hardworking, no
nonsense men who helped him. If not for them, he and
Amanda would probably be destined to live at the
parsonage for many more years to come.

There were eight homes to erect all total. Five were
free standing: his and Amanda's, Gabriel and Riley's,
Rising Sun and Falling Star's, Dawn and Messai's, and
that of the McCrea family. Three others were attached
to businesses. Dr. Sean O'Clarity's home was to be
attached to the back of his office, Edmond and Murial
Dodd's home, attached to his law office, and Maggie
Mulligan's house, attached to the general store.

From that point the stables, sheep barn, hired
hands, and horse handler's quarters would be built, as

well as the church—with its social center, and the schoolhouse. Feverishly the men worked, and the women supplied food, water, and medical attention, as needed. Even the older children were busy, pushing wheelbarrows full of dirt and stones to and fro, and taking tools from one building site to another.

It was the morning of June twenty-first, Amelia's seventieth birthday. He and Amanda stopped to pay their respects at her grave. Amanda bought a small bouquet of roses to place by the headstone.

"Until I found her diary, she was almost lost to me. So many years have gone by since I've seen her; I was beginning to forget things." Amanda arranged the roses into the dirt.

"Aye, I suppose reading her written words has a way of bringing her somewhat back to life." He grasped her hand and helped her to stand.

"It does, very strongly, in fact," she agreed. "I'm finding it hard to put the journal down." She paused. "My mother died so young, only thirty-three years old. I had three children when I was the same age and looking forward to so many years ahead...to watch them grow, to grow old myself. It's totally unfair as to how my mother's life was cut so short."

Josh concluded her late night reading was thus the reason she appeared very tired, basically worn out. And rightly so, as she cooked and prepared food early in the morning to share at Eagle's Landing. If she wasn't bringing water to everyone or serving food, she was dealing with sunburn, heatstroke, or bandaging wounds. She helped with the children and sanded down or painted the furniture Vernon Washburn built from leftover lumber. And then instead of taking her slumber once at the parsonage and regrouping for the next day, she took to reading her mother's journal all night.

He frowned. "Which leads me to believe you're not receiving a proper night's sleep, after doing so much on the property by day. I'm always waking to find you sitting in the corner with the lantern."

She shrugged. "It becomes hard not to see what will happen next, much like a good novel. Though, I know the outcome, I didn't know what transpired before. My mother never spoke of her time in England. Finally, I'm finding out."

He caressed the side of her face. "Promise me you will cut down on the work and the hours spent finding out to allow yourself more time to rest."

She moved her face to kiss the palm of his hand. "I promise to try."

They separated ways for the day, he to work with Curly, Ernie, and Oscar and she to work with the women. The sun blazed high in the sky at the noon hour. The soft, warmish breezes of spring, slowly being replaced by the dry, hot heat of summer. Sweat trickled into his eyes and down his back, his throat was parched, and his stomach cried out in rumbles for food.

Curly, who was working beside him, began to laugh. "Yer belly sounds like mine feels."

Oscar, overhearing their conversation, added, "I say it's 'bout time we got us some grub."

"Aye, I'd say that's a capital idea, old chap," he agreed.

As he approached the meal table, which was set up by the wickiups lining the creek, he looked for Amanda. Usually she had a plate of cheese, a few slabs of cold meat, and a slice of bread waiting for him, along with a canteen of fresh, cool water. It was the time of the day he looked forward to the most, not so much for the food but to be able to talk with his wife. Their playful banter always reinforced his energy, something he needed to finish out the day. But today she was nowhere in sight.

Spotting Vernon, he made his way beside him for a further inquiry. "Is Amanda in the barn, sanding, or painting furniture?"

"Nope, not today," Vernon confirmed.

He then caught up with Riley, sitting on a stump reading to the younger children gathered at her feet. "Have you seen my wife?"

Riley lifted her gaze from the book. "Aye, she's been taken to Owl Woman and Little Elk's wickiup."

His heart took a sudden plunge to his toes. "Taken...why, and by whom?"

"She became ill and collapsed," Riley said. "Dr. O'Clarity carried her into Owl Women's wickiup. They are both with her now."

He took off at a run, his breath catching in his throat, fear for her wellbeing choking him. Why was she ill? What could be the problem? Whatever the case, he would be by her side, care day and night for her until she was well again. He would take her to the best doctors; do whatever it took to find a cure, because he couldn't lose her. By God, he wouldn't be able to live on without her.

By the time he was upon Owl Woman's dwelling, he had worked himself into a frenzy. Sick to his stomach with fear, he rushed into the wickiup. With wide eyes he looked around the dwelling, finding his wife lying on a heap of blankets, eyes closed, face pale.

Owl Woman sat beside her, placing a wet compress upon Amanda's forehead. Dr. Sean O'Clarity closed up his black bag and made his way toward him.

"She'll be fine, Josh. She's just resting comfortably now." Sean placed a restraining hand upon his arm. "I've given her something to make her sleep. She'll be out for a few hours."

"Was it heatstroke?" He pushed the doctor aside and made his way to kneel beside his wife.

"No heatstroke," Owl Woman said.

"What...what then?" his voice cracked, as he surveyed Amanda's peaked visage. With a trembling hand, he reached for one of hers, bringing it to his lips to bestow a gentle kiss upon her knuckles.

"I did not think she could get...not again...not now..." Owl Woman shook her head.

Josh turned to Sean, feeling on the verge of hysterics. "What's wrong with her, Dr. O'Clarity? What did she get?"

Sean ran a hand through his russet curls and sighed. "Well, 'tis a fact, sir, your wife has gotten with child. You, my man, are goin' to be a father."

His ears began to ring; the blood drained from his head. "A fath...a father?" he heard himself say, felt his tongue form the words, yet his brain couldn't fathom the idea.

"Aye, sir," Sean confirmed. "I'd say Amanda's into her eighth week."

"Expecting—she's expecting—I'm going to be a father." His thoughts rattled; his fingers grew numb.

"Aye, Josh," Sean said.

Owl Woman grunted. "Must have happened on that *honeymoon* you took her on, time fits right."

228

The elder woman was correct, as it had been eight weeks since their wedding night. But he hadn't even dreamed of, had a notion whatsoever Amanda would be able to... "We're having a baby."

Sean neared him and leaned down to give his arm a reassuring pat. "And all is well."

"Right now he does not look so well to me," Owl Woman remarked.

"Take a deep breath." The doctor grabbed him by the shoulders. "And get a grip, man. 'Tis a grand and marvelous thing that's happenin'."

"Aye, aye, it's a miracle...a bloody miracle." Josh's body trembled while thoughts of Abraham and Sarah swirled around in his head.

"Aye, 'tis at that, but you need to get a hold o' yourself, my friend," Sean warned.

The last thing he heard, before everything went black, was Owl Woman saying, "Looks like you will need to open up that black bag once more, Doc, and use those smelling salts of yours again. I will fetch another wet cloth."

Chapter Twenty-Four

"I feel like a bird whose wings have been clipped and left to rot in a cage like a prisoner," Amanda snapped, hands on hips.

"You're not a prisoner, Amanda," Josh cajoled. "No doors are locking you in a room."

She frowned. "No, not specifically. But you and my son have made it known loud and clear your wish to keep me here." She gestured with a wave of her hand around their bedroom. "Safe and sound in this parsonage, and far away from the building site."

He ran a hand through his hair. "Can't you try to understand anything from our prospective? Gabriel is now frantic for the health of two women he loves, and I am beside myself with fear I will lose the only woman I ever loved, if she doesn't take care of herself."

The two men in her life were totally overreacting. "Oh for pity's sake, Josh. I'm only having a baby which I have done three times before in worse conditions and with far less convenience."

"And at a much younger time in your life."

She narrowed her eyes. "Are you calling me old?"

"Nay—nay, only that now you are a...a..." He groped for the right words, then finally settled on, "A well-seasoned expectant mother."

She broke out in hearty laughter. "Why, you're just a silver-tongued devil, aren't you?"

He frowned. "What do you mean?"

She searched his handsome face, admiring the even features. "I'm just impressed, is all, the way you can sprout out diplomatic verbal responses like that. Cultivated, no doubt, from preaching all these years on the pulpit."

He chuckled. "Aye, well, some habits are hard to break."

She sighed. "I fully realize I'm a lot more *well-seasoned*," she admitted, emphasizing his words, "than before, but my body is healthy. And I am not so daft as to think I can do all the things I did in my earlier days while expecting a child. But I see no reason this birth will be any different than the previous ones." She crossed her arms over her chest. "And keeping me inactive and hidden away isn't going to be good physically or mentally for me or this baby."

He neared her cautiously as though she'd bite his head off, much like a female praying mantis would her mate. The thought made her stifle a smile.

"You're not hidden away, nor does anyone expect you to take to your bed. But lately you've run yourself ragged. Until you replenish your body, get some rest, regain your strength, it is best you stay away from the rugged and hot days you were experiencing at the building site."

"Josh, all will be fine...I'm fine. You and Gabriel just need to believe..."

"Please, Amanda," he interrupted, his blue eyes moistening. "I couldn't bear it if anything happened to you and the baby. I've waited...wanted for so long a wife and family. To have it now and lose it..." His voice cracked with emotion.

"Oh, my darling Joshua." She approached him, enveloping his face between her hands. "You aren't going to lose either of us. Trust me on this. I do know my own body and its limits."

She entwined her fingers in his hair and brought his head down to rest on her shoulder. Immediately he responded, clutching her in a loving embrace. Then, to her great surprise, he began to sob. Her heart went out to him, and suddenly she understood the ferocity to which this man loved her...what she meant—how much the child growing beneath her heart meant to him. And what he meant to her became a stark clarity. After all he'd done for her throughout the years, his devotion, love, loyalty, and the way she could depend on him...what would it hurt to appease him now?

"Josh, I will do as you ask, so fear no longer," she conceded. "I will rest, and I promise to take it easy."

He pulled back to meet her gaze, relief glistening in his eyes. Gently she wiped away his tears with the palms of her hands. Then she kissed him, deep and long so he would have no doubts about the truth of her words or her love and respect for him.

"I love you, Amanda, with every ounce of breath in my body."

"As I do you," she said, sincerely meaning every word. "And I hope you will remember your heartfelt pledge after you realize my current condition has just doubled your labor."

He arched a brow. "How has it managed to do that?"

"The second bedroom in the cottage's floor plan can no longer serve as a guest room. Now, that room must be for the baby." She grinned. "So, I'm afraid, my darling, since it is not possible to add a room down, you will need to add a loft up, and building a two-story home will definitely double your labor."

"Bloody hell, you're right," he playfully cursed, then leaned in to kiss her again.

Once the men departed for the day's work, she made her way to the kitchen to join Sylvie for a cup of tea. To her surprise, Riley beat her to it.

"Is everything well with you and the baby, Riley?"

The younger woman smiled and caressed the small mound of her belly. "Aye, couldn't be better."

"Then why are you not with Gabriel." Amanda grabbed a mug and spooned in a few tea leaves.

"I just got to thinking how upset I was making my husband, trudging around all day in the heat, heat I'm not really used to. He's right; all the bending, lifting, carrying, serving can't be good for the baby. And truthfully it's wearing me out as well."

"I told her this mournin' you'd be right happy for the company. And so would I," Sylvie added. "Neither of ya should be workin' out there all day beneath the blazin' sun, breathin' in all that there sand, sawdust, and paint fumes, anyway."

She added water to her cup from the kettle on the stove, stirred the brew, and joined the other two women at the table. "No, I suppose not. After all, we are looking after someone other than ourselves." She patted Riley's hand.

For a while no one spoke, each woman sipped their tea, lost in their own thoughts. The quiet household adding to the tranquility.

Then Sylvie broke the silence. "How in tarnation did you get yourself in the family way?"

Amanda nearly choked on her tea.

Riley giggled. "The usual approach, I would presume."

"Ya know what I mean," Sylvie scowled.

"Yes, I know what you mean." Amanda put her cup down.

"Well?"

Amanda shook her head. "I'm just as stumped, Sylvie. For almost three years my monthly courses have been irregular. I would miss months on end, then my woman's time would return, only to disappear for several months again. My blood issue stopped completely about nine or ten months ago. And when nothing ever happened with Proud Eagle, I truly believed I was past my child-bearing years. That's the reason I hadn't a notion I conceived." She sighed. "No one could have been more shocked than me." She rubbed her temples with the pads of her fingers. "So much has changed. Only seven months ago I was the wife of a man I was wed to for thirty years. Now I am married to another man, and I'm having his baby." She sighed again. "I just wish things would slow down enough for me to catch up."

"Ah, well, the good Lord's got His reasons for everythin', I reckon," Sylvie mused. "Perhaps this baby is an answer to a prayer?"

She frowned. "Whose prayer?"

"Why, Josh's, of course. Last night I overheard him tellin' Ben how long and hard he's prayed for a wife he was truly in love with, and a family," Sylvie said. "And it's kinda nice, I'd say, the two of ya havin' yer babies together."

"Just think, you'll be a mother for the fourth time

and a fifth-time grandmother. I'll be a first-time mother and a third-time sister-in-law. And Gabriel will be a very older big brother," Riley reflected.

"Not to mention my baby will be your baby's aunt or uncle." She touched her own stomach.

"As long as neither of ya are yer own grammaw, you'll be fine," Sylvie chimed in.

That remark got them all laughing.

"Say, I've just had a thought," Sylvie shared, her large features breaking into a sparkling smile. "If I reckon right, I've got a trunk in the attic filled with baby patterns for sewin' clothes. And I do believe along with the patterns, there's instructions on how to knit a blanket, sweater, bonnet, and booties...as well as knittin' needles of all sizes. Since I loved and enjoyed makin' clothes for my own daughter, maybe ya two would enjoy it, too?"

Riley's face brightened. "I think that's a capital idea."

"Well, then what do ya gals say to takin' a walk across the road to the general store, purchasin' fabric, yarn, buttons, and other such do-dads, then comin' back here, bustin' out my trusty sewing machine, and whippin' up a wardrobe for these two youngin's?"

The suggestion brought Amanda the most delightful bout of happiness. Leave it to Sylvie to always be there for her, turning what could be a compromising situation into a joyous event. "I say, my dear friend, I don't know what I would do without you, and what are we waiting for?"

"My sentiments exactly," Riley agreed.

Sylvie stood, collected all the mugs, and put them into the sink. "Well then, let's get crackin'. We've got lots to do."

At Sweeny's General Store and Dry Goods, they ran into Flora Remington. Amanda knew Flora and Vernon were getting on famously, as Washburn kept her informed while the two of them worked on his furniture creations. He seemed happy, content, and with Flora by his side and all the new neighbors on the property, Vernon was anything but a lonely man.

Since Amanda had been at the building site by day and Flora visited the property in the evenings or on the weekend, the two kept missing each other. As a result they hadn't talked much, and they both had such marvelous news to share.

"I'm with child," she announced. "Eight weeks already, can you imagine?"

Flora's plump face, first shocked, blossomed into a full smile. "Not something planned, I gather."

"No, not at all. A miracle, actually, as I truly believed my chances were highly improbable."

"But obviously not impossible," Flora commented.

"Evidently. The entire situation is so uncanny. I mean, my odds were anything but great."

"Maybe so, but it doesn't make it any less a reality," Flora returned.

"So true, and since my daughter-in-law," she said, gesturing to Riley standing beside her, "is in the same condition; we need to make baby clothes. Thus bringing us to why we're in the store."

"How wonderful." Flora turned her attention to Riley. "I congratulate you both, but in truth it must be the way the position of the moon is situated, or some such phenomenon as that," she guessed. "As my daughter-in-law, Adelaide is also expecting. She is due in three months."

"Congratulations to you as well," she offered. "Will you be closing the shop and taking a trip to New York City to be with her?"

"No, as a matter of fact, Clay, my son, has decided to return to Willow Creek. The rush and chaos of the city isn't where the two of them want to rear their child. And as luck would have it, Mr. Cargraves at the bank is retiring. When I informed him of my son's return, he decided to turn his position over to Clay. Stanley Cargraves is an old and dear friend of my late husband," Flora explained. "He's watched my son grow up and knows he's an honest young man. Stanley would trust no one else but Clay to take over his duties."

"Then Adelaide can help you in the shop," she concurred.

"Adelaide will be running the shop," Flora said. "The place doesn't need two shopkeepers. Besides, the living quarters would be way too cramped, especially after the baby is born."

Amanda frowned. "Then where will you live?"

"At Eagle's Landing, with my soon-to-be husband, Vernon," she beamed.

She gasped. "When is the wedding?"

"In three weeks, when Clay and Adelaide arrive." Then Flora turned to Sylvie. "We would like to meet with Reverend Newcomb on Saturday to plan the nuptial ceremony."

Sylvie nodded. "I'll tell him yer comin'. How's around four sound? Then after ya two can join us for dinner."

"Oh, please, there's no need for you to go to any trouble," Flora said.

"No trouble at all, Flora," Sylvie reassured her. "I'd be right pleased for yer company."

"Then, I accept," Flora agreed. "And we'll be at the parsonage by four."

"And have you two planned any sort of celebration after the church ceremony?" Amanda probed.

"Clay and Adelaide want to take us out for just a private, quiet dinner at the hotel restaurant, whereby after Vernon and I will remain for a night or two." Flora's cheeks blushed pink.

Amanda reached out to affectionately squeeze the other woman's hand. "It all sounds lovely. Josh and I spent our wedding night there, and you will be completely enchanted by the honeymoon suite."

"Of course, you are all welcome to join us at the church ceremony," Flora invited. "As well as those at Eagle's Landing. As soon as we have established a date, we will spread the news."

"Josh and I wouldn't miss it for anything."

"Gabriel and I would be honored," Riley added.

"Just think of it," Flora said. "Soon, we'll all be neighbors."

She hugged her friend. "Perhaps, more like family."

"Oh, my sweet Amanda, I truly love the sound of that," Flora approved.

The afternoon fled by, as they lingered over the material choices. There were some with baby ducks swimming in a pond, bunnies munching on carrots or smelling flowers, teddy bears eating honey while comical looking bees circled their heads, and puppies and kittens chasing butterflies. Soft hues, like yellow, green, and white were chosen—acceptable shades for either a boy or a girl. Between Riley and Amanda both needing such colors for their baby's outfits, Sweeny's was just about bought out.

Sylvie was the button expert, knew which ones were easier to sew on and lasted the longest. She also chose the various ribbons, lacing, and thread needed to complement their creations.

After their shopping excursion, they sat at the soda counter for an ice cream. Amanda chose a butterscotch flavor, topped with chocolate syrup and chopped walnuts. As she spooned the delicious, refreshing treat into her mouth, she groaned with delight. The sweet, sticky coolness melted on her tongue, slipped down her throat, and pleased her belly. "I remember when I was carrying Gabriel I constantly craved corn bread, couldn't make enough of the stuff. For Raven I craved squash." She turned to Sylvie. "Remember when I expected Sunny, my yen was for tomatoes? Which you grew a bountiful crop of in your garden."

"Yup, I recollect. We had tomatoes comin' out of our ears," Sylvie said.

Amanda smiled fondly. "You and Ben would travel to the village with a basket full, just for my pleasure alone. No one dared to get between me and those tomatoes."

"When I was expectin' my daughter Sarah Joy I had a hankerin' for griddle cakes topped with molasses," Sylvie remembered. "I'd turn the jar over the cakes and watched eagerly, hungrily at the molasses as it dripped out in a slow stream." She laughed. "Ben would sit and stare at me with the most peculiar look upon his face."

"I've taken a shine to lemon drops," Riley

confessed. "Sweeny sells nice, big round ones, so wonderfully sour they pucker your mouth up into a perfect bow-shape. Gabriel supplied me with a large bag full, since I get the desire for one at the oddest times. He can't stand to look at me while I'm sucking on one, though. Watching makes his eyes water."

On their way back to the parsonage with their purchases, Riley giggled. "I think Flora is right."

She frowned. "About what?"

"The position of the moon, as there certainly is a lot of love in the air with all the baby-making and marriages," Riley said.

"Who else is expecting?"

"Sure as tootin' it ain't me," Sylvie quipped.

Riley giggled again. "Nay, not a baby this time, but another marriage."

"Who's tyin' the knot now?" Sylvie said.

"The Aussie and Maggie. He proposed last night, and she agreed," Riley said.

Amanda stifled a smile, as she remembered the compromising position she'd accidentally walked in on. "Have they set a date?"

"Nay, but I believe it will be soon." Riley followed Sylvie up the porch stairs.

"Not soon enough," she whispered to herself.

Chapter Twenty-Five

Amanda enjoyed making baby outfits with Sylvie and Riley. Rising Sun and her daughter, Dawn, stayed occasionally to help them, as did Maggie. Even Flora stopped by to lend a helping hand. Flora and Maggie talked about their up and coming nuptials with Flora's now only ten days away. Maggie and Eli were set to take their vows within a month's time which was when their dwelling and storefront would be finished. Flora offered to help Maggie manage the small general store.

Amanda thought this was a most fortunate offer especially with the way Eli and Maggie couldn't stay away from each other. No doubt Maggie would be the next woman to be expecting a baby. When that time came, Maggie would really need Flora to step in and run things for a while.

"I can't get over how tiny they are." Josh marveled over a baby nightgown one morning before leaving for Eagle's Landing. He frowned as he fingered a sleeve. "I fear, just while holding this child I'll cause harm."

"You'll get used to it," she reassured him. "Soon you won't think twice about dressing, changing, and washing our baby's bottom."

His eyes widened. "Me...I'll be cleaning a dirty bum?"

She placed her hands on her hips. "And why not? You are this baby's parent, too."

He arched a brow. "I just didn't think the man...the father did such things. In England the nanny takes care of those matters."

"Do you plan for us to have a nanny?"

"I hadn't thought much about it, I presume. That sort of thing is usually left up to the wife." He reached for a pair of booties. Sticking a finger into each small sock, he pretended to imitate a walking motion.

"Well, this isn't England, and I don't care to hire a nanny. I've raised three lovely, intelligent, and wonderful children without a nanny, so I believe I'm up for the task a fourth time." She removed the booties from his fingers and placed them back in the basket.

His lips thinned. "So, then, I assume I'm still in line to help with nappy duty."

She frowned. "Nappy duty?"

"Aye, the cloth you wrap the baby's bum with to catch all the mess," he explained, crinkling his nose.

"You mean diapers?" she corrected.

He scowled. "Diapers—nappies, what's in a name?"

She giggled, recognizing the famous phrase from Shakespeare's *Romeo and Juliet*. "Something that will never smell as sweet."

He joined in on her mirth. "Aye, this nappy part I'm not so anxious for." He pulled her close and kissed her gently. "But I will take it like a man; do my part to be the best father a son could have."

"Or a daughter," she whispered against his lips.

"Aye, or a daughter," he softly agreed.

After Josh left for Eagle's Landing, she helped Sylvie with the housework, did a bit more sewing, and ate lunch. Upon retreating to her bedroom to rest, she spotted her mother's journal. She had been so busy making baby clothes, she forgot all about her newly found treasure. Picking up the journal from its place on the dresser, she opened to the page where she last left off, and began to read.

*Tuesday, June 21, 1842*

*Today I am seventeen, and I woke with anticipation as to what might be planned. Father said he had a surprise for me...a guest I would be happy to meet.*

*At seven in the evening, Ida came to my bedchamber to inform me my special guest had arrived. He was waiting for me, along with Father, in the library. My heart raced, and I had all to do NOT to run down the stairs like an excited child. Once at the door, I hesitated before knocking—hoping to recognize the deep, smooth voice speaking to my father.*

*I frowned as my father began listing my attributes...as though I were a horse up for auction. Should I expect then, when I enter the library, for him to show our guest my good teeth, straight spine, and long legs? And why was any of this being said in the first place?*

*Then, to my humiliation, my father pointed out my willfulness and added, "I give you my permission to deal with my daughter thusly when she becomes your responsibility, and the need arises. I find a good, sound paddling or the occasional birching to the bared bum works wonders."*

*"I do not beat women, sir," the guest*

*replied, his tone rather indignant with such a thought.*

*"Then Mr. Rawlings, I pity you, for unless you learn to control your wife, you can forget about maintaining any peace or power in your home," my father snapped. "For a wife to respect her husband, she must fear him. And above all realize she is to please and obey him in everything he asks."*

*I gasped. Howard Rawlings! Our guest was my intended. I turned to run back upstairs to my chamber, where I planned to feign a headache and remain until the morrow...but Hendricks, my father's gentlemen's gentleman and personal spy, caught me by the arm. Then, opening the door he announced me as though I were being presented to the crown.*

*Howard Rawlings turned to face me. He was a pleasant looking man in his late twenties, with even features. Tall, thin, smartly dressed in a dark blue suite, his large brown eyes surveyed me.*

*Politely tilting a head cropped with thick, chestnut colored hair, he smiled. "My pleasure, Miss Bentley."*

*I curtsied, the heat rising to burn my face. "Mine, as well, Mr. Rawlings."*

*My father beamed with delight, nearing me and taking my arm to escort me fully into the room. "I'm so pleased for this evening. My only regret is my dear friend, Winston...God rest his soul, is not here to join us—as it was both of our wishes to have our children wed one another."*

*"Aye, he would have derived much satisfaction," Howard quipped. Then sighed and added, "He spoke of the contract between you often. In fact, he wouldn't let me forget it."*

*I detected a note of sarcasm in his tone, and wondered if Howard—like me—was dreading this union as well. Perhaps it might be beneficial to both our causes, if I were to inform him of my willingness to dissolve the agreement our father's made on our behalf. But it would have to be done in private, and the chances of us being allowed unchaperoned in a room together, was highly improbable.*

*All through dinner I waited for the opportunity, and then an opening presented itself.*

*"Shall we retire to my den, Howard, for a cigar and a brandy?" my father offered.*

*"Father, give me a moment to go on ahead, so I might pour a glass of brandy for you and Mr. Rawlings," I said, casting a quick smile toward our guest. "And make ready the cigars," I added sweetly.*

*I stood, and made haste to the den. Closing the double doors behind me, I rushed to my father's desk, reached for a small slab of paper, and scribbled with the quill a note:*

*"I Will Be At The Side-Lawn Garden Fountain Later This Evening, At Nine Sharp. Meet Me There....Urgent We Talk!"*

*Shoving the note under my cuff, I*

*prepared the brandy and the cigars just in time for my father and Mr. Rawlings to enter the room.*

*I called upon my manners, serving our guest first. I handed Mr. Rawlings a class of brandy, but when I gave him the cigar, I slipped the note with it, into his hand. Our eyes locked. For a moment I feared I'd read him wrong. Silently I prayed, hoping against hope, a man who did not believe in beating a woman, wouldn't throw her to the wolves either.*

*To my great relief, Mr. Rawlings kept the note hidden in his hand, cast me a gracious smile and said, "Thank you, Miss Bentley."*

*After I finished serving both men, and lighting each of their cigars from the flame of a nearby candle, I bid then a courteous goodnight.*

*At the allotted time, I snuck back downstairs and out the kitchen door. What excuse Howard Rawlings made to my father for wanting to stroll alone in the gardens, I don't know—and didn't care. All that mattered to me was the fact he was standing beside the water fountain, a lit lantern by his feet, in the side-lawn garden at the precise time I requested.*

*I stayed in the shadows, out of sight, should my father chance to look out the solarium windows. "Thank you, sir, for doing as I asked."*

*He kept his eyes ahead, puffing on the*

*cigar. "And why have you summoned me here, Miss Bentley."*

*There was no easy way to put it, so I spoke frankly. "I do not wish to marry you, Mr. Rawlings, though you seem to be a nice enough chap," I added, not wanting to offend him too awfully much.*

*He chuckled. "Well, I don't want to marry you either, Miss Bentley." He walked over to a nearby rose bush, and bent to smell the blooms. "Quite frankly, you've been a thorn in my side since the day you were born. You see," he went on to explain, "I am already in love with Millie Dansworth...have been for over two years. And if it weren't for the bloody contract my father made with yours, I'd already be wed to her and perhaps even have an heir by now."*

*My heart soared. "I am so very pleased to hear this, sir. I hope you and Millie Dansworth will be extremely happy together."*

*"Well, you see, Miss Bentley, your father will not allow that to be possible," he said.*

*"How can he prevent you?" I probed, my relief of a moment ago slipping.*

*"By providing his copy of the contract in a court of law," he explained. "Should I relinquish my end of the agreement, Wilson Bentley will ruin me...sue me for everything I own as well as smear my name. I will be run out of my profession and this town."*

*I gasped. "Nay, nay, that cannot be."*

*"I swear to you it is the truth," he said*

*sadly.*

*I felt sick, the nausea rising in my throat. I swallowed it down hard, and took a deep breath. "What if I relinquish my end?"*

*He chuckled sardonically. "Your father isn't ready to allow you to forfeit."*

*"I didn't say he would allow—I said I would relinquish," I countered.*

*He almost turned to look at me, then caught himself. "And how do you expect to manage this on your own?"*

*"I don't," I said. "I will need your help."*

*He made his way back to the water fountain. "And how exactly would I go about helping you, Miss Bentley."*

*"I wish to travel to America, Mr. Rawlings. Pay for my passage, and I will be gone from England, from this arrangement, and you will be freed from the contract. Since it will be my fault the agreement was broken, and you will be the party scorned, my father will not have legal basis to harm you. Then you will be able to marry Millie," I explained.*

*"As tempting as your offer is, I cannot allow it," he said.*

*I felt the tears burn the back of my throat. "I would agree to pay you back, somehow."*

*"I don't care a fig about the bloody money, Miss Bentley. I am wealthy enough to purchase several passages to the colonies, if I so desire," he said. "But in good conscience I cannot allow an innocent young woman, even a willful and stubborn one as you, to travel to*

*any destination...especially an untamed one, alone," he interrupted.*

*"So, instead you'd condemn us to a life of unhappiness?" I snapped.*

*"Nay, you aren't listening to what I am saying," he scolded. "I said, I would not allow you to travel alone. But should you be properly escorted, I am all for the idea."*

*I folded my arms across my chest, "I'm listening."*

*"My friend, Jacob Jennings and his wife, Katrina, will be sailing in two weeks to the colonies. They are planning to open a school in Texas. I'm sure they'd welcome another teacher to help them. Since your father has boasted you can read, write, and cypher, I'd say you are quite prepared to fill the position. But we need to work fast on the matter."*

*I listened to his plan.*

*"On Sunday, the twenty-sixth day of June, I will have a carriage waiting for you at midnight, behind the large deserted stable down the road."*

*It will take you into London—to where the Jenningses will be staying," he explained. "You will wait with them until departure on Tuesday, the eighth of July. I will leave your passage there for you, and an ample stipend to sustain you on your journey."*

*I wanted to run over and hug him but dared not emerge from the shadows, just in case my father watched. "I thank you with all of my heart, Mr. Rawlings."*

*"As I do, you, Miss Bentley,"* he countered. *"Oh, and one more thing."*

*"Aye,"* I said, fearing he'd wage a hefty stipulation.

He reached down to retrieve the lantern, readying himself to return to the manor. *"I hope we never set eyes upon each other again."*

*"As do, I, Mr. Rawlings, as do I,"* I agreed.

****

*Thursday, June 23, 1842*
I went about the house saying silent *"goodbyes"* to everyone. It very well might be the last time I set eyes on any of them.

I wish I could take Kaylena and Mother with me, free them from a life with Father. But that would be impossible, so I must wipe the thought from my mind and concentrate on moving forward myself. All of this is a bittersweet situation.

****

*Friday, June 24, 1842*
This morning Father called me into his den with the news he was sending me early on Sunday morning, the twenty-sixth of June, to visit with his sister, (my Aunt Winifred), in Seahaven, as she's offered to sew my wedding trousseau. This news sank my heart to my toes, as I knew of my other scheduled departure on Sunday night. When I tried to persuade him to send me on Monday instead, he got angry at my exuberant protests and sent me to my

*room.*

*I climbed the stairs with heavy feet, knowing Ida would be sent up shortly to redden my bum.*

*I waited and waited. Aggie brought me my dinner on a tray—I ate—and waited further. Still Ida hadn't arrived to dole out my punishment. When the hallway clock, struck midnight, I was awakened abruptly to find Father standing over me with a lit candle in one hand and a birching rod in the other. He reeked of brandy.*

*"Though your mother has convinced me to send you to Seahaven on Monday, I will not be undermined by your insolence," he growled, setting the candle on the bedside table.*

*Before I could say a word, Father grabbed me by the hair and pulled me from the bed, striking me across the back with the birching stick. The sudden shock of pain brought me to my knees. He then reached for the collar of my nightgown and ripped the material down the middle. The back of the garment fell apart, exposing me to his view. Humiliation stung my eyes, and I scrambled to cover myself with a sheet from the bed, but another blow to my naked flesh paralyzed me. I fell to my knees, and Father proceeded to whip me like a dog—across my shoulders, down my spine, on my bum and against my thighs. Over and over he swung the stick, until the pain was too much to bear. I collapsed upon my stomach, screaming, sobbing, pleading for him to stop.*

*It was Hendricks who came to my aid, pulling Father aside. Then my mother ran into my room next, screamed when she caught a glimpse of my wounds, and fell down on her knees beside me.*

*"Get him out of here," Mother demanded of Hendricks. "Then find Aggie and Ida, and send them to me immediately."*

*Hendricks hurried to obey her, shutting the door behind him.*

*I glanced up into my mother's eyes. Tears welled heavy in her saddened gaze, and streamed down her pale, strained face. "Never again," she mumbled over and over.*

*I tried to stand, but the pain was too great. It was then I lost control of my bladder, wetting myself and the floor. From that point on I don't remember much. Just bits and pieces—glimpsing Aggie, Mother, and Ida caring for me...washing me, applying salve and bandages to my wounds.*

\*\*\*\*

*Sunday, June 26, 1842*

*I've been locked in my room all day, and demanded to remain so until I am to leave for Seahaven early on Monday morning. But at the hour of eleven Mother entered the room. In her hands she carried a satchel and a small, lit candle. "Hurry, now, we must get you dressed as fast as you can muster," she whispered."*

*I gasped. "You know?"*

*"Aye, I followed you out to the garden on Tuesday night, and overheard the whole conversation between you and Mr. Rawlings,"* she admitted.

*"Is this why you convinced Father to let me leave for Seahaven tomorrow?"*

*She nodded.*

*"Come with me, Mother,"* I pleaded.

*She sighed heavily. "You know that's not possible, Amelia."*

*"But you and Kaylena are also in danger here."* I took my mother's hands in mine. *"How can I, in good conscience, leave the two people I love the most behind?"*

*"If you stay our fates will not change, only yours will also be miserable. At least, knowing you've escaped to follow your heart, my spirit can rest in peace,"* she said, taking me into her frail embrace. Then pulling back, she reached for the satchel. *"I've packed all you will need, and added my wedding dress— for that special day I know you will have. I won't be there to see it, but you will still be able to wear the gown my grandmother and mother wore before me—making the tradition live on. Along with the gown and veil, I've packed the family Bible and a quilt I made for your future marriage bed. When you sleep beneath it, think of me."*

*"What about father and Hendricks, they will see us,"* I worried.

*"Nay, your father is full of the brandy and snoring loudly in his bed. And tonight is*

*Sunday—remember? Hendrick's night off."
She walked with me as far as the lower garden
path. "God speed, my darling, and know
always—wherever you are and whatever you
are doing, I love you forever."*

*I hugged and kissed her, tears flowing
down my cheeks, to my neck, and settling on
the collar of my blouse. It would be the last
time I'd ever set my eyes on Cornelia
Bentley—the last time I'd hear her voice. "I
love you, too, Mother," I whispered. I forced
myself not to look back as I made my way,
painfully down the long path, holding the
candle so I could find my way to the deserted
stables at the end of the road, and to where
Mr. Rawlings' carriage waited.*

\*\*\*\*

*Monday, June 27, 1842*
*London*
*I sighed with immense relief when we
pulled into London around one in the
afternoon on Monday. It was Anna Jennings's
(Jacob's mother) home we stopped at. Anna
was a lovely woman, very grandmotherly—the
type of grandmother I always wished for. Both
Jacob (who was rather tall, thin, dark, and
pleasant to the eye) and Katrina (small blonde,
large blue eyes and a sweet smile) were in
their late twenties, kind, friendly, and very
happy to have me along on their journey.*

\*\*\*\*

*Tuesday, June 28, 1842*
*We broke our fast early, bid old Mrs.*

*Jennings goodbye by the time the hall clock struck seven in the morning (there was a lot of crying, hugging, and kissing), and climbed into another carriage (much bigger than the last I traveled in) to begin our journey to Liverpool, where we will board the* VICTORY *to America.*

\*\*\*\*

*Thursday, July 7, 1842*
*Liverpool*
*I have not been able to write an entry all these days, as access to a pen and ink has been hard to come by. Tomorrow we leave early for port.*

\*\*\*\*

*Friday, July 8, 1842*
*The* VICTORY *is the biggest ship I'd ever seen—in truth, the only ship up close, as I've only seen sailing vessels from afar in Brighton. My cabin is small, but as long as the ship stays afloat and brings me safely to America, I shan't complain.*

\*\*\*\*

*Monday, August 8, 1842*
*Boston*
*We've arrived in Boston, Massachusetts. When I disembarked from the* VICTORY *and stepped onto American soil, I knelt to kiss the ground—blessed to have made it to my destination and happy to have the earth beneath my feet. Never will I step foot upon the decks of a ship again.*

*We were brought to the home of Roger*

*and Emma Wiggins, Jacob's cousin and his wife. Their little girl, Beckanne, is Kaylena's age with waist-length braids the same color. She reminds me so much of my dear little sibling, that seeing her brings tears to my eyes. I have never been so content, nor felt so happy and alive as I do now. We will be staying in Boston with the Wigginses until the spring of 1843. Texas is a six month journey by wagon train through untamed land. To travel now would find us only midway by winter, adding to the hardships we could face. To earn my keep, I will be Beckanne's governess and tuitor. Bravo! I'm in America, and I've secured a position.*

****

*Friday, August 12, 1842*

*I've sent a letter off today to my dear friend, Lucinda Collins, telling her only that Father agreed to send me overseas. I mentioned our falling out...the beating in detail I received before he agreed, and nothing further. For this reason I asked her to only share my correspondence with my mother. In turn, I asked for news from Brighton and Collins Stead. I know Lucinda will be discreet, keeping secret my letters and whereabouts. God, I miss them so!*

In truth—after reading all Amelia endured at the hands of Wilson Bentley, Amanda was glad her grandfather was dead. And if it weren't for Cornelia Bentley and Howard Rawlings, she would not be here. How she wished she could have met her grandmother.

And what ever happened to Mr. Rawlings? Was he still alive today? And if so, where was he now? Did he have the happy life he'd hoped for with Millie Dansworth...did they have a family together?

And how she admired her mother, even more so then before. Amelia Bentley had courage. What a chance she took confiding in Howard, a man she barely knew. She had strength, enduring horrible beatings as she did. And amongst all of this, she had to face leaving her beloved mother and sister. But this was what had to happen if she was determined to be free from her father's brutish binds—and travel to America.

"Thank you, Mr. Rawlings, for being a nice man and helping my mother...and I love you, Grandmother," she whispered, suddenly appreciating two people she never knew.

She closed the journal just as Josh opened the bedroom door. Without realizing it, she'd read away the rest of the day.

She placed the journal aside and stood. "I lost track of time, and since you're back from the site, it must be the dinner hour," she said, her body crying out for food.

He nodded. "Sylvie has it ready, but first I've some good news." He smiled. "We should be able to move into our home in three weeks' time."

She went to him, throwing her arms around his neck and giving him a big kiss. "Home," she whispered wistfully. "Doesn't that sound grand?"

"Aye." He embraced her around the waist. "Grand indeed."

Chapter Twenty-Six

Josh thought the summer had flown by, in spite of the long hours of hard work that went with it. Flora married Vernon, and Maggie wed Eli, all the homes were built, and a few finishing touches were all that was needed on the church, stable, general store, and schoolhouse. Street paths were made and named. Their home, for example, sat on the corner of Amelia Lane and Ethan Drive. Other locations in Eagle's Landing were called Eagle Parkway—the main street and business district; Gregory Avenue, Cornelia Court, Creek View Manor—where all the wickiups sat, and White Dove Road.

Riley was due to give birth in two months, her swollen appearance making each day more difficult to maneuver. And Amanda, now into her fifth month, toted a rather round, full belly as well. He loved looking at her naked body, the breasts so full and heavy—pink peaks engorged, her bum so round and inviting, and the beautiful swell of his child beneath her heart.

She fixed their home in soft, cozy shades. The parlor was done in various hues of blue. The chosen color graced the settee and four upholstered chairs. Another area was set aside for his desk and bookshelves, a braided rug placed upon the hardwood floors. Drapery, curtains, and other window fixtures complemented the décor of each room. The icebox, cast iron stove, indoor sink, tub pumps, and outhouse privy were a tremendous convenience. Not to have to fetch water from a well, relieve yourself behind a bush, or bathe in a creek pleased his wife to great capacity.

The kitchen was at the center of the home, the main fireplace situated in the dining area. The table was placed in the exact location as it was when Amanda lived in the old house as a child. Amanda liked this room the most and sat there with a cup of tea, writing letters to Raven and Sunny, sewing, or enjoying late night cravings of toasted bread smothered with honey. The baby's nursery was beside theirs, done in cream and lavender; and a large loft, furnished with several beds, night tables, and a few dressers was ready for Raven and Sunny's visits.

But it was their bedchamber he favored, done in a deep wine and beige. An oak wood canopy bed, matching night tables, dresser, and vanity table with a mirror, as well as two cushioned arm chairs finished it nicely. Here he could eliminate his body from every stitch of clothing, lie upon the bed naked as the day he was born, with legs askew and hands beneath his head. And his beautiful wife would caress him, suckle him, bring his loins to a most pleasurable state, then spread her own limbs for him to release his passion within her.

An early fall rain shower fell on this night, softly pelting the roof. "Ah, a female rain," Amanda commented. She was lying naked beside him, her body full with his child.

"Why do you call it so?"

She smiled fondly. "Because it falls softly, gently, nurturing the earth, quenching its thirst, as a mother does a child." She turned to meet his gaze. "Or a wife does for her husband."

He turned onto his side to face her, propping his head upon one hand. The other reached out to caress one of her breasts, so engorged, blue veins made little paths against her creamy flesh. "Are you sore here?"

"Sometimes," she whispered.

"Will it hurt too much then, if I suckle you?" The tip of a finger rubbed tenderly over an erect nipple.

"Not if you are kind."

"As I shall always be with you, my love." He leaned to take the peak into his mouth. He drew on it tenderly, caressing it with the tip of his tongue.

She groaned with pleasure. "You are assisting the milk to come. By the time the baby is born, I will have no trouble nursing."

He pulled back, raising his gaze to meet hers. "Will you allow me to have a taste as well?"

"Anytime you wish," she said dreamily, her eyes half closed—relaxed. "It's very sweet."

"Like you." He moved his hand to stroke her rounded belly, the navel protruding. The babe kicked at that moment, making them both laugh. "I so very much love when that happens."

"Move your hand lower." She spread her thighs.

He complied, teasing the soft nub within her valley with a fingertip. She grew moist with his feather-like flicks.

"Faster," was her breathless command.

Again he complied, taking immense pleasure in watching her body pulsate with the desire he brought forth. With her knees bent and legs spread, she was fully exposed to his view—vulnerable to his touch, and he was thrilled with the privilege to freely bring her yearnings to fruition. Slipping a finger now deep inside of her, he felt the hot, wet walls of her womanhood quiver as he moved in and out. When he penetrated her bum, her hips rocked with the rhythm of his touch. He teased her until his foreplay drove her into delicious spasms. She climaxed around his fingers, moaning and gasping with pure ecstasy.

"Good God, woman, you allow me to be so outrageously free with your body." He mounted her carefully for his own release. Holding his weight upon his elbows, as not to hurt her, he filled her with his juices and took enormous gratification expelling every ounce.

As they lay spent and entwined, he wished he were twenty years younger. If so, he'd have the stamina to never allow this woman to leave his bed.

She snuggled her face beneath his chin. "Josh, do you know what I crave for...what I'd love you to do for me this very moment?"

He smiled to himself, mustering whatever reserve he had left, making ready to lick her, watch again as she gloriously shattered. "What would that be, love?"

She sighed and curled against him. "Would you...could you...?"

"Aye," he interrupted breathlessly, his anticipation mounting.

"Do you mind terribly..."

His loins grew hot and hard. "Whatever you ask of me, I'll do."

"Please then, would you make me a plate of toast and honey." She pulled back to plant a tender kiss on the side of his mouth and flashed him the most irresistible smile.

He playfully pinched her bum and chuckled when she let out a diminutive squeal. "Aye, for you I'll do even that, my love."

\*\*\*\*

After living in a wickiup with only a door-flap as a barrier between the inside and out, Amanda loved the fact she had an actual door to bolt at night. She felt safe, protected, and the heavy portal kept the cool October nights from penetrating her home and critters from making their way freely into her bed or rummaging through her belongings.

To have real furniture to sit upon was also pure joy. The upholstered chairs in her parlor were the most comfortable to lounge in, especially with a sore back from carrying a full load up front. And what heaven it was to soak in a tub, the water gathered from an indoor pump, which could be warmed efficiently on a cast-iron wood burning stove instead of an open fire. She was able to drain the tub simply by pulling the plug from the drain hole.

And she adored her clothes washing machine. Being able to use a crank to rotate and wash the clothes, then wring them out using the wringer device attached before hanging them on a clothes line to dry, was far better than beating them clean upon a rock and hanging them on tree limbs. What once was back breaking work, done now in half the time, and in the privacy of her home.

Vernon had built her a cedar chest, and in it she stored her father's violin, the family Bible, and her mother's journal which she hadn't read in quite a while. With all the excitement of moving into and furnishing their home, she hadn't had time to read the diary further. But now, alone because Josh was helping with the sheep barn, and sitting by the fire sipping a cup of ginger tea, she decided to visit Amelia's world until she needed to start the evening meal.

*Saturday, September 3, 1842*

*I've been so busy with my duties as governess and tutor, I haven't had time for entering even one word in my journal. Beckanne is a handful, but a delightful one at that. She's so intelligent and eager to learn, it makes teaching her a pleasure. But today we put aside the books and went to a festival.*

*As I walked the fair holding Beckanne's hand, I was drawn to where I heard someone playing the violin. I found the minstrel only down the street. A young man with honey-colored hair and huge, pale blue eyes was sitting upon a crate, playing a song. When he'd finished the tune, his gaze met mine. And for an instant all the sounds surrounding me ceased. And then a very strange thing happened. My body heated, and a funny tingling began in the very pit of my stomach.*

*The young man swallowed hard, as though he were feeling the same sensations. Clearing his throat, he said, "Where have you been?"*

*His question stumped me, for it was asked as though he was looking for me for some time—when in fact, we were complete strangers. But what happened next was even odder. My reply was, "It matters not, for I'm here now."*

He bowed politely. "My name is Ethan Gregory, all the way from Joliet, Illinois. Born and raised in Jefferson County."

"Well, Mr. Gregory, ye are very bold," Beckanne chafed. Then turning her attention to me, she said, "Come, Miss Amelia, father will wonder where we've been."

"And do you have a last name, Miss Amelia," Mr. Gregory pressed.

"She does, but it is not of any concern to ye, sir," Beckanne snapped, pulling on my hand to leave.

"Bentley...Amelia Bentley from Brighton, England, sir," I choked out.

Mr. Gregory tipped his head politely again. "My pleasure, Miss Bentley."

I curtsied. "Mine, as well, Mr. Gregory."

"Come, Miss Amelia," Beckanne pleaded, pulling me harder. "Father will be worried and not pleased ye are speaking to a stranger."

I allowed her this time to break me away from the violin player. However, I've thought of nothing else but our peculiar meeting and his captivating blue eyes, ever since.

****

*Sunday, September 18, 1842*

After church this afternoon, we were all gathered at the table for our midday meal, when there was a rap at the front door. Roger went to see who it was coming to call, and within a few moments returned to the dining room.

*"Ye have a visitor, Amelia," he said.*

*Katrina told Jacob to go with me to the parlor, and there we saw Ethan Gregory standing by the windows. He looked shockingly handsome in his Sunday best—a dark gray, three-piece suit and shiny black shoes. His smile, revealing even white teeth, dazzled me. I found myself smiling as well.*

*"Good afternoon, Miss Bentley," he said.*

*"Mr. Gregory," I countered, feeling my insides quiver.*

*"Good day, old chap," Jacob chimed in, extending a hand in greeting. Ethan shook Jacob's hand. "I'm Jacob Jennings from London, England."*

*Ethan cleared his throat. "My name is Ethan Gregory, from Joliet, Illinois."*

*After Jacob introduced himself he inquired, "And what is your business in Boston, Mr. Gregory?"*

*"I'm one of the wagon train guides, sir. The next group I'll be escorting out west will be in April. For now, I work at the docks."*

*"I believe, then you will be escorting my wife, Miss Amelia, and myself on our way to Texas," Jacob explained.*

*This news made Ethan smile. "I shall enjoy my last wagon train journey."*

*"And then, will you return to your family in Missouri, Mr. Gregory?" Jacob probed further.*

*"No, sir, I'm headed out west. Last time I was there, I bought myself fifty-seven acres of*

*land in the Arizona territory, near Willow Creek."*

*"And what's your business here today, Mr. Gregory?" Jacob said.*

*His smile deepened. "I've come to ask Miss Bentley's father if I might court her." Ethan met Jacob's gaze. "Would you please inform him of my visit, sir?"*

*"Nay, Mr. Gregory, I cannot, for Mr. Bentley still resides in England. But I'm Amelia's guardian," he finally said. "So you may address your request to me."*

*Ethan squared his broad shoulders. "Then, Mr. Jennings, may I have your permission to court Amelia?"*

*Jacob thought for a moment, then turned to look in my direction. "Well, Mr. Gregory, I'd say that's entirely up to Amelia." Never in my life have I been given a voice on my own behalf.*

*"Aye...aye, I should like to court Mr. Gregory."*

*Jacob turned back to Ethan. "There now, old chap, you have her answer."*

*My knees trembled.*

*"And where would you be taking her, Mr. Gregory?" Jacob probed.*

*"The Wharf Eatery, sir. They serve a delicious salmon meal there on Wednesday at five," Ethan said.*

*"Then she will see you on Wednesday, at the hour of five, and you shall have her home by the decent hour of eight," Jacob said.*

*Ethan nodded.*

*"I trust you will be respectful toward the lady?" Jacob replied sharply.*

*"I shall guard her with my life, sir," Ethan promised.*

*Jacob nodded satisfied. "Now, Amelia, please see Mr. Gregory to the door," he said before taking his leave to the dining room.*

*The two of us walked in silence to the foyer. I opened the door, and smiled. "Thank you for the invite, Mr. Gregory."*

*"Would you call me Ethan?" he said, his spicy cologne playing havoc with my senses.*

*"If you will call me Amelia," I said.*

*"I was hoping you'd say that." Then he cast me a dazzling smile and whispered. "Amelia, I think you twinkle when you smile, and it's completely captivated me, so here and now I want you to know, you are the prettiest woman I ever set my eyes upon. And from this very moment forward, the only woman I ever want to see." With such a declaration said, he strode down the front steps and out to the road.*

*I closed the front door, braced my back against the wood, sighed heavily and twinkled.*

Amanda wished she could have read more, learn how her parents' first date turned out. But from this point on several pages were destroyed. She wiped the tears from her eyes and sat in quiet contemplation. Through her mother's words she was able to get a good glimpse of how her parents met—how smitten they were with each other at first glance.

"You two were always meant to be together," she whispered to herself.

Not Wilson Bentley or the vast ocean between their worlds could keep them apart. And now they're together once again, in heaven.

When Josh arrived home, and they sat down to dinner, she asked him, "When was it that you fell in love with me?" It was a question she was able to have an answer to, now that they were married.

He put his fork down and folded his hands in front of him. "You had just turned seventeen, coming to help Grace with the Easter pie sale. You wore a blue dress, trimmed with white, and one of Grace's aprons to keep it clean. But it did little good, because you were covered in flour...smudges on your nose and cheeks...streaks of it even in the pale curls that framed your beautiful face. I watched from the kitchen doorway, and at that moment I knew I loved you— would love you for the rest of my life."

"Did you go to my father, tell him your feelings. I mean, my mother was only seventeen when she married my father. I remember her telling me she had four more months to go until she turned eighteen when they wed," she said.

"Nay, I didn't think Ethan would appreciate hearing I had feelings for his daughter. He was a protective father, and since your mother died, you were all he had left in the world. I knew he'd deny my request to court you. So, I decided to hold off, wait another year. But then the Chiricahuas attacked your father and killed him. And when I asked for your hand in marriage, it came out wrong, you believing I only wanted to marry you to take care of you." He smiled.

"And because you are a stubborn and willful woman, bent on returning to the farm and keeping it going as tribute to your father, you put my proposal off, asking for more time to think it over."

"But then I found Proud Eagle one night, wounded in my yard," she filled in. "And the rest is history."

He sighed, reaching for his cup of tea and taking a sip. "Aye." He frowned, remaining silent for a moment, as though he was thinking whether or not to speak his next words. "I often wonder," he began. "If you hadn't found Proud Eagle as you did, if you would have accepted my proposal."

She reached over and covered his hand with her own. "The answer is, yes—I would have married you. I had planned on accepting your offer."

"Because you were alone and without your father?"

"No, because I loved you," she whispered. "I loved you always, as a good family friend. But when Papa died and you proposed, I started to think things over, began to feel differently, until..." she let the rest ride.

He smiled. "It isn't important now. You are my wife, and soon you will give birth to our child. We were meant to be, just not on my terms. It was God's timing that mattered."

"And what will be—will be," she concluded.

Chapter Twenty-Seven

Riley went into labor early on a cold, November morning. They were awakened before dawn by Gabriel and rushed next door to be with Riley while he fetched Owl Woman and Doc O'Clarity. It was rather uncanny the way Sean and Owl Woman pooled their experience, helping and healing others using a mixture of science and nature. The combination, thus far worked. He hoped it continued.

As the mantel clock struck noon, Josh sat in the parlor with Gabriel, who paced like a pregnant duck. The doctor, Owl Woman, and Amanda were with Riley, their encouraging words could be heard through the bedroom door as well as her grunt or groan of pain.

"I want to be in there with her. I should be by her side." Gabriel ran his hands through his hair. "Wait—wait until it's your time with my mother." He pointed a finger at Josh. "You will go mad as well."

"I doubt that not one bit, Gabriel. But until you are called into the room, you must accept what's happening and be patient."

Finally Amanda opened the bedroom door, her own belly swollen with the last stages of pregnancy. She looked exhausted, and Josh suddenly felt protective toward her, concerned for his wife's well-being.

"Gabriel," was the only word she said, and he all but flew into the bedroom.

More grunting, groaning, then screaming could be heard for at least another hour. Finally, around two in the afternoon, a baby wailed—long and loud.

"Praise and thank you, God," Josh whispered to himself.

Amanda opened the door shortly after, looking totally spent and worn out. He helped her over to a chair. She sighed heavily. "It's a boy—we have a grandson—and he's perfect. Already he has a head full of dark hair, just as Gabriel did when he was born. They've decided to name him after my father— Ethan...Ethan Soaring Eagle."

"And Riley?"

"She is well, all is well." She rubbed her eyes with the palms of her hands. "I believe even my son will make it."

He chuckled. "Then, in view of this, let me take you home. You can put your feet up; I'll make you lunch and a cup of tea." He arched a brow. "Possibly a nap might be in order for the both of us."

She caressed his face. "That sounds heavenly."

On the way to their house, they spotted Rising Star waiting patiently under a nearby tree. "What news have you for me?"

"It's a boy," Amanda said with a big smile. "And they've named him Ethan Soaring Eagle."

Rising Star returned the smile, nodded, and took off running toward the creek. In no time drums could be heard, and the tribespeople began to chant the baby's name. The first baby born at Eagle's Landing along with the word *Yuma*.

He frowned. "What are they saying?"

"*Yuma* is the Apache word meaning the Chief's

271

son," she explained.

When they got into their house, he fed her as he promised, then helped her off with her shoes and clothes. Once she was comfortably settled into bed, he disrobed and climbed in beside her.

Pulling her close, he kissed her forehead and whispered. "Rest now, Grandmamma."

She giggled, snuggling closer, "You too, Grandpapa."

He smiled to himself. In less than a year's time he'd become a husband, a grandfather, and soon he'd be a father. Life was good.

\*\*\*\*

Amanda woke to darkness. Josh stirred beside her, placing a hand over her swollen belly and caressing it with tender strokes.

"I'd say we've taken more than a little nap," he whispered.

She stretched her legs. "What time do you think it is?"

He moved to sit up. "I'll light a lantern and find out."

"No." She placed a restraining hand upon his arm. "Stay here with me."

Suddenly every sinew of her being ached for his kiss, his touch, and the intimate release of her hunger. As though he read her mind, he reached out and gently played with one of her nipples. Involuntarily it stiffened, causing a warm and pleasing sensation between her thighs. His touch danced between them, coaxing and teasing, seeking the silken crevice for her ultimate pleasure. She opened to his touch like a flower and with each flick of his finger against her slippery bud, she trembled. Arching her spine, she pressed herself into his massage and groaned, growing all the more delighted with the shimmering darts of passion igniting throughout her body. Then she braced herself for the pleasurable release that would soon follow. Wider she opened, her legs bent, heels pressed into the mattress, and submitted to the ecstasy.

"Amanda," he whispered, a glint of excitement edging his tone. "The sweet angles of your body beckon me, heating every fiber of my being."

He leaned closer to her, and she felt his growing, hard loins against her thigh. Desire washed through her with evident intensity. She reached down and gripped his stiffening member, gently pumping it up and down. His engorgement grew, its tip wet and sticky with his fervor. His moan of delight caused her own loins again to throb, and her body ached even more now with longing. Her pulse raced as their needs meshed, their bodies engulfed in heightened senses. She was intoxicated with desire.

The catch in her throat left her tone breathless. "Enter me now, as I need you to fill me with your love." He moved over her, penetrating her flesh. The length of him slid easily as he pushed himself into the warmth and depth of her body. With his hot and hard arousal filling her, tight inside of her, she clenched around him...feeling the force of his passion flow into her, in total completeness.

Chapter Twenty-Eight

*Eagle's Landing, Arizona*
*January 1896*

The weeks flew by, and Amanda's husband tried his best to keep her from doing too much. But she couldn't be stopped. In fact she just about threw her whole heart and soul into making the first Thanksgiving for Riley, Maggie, Eli, and the Irish folks an experience to remember.

Then Christmas followed, and the holiday baking, cleaning, and decorating took over most of her days. But everyone enjoyed a wonderful meal, and she did have lots of help with it all. Sylvie was a constant blessing with the preparations. Amanda imagined, after having a house full of guests, Sylvie's home must now seem very quiet and lonely.

The second week into the New Year, Eagle's Landing was finally registered by law and considered an active, thriving town. It would be placed on the map like Willow Creek, Baker's Corners, and other neighboring cities of Arizona.

Edmond Dodd brought them the news. "In fact your baby will legally be the first child born at Eagle's Landing." Then he smiled and added. "Besides the amazing way this town was founded, the Holmes' baby's birth will be recorded as another fact to go down in the town's history."

As everyone settled into winter, so did she, and most days she did nothing but wobble like a stuffed turkey from the bedroom, to the kitchen, then the parlor, and back to the bedroom. With the festivities behind her, and the need to gather her strength for the birth ahead of her, she decided to dive once more into her mother's journal.

*Thursday, December 8, 1842*

*I've received a letter from my dear friend, Lucinda. And though I opened it with anticipation of news from home, when I read it, my mood changed. My dear, sweet mother, Cornelia Cassia Bentley, had passed away. My heart is broken in two. The letter indicates she died a month ago. And I couldn't help but wonder, was it while I laughed and enjoyed an evening with Ethan that my mother took her last breath? What was I doing the moment she departed from this world? And what about my little sister, Kaylena? How is she holding up? I could only hope Aggie was there for her, in my place.*

\*\*\*\*

*Sunday, December 25, 1842*

*Mr. Ethan Gregory proposed marriage to me today. We were all gathered around the dining room table, enjoying Christmas dinner, when he stood, got down on one knee in front of the entire household, and asked for my hand in marriage. Of course, I agreed. The only thing that could make this day even more wonderful then it was is if Mother could be here. I hoped, in spirit she was with me, knowing how happy and in love I am.*

\*\*\*\*

*Sunday, February 12, 1843*

*Today was my wedding day. At seven this evening, I married Ethan Gregory at the Pine Street Chapel, wearing Mother's gown and veil. He placed his grandmother's gold wedding band upon my finger, and I in turn, placed his grandfather's wedding band upon his finger. Dinner at The Wharf Eatery followed; attended by the Jenningses, the Wigginses, and a few chaps (and their wives) Ethan worked the docks with. Then we mounted the stairs, to the room above the eatery Ethan rented for our wedding night. As I write this entry, my husband sleeps soundly in the bed, while I sit at a small table in front of the fire. I am too full of emotion to join him in slumber.*

*As we made ready for bed, he helped to remove my gown. When he raised my shift over my head, he froze. "Who has done this to you," he snapped.*

*Instantly I realized he was referring to the birching scars across my back. Pulling away from him, I covered my nakedness with a blanket from the bed and went to stand by the fireplace. Miserably I stared into the flames. "My father," I said, too ashamed to meet his gaze.*

*"Mother of God," he gasped. "What man would beat his daughter..."*

*"It's what he did," I interrupted. "It was his way, to beat me or have me beaten whenever he thought I needed it," I explained, still not able to face him.*

*"You know, don't you, if he were here before me, I'd have no choice but to kill him." He moved closer to where I stood.*

*"And I would choose to let you," I replied in return.*

*He placed his hand on my shoulder. "No one will ever touch you in such a way again, Amelia. You have my word on that. You also have nothing to fear from me. I don't beat women."*

*His words suddenly reminded me of Howard Rawlings, as he declared the same.*

*"Nor do I beat children," he added. He turned me around to face him. "Love is kind, Amelia. And I love you with everything inside of me."*

*I smiled, my heart rejoicing. I dropped the blanket I held around me, standing naked before him. "I believe I would like you to show me how much you love me, Ethan."*

\*\*\*\*

*Monday, April 10, 1843*

*I sent one last letter off to Lucinda, for we are on our way to Texas. I cried when I said my goodbyes to the Wigginses, especially my precious, little Beckanne. I fear I shall never see them again. They are good people, loving me like their own. I shall miss them with all my heart.*

****

*Wednesday, May 24, 1843*
*The nights are rainy and cold. I am thankful to have Ethan's warm body to curl up next to. There's lots of mud for the wagons to get through. The road is thick with the sodden earth, preventing the large wheels from turning. Several times we get stuck. The going is tough. I am cold, wet, tired, and running out of ink.*

****

*Sunday, October 8, 1843*
*Dry Gulch*
*I cannot believe we are finally in Texas, a small town called Dry Gulch. The land is vast, bare except for the handful of red-roof, adobe homes dotting the small town here and there. We will begin to build the school Jacob and Katrina have come to start. Ethan and I will stay until the spring, since I promised the Jenningses I'd help them with their school, as was the original plan—my commitment to them.*

****

*Monday, December 25, 1843*
*Christmas has arrived. Katrina announced she is with child. I am so pleased for them both, as they've been married eight years now with no children. It gives me hope for Ethan and I—married a year in two more months and still we are childless. Ethan says the good Lord is waiting until we are home in Arizona, before he makes us parents. I pray he*

*is right.*

\*\*\*\*

*Tuesday, April 16, 1844*

*I bid my beloved Katrina and Jacob a fond farewell. When I will see them again—if ever—I don't know. This land is wide and untamed. Traveling to and fro is not easy. After I hug and kiss Katrina, I place my hand upon her belly, which is just starting to swell. Perhaps, touching her baby-mound will bestow a blessing upon my own womb. I visit the school I helped to establish one more time, hug all the children, and then we are on our way.*

*Farewell to Dry Gulch!*

\*\*\*\*

*Friday, August 23, 1843*
*Willow Creek, Arizona Territory*

*We are home—in Willow Creek. The town is small...not really a town by England's standards. Our home is but two rooms, a bedroom and a room where kitchen and parlor are combined. It is hot, dry, and quiet. Ethan is working on building a church with several of the town's men. I am conducting school for five students in a small room behind the general store. Now that we've arrived at our home, I pray I am blessed with a son or daughter.*

Again Amanda noticed pages destroyed or missing. By now a low, constant pain in her back bothered her. But she read one more entry, made almost three years later.

\*\*\*\*

*Thursday, June 4, 1846*

*We were on our way home from town this afternoon—had to buy flour and sugar, when we had a pleasant encounter. The jostling wagon makes me sick, now that I am six months along with child. Finally the Lord has answered our prayers. So, we have to stop frequently along the way, thus why we had the chance meeting. I knew who he was instantly, remembering his face from all the times I saw it in a painting at Glenshire, Sussex. The shock of white hair sweeping across his temple, the large blue eyes, it could be nay other than Lord Silas Collins. And he was walking along a wooded path, holding the hand of a little boy, who appeared to be about three or four years old.*

*"Lord Collins," I shouted.*

*He frowned, making his way closer to our wagon. "And who might it be that calls me thus?"*

*I introduced myself. "I am Amelia Bentley Gregory, and this is my husband, Ethan." I gestured to Ethan sitting beside me. "I am a friend of your niece, Lucinda Collins, and I've looked upon your portrait at Collins Stead more times than I remember."*

*Lord Collins chuckled. "I'd quite forgotten about that dreadful portrait I share with my brother, Sherman." He searched my face. "And what, by God, brings a wisp of a lady such as yourself, to these parts?"*

*"You, my Lord," I said.*

*He arched a bushy brow. "My good woman, I scarcely know you, how would I have been an influence?"*

*"Your letters to your family sparked my interest to come to America, and then travel out west with my husband." I then briefly filled him in on my journey.*

*He turned to glance down at the little boy who held fast to his hand. "Do you hear that, Peter? I've become somewhat of a legend to this lady."*

*The little boy smiled at me, and I fell in love with him on the spot.*

*"This must be your grandson." I remembered from a letter I had read many years ago at Lucinda's eighteenth birthday party. Silas mentioned he was to be a grandfather in six months' time.*

*"Aye, that he is." He hoisted the boy to stand on the wagon runner. "I call him Peter. But his tribespeople call him Proud Eagle. And one day he will be the chief, taking over for his father, as is the Apache custom."*

*The boy was a handsome child, large dark eyes and thick black hair that fell to the collar of his buckskin shirt. "Are you as adventurous as your grandpapa?"*

*"One day, me a warrior," Peter Proud Eagle exclaimed proudly.*

*I laughed. "I'm sure you will be excellent at it as well."*

*Then the child reached forward to touch a*

*lock of my hair. "Holos," he whispered, examining the strand like it was a precious jewel.*

*I frowned. "What is holos?"*

*"The Apache word for sun," Lord Collins explained.*

*"Holos," the child repeated.*

*"Aye, you're correct, young Peter. Her hair is like the color of the sun," Lord Collins agreed. "Forgive him; he has never seen a lady with golden hair." He gently released the boy's hold on a wayward curl and lifted the child onto his shoulders. "Come, my fine chap, we must get you back to the village before your mother worries." And to me he said, "My best wishes to you both."*

*As we pulled away I heard the child call out. "Bye, bye, Golden Lady."*

*And then the strangest thing occurred. When I turned to wave to the boy, the babe I carried beneath my heart, jumped inside me.*

Amanda sat numbed. Her mother had never mentioned this meeting. She would have remembered if Amelia had. And all this time—all the years she spent as Proud Eagle's wife, Amanda often wished her mother could have met him. Only to discover now—in truth—she already had.

Little did Amelia Gregory know, eighteen years later the little Apache boy she met along the road walking with Silas Collins, would grow up to be the strong and loving warrior who would marry the baby she carried.

And what of Proud Eagle? He was just a small boy

when he met Amelia. No doubt, too small to recollect the encounter. But could he have somehow stored away the event in his mind, to have it flicker a light of remembrance when he met Amanda? For a moment she called to mind the first time they introduced each other, after she'd found him injured and helped him to the barn in order to clean his wounds and give him something to eat.

*His large black eyes searched her face. "What are you called?"*

*The tenderness in his expression amazed her. "I am Amanda...Amanda Gregory."*

*His gaze boldly observed her hair. "Golden Lady fits you better," he whispered, than continued to eat his meal.*

A tear trickled down her cheek as she closed the journal, leaving the past again. Both of them were gone now, and neither of them would ever know the circle of life they were a part of. "We are all entwined; fate has brought us all together to be a family." Stretching her aching back, she glanced at the mantel clock, shocked at the time. "Good heavens, the day passes so quickly when I take up reading Mamma's journal."

She needed to start dinner for Josh. He'd be starving when he returned from helping Mickey McCrea at the stables. But when she stood, something burst from deep inside of her and cascaded down her legs. When she glanced at her feet, she was standing in a puddle.

Her water broke!

Chapter Twenty-Nine

Josh was rubbing down Gorgan, a beautiful chestnut mare when Gabriel came into the stable.

Making his way to where he stood, Gabriel reached out to stroke the animal. "A fine mount, would you not agree?"

"Aye." He took a moment to admire the beast. "She will breed well, I am told."

Gabriel nodded. "Mickey knows his horses." He took a deep breath, expanding his chest. "Now that Eagle's Landing is a legal, functioning town, and my wife has given birth, I am only waiting for my mother to deliver your baby. Once all is well with her, I will set Mickey McCrea to work at his second job."

His heart raced. "Many folks from neighboring towns hold great respect for you because of the jobs you've given them, as you hoped. So, you have a much better chance, after finding the culprit, of bringing him to justice for his crimes."

Gabriel frowned. "That was my first intent when I hired the others, but since then I have gotten to know many well from working so closely with them. The three men who helped you, plus the two that assisted me have asked if they could build homes for themselves at Eagle's Landing."

He arched a brow. "And have you agreed?"

Gabriel nodded. "I've already allowed them to

284

break ground and begin because I see them as good people, hardworking, and they have much to contribute to the town. Oscar Hunt is a goat farmer, and he could help Eli with the sheep. Oscar's wife is a seamstress. She can sew clothes to put on consignment in Eagle's Landing's General Store. Ernie Grant and Curly Blackwell are excellent horsemen and would be of much help to Mickey. Ernie's wife makes hats and Oscar's wife bakes delicious pies and cakes, also store merchandise. The two men who worked with me, Hudson and Brewster Cooper, are brothers. Brewster makes saddles and other leather items, and Hudson is a shoemaker. His wife, Rowena is a healer, knows how to grow and use herbs. Brewster's wife, Gretchen, is a candle maker. With all these skills, our town will prosper. And between all of these families, there are sixteen children; eleven of them are of the age to attend our school."

"And yet still there lies the fact if these folks are a part of this town, they will stand by you when you need them, too," he added.

Gabriel nodded again. "I will tell you when I have made my move, set McCrea onto this varmint's trail. I think we will all need to watch our backs, then...and watch out for our women. Whoever murdered my father, when exposed, will be out for revenge." He pulled a watch attached to a silver chain from the pocket of his buckskin vest. "But for now everything remains the same, and I must get myself home, as Riley will have the evening meal ready."

Josh frowned. "I should make my way home as well."

A chill in the air had him raising his collar and

pushing his hands into his jacket pockets. He greeted Doc O'Clarity as he drove a wagon past him. Upon the seat beside him sat a boy about twelve.

"Where are you off to at this hour?"

"The Simpson farm about a mile away," Sean said. "Nick here"—he pointed to the boy—"came to fetch me. His mother's in labor."

He smiled. "Ah, your first patient outside of Eagle's Landing?"

Doc returned the smile. "Aye, it appears so, my friend."

He greeted a few others on his walk home, inhaling Arizona's crisp, winter air. The thought of a warm meal and sitting around the fire with his wife put a bounce into his step.

When he arrived home, he hung his jacket on a peg and found her on her hands and knees in the kitchen, wiping up a puddle of water on the floor. Nearing her, he took her by the arm and helped her to stand. "Here, let me do that." He took the rag from her and cleaned up what remained of the mess, then tossed the rag into the sink to be rinsed. "What did you spill?"

"Nothing," she gasped.

He turned to find her leaning against the wall, face pale. He frowned. "Amanda, what's wrong?"

She put a hand on her stomach, caressing the large mound. "My water broke, Josh. And I need you to fetch Doc O'Clarity and Owl Woman."

For a moment he froze. With wide eyes he stared at his wife like she'd suddenly grown two heads. "You're having...the baby is coming...now, tonight?"

She nodded. "Please, hurry."

He swallowed hard. "But Doc just left."

Panic rounded her eyes, and she began to tremble. "Left—left for where?"

He neared her, as she looked like she might collapse. "The Simpson farm, about a mile away. It seems Mrs. Simpson's decided to have her baby tonight as well."

She reached for his arm, digging her nails into his jacket sleeve. "Then fetch Owl Woman and Rising Sun."

"Let me get you into bed first." He gathered her into his arms and carried her into their bedroom.

Once he had her settled, he raced next door to Rising Sun's house.

When Rising Sun heard Amanda was in labor and Doc O'Clarity had gone on another house call, she rushed around gathering clean towels, a sharp knife, and a ball of string. "You and I will return to Golden Lady, and Falling Star will fetch Owl Woman and my daughter, Dawn."

"I don't know the first thing about..."

"I will tell you," Rising Sun interrupted. "Just stay calm and do everything I say."

He nodded, as he was not about to quarrel.

When they entered the bedroom, they found Amanda crouching at the foot of the bed, holding onto the rails. She was bare-footed, her bloomers were off, and her skirt was tied up around her waist.

"My love," he choked out hoarsely. "Let me help you back into bed."

"No," Rising Sun snapped. "This is how she will give birth."

He inhaled sharply. "Here? Crouching like this?"

"Yes, it is our way...much easier to push out the

287

baby," Rising Sun explained.

"Where is Owl Woman?" Amanda gasped.

"She comes, Golden Lady, as well as Dawn," Rising Sun reassured her. "Falling Star has gone for them." She turned to Josh. "Help me rid her of these clothes."

With trembling fingers, he freed the buttons on her blouse, and together he and Rising Sun removed every stitch of clothing his wife wore. Naked now, she crouched, pushing, breathing hard, panting...legs spread and shaking.

"Take her arm, as I do," Rising Sun instructed, showing him how to brace Amanda beneath her arm pit, assisting her to remain on her feet.

Owl Woman rushed into the room, Dawn at her heels, shutting the door behind her. Immediately Owl Woman got to work, placing a clean towel down on the floor between Amanda's legs and squatting herself to get a look. Reaching out, she probed between Amanda's thighs with two fingers, then nodded satisfied. "This one will come fast," she announced.

"Not fast enough," Amanda moaned. "My body hasn't given birth in twenty years, so I hope it holds up."

"Well, my friend, your body must remember what to do, or you would not be in this situation," Rising Sun teased.

A sharp pain struck her. She threw her head back and moaned.

"Wouldn't it be more comfortable for her to be lying in the bed," he suggested.

"No," the four women snapped simultaneously.

"I will boil water." Dawn left for the kitchen.

Sweat poured off Amanda, wetting her forehead, cheeks, breasts, and belly. The veins at her temples and down her neck stuck out as she strained to push the baby from her body. With each horrendous pain she cried out, trembling as she endured the process over and over again. Her suffering drove him sick with worry, beads of perspiration trickling down his own face.

Dawn returned with a basin of water and several clean cloths. Wetting one, she washed Amanda's back, neck, and breasts. "This will cool her down."

Amanda's pain continued. With each spasm he ached with sympathy. Never did he have an inkling of what a woman in labor underwent. "God save us, how long can she go on like this?"

"As long as it takes, holy man," Owl Woman quipped.

"Is there nothing to give her for the pain?" His own stomach clenched as he watched his wife's torment.

"Nothing can take this much away." Owl Woman knelt to check again between Amanda's thighs. "Push now, Golden Lady. I see the head."

Amanda was beet red with agony, pushing and grunting. Then with a long, primal howl that curdled his blood and made all the hairs on his flesh stand on end, she forced the head out from her womb. Owl Woman reached up and eased the baby free.

The midwife tied off the cord with the string before cutting it with the knife. "It is a girl child." She breathed into the baby's face.

Moments later the afterbirth fell from Amanda's body, and then a rush of blood. Dawn, efficient and calm, began to clean the floor.

"A daughter, we have a daughter," Amanda

whispered.

"Aye, a daughter," he repeated somewhat in shock. And then he heard the baby cry, and his own tears fell from his eyes.

"Get her in the bed now," Owl Woman demanded, wrapping the baby in a blanket.

He gathered her in his arms while Rising Sun ran to cover the mattress with several towels. Dawn removed the soiled clothes and took the basin to be refilled with fresh, clean water.

Exhausted, Amanda collapsed against him. As he carried her to the bed, he kissed her forehead.

"Thank you, my sweet love, for this child," he said, his voice cracking with emotion.

Rising Sun hurried to Amanda, wiping her face and neck with a dry cloth.

Dawn returned to the bedroom with a clean basin of warm water and placed it on the bed side table. Picking up a towel from the pile she brought, she dipped it into the water and began to wash Amanda between her thighs. Rising Sun helped. Again and again they washed, but the blood poured from her, heavily. It soaked the towels beneath Amanda's body.

"Too much blood comes," Rising Sun said, a concerned frown creasing her brow.

Owl Woman assessed the situation as she placed the baby into Amanda's arms. "Good for the baby to suckle here," she said, indicating the breast. "To heal down there," she added, referring to his wife's womanhood.

Weak and pale, Amanda pulled the child to her to nurse. But the blood kept coming. She grew paler, her breathing shallow, her eyes closed. Owl Woman took the sleeping baby from her and placed her in the cradle.

Fear rioted within him. "She needs a doctor...my wife needs a doctor." He hurried from the bedroom and out to the front door, ready to ride to Willow Creek for the doctor there. But as he opened the front door, he ran smack into Sean O'Clarity and Falling Star.

"The tribespeople are lined all along the main road, waiting for me. I was told to come here," Sean said.

"She's already had the baby, but she's hemorrhaging." His heart pounded in his ears.

Doctor O'Clarity rushed past him with his medical bag in his hand, to the bedroom, and shut the door behind him. Josh stood looking at the closed portal, scared, confused, tired. He ran a hand through his hair, tormented.

Falling Star rested a hand upon his shoulder. "Best to stay here. Let those who know what they are doing, do their work."

"But she might need me." He remembered how weak and pale she looked.

"What she needs is for you to be strong, give the doctor and Owl Woman a chance to help her without you getting in the way." Falling Star took Josh by the arm, leading him to the table. "Come, sit." Then Falling Star reached for a bottle of wine and two glasses Amanda had ready for the evening meal. He poured them each a glass and handed one to Josh. "Drink the wine, it will help."

"The only thing that will help is if her bleeding stops." He threw the sweet liquid down his throat and swallowed hard.

"You could pray," Falling Star suggested.

He frowned. "What?"

"You are a holy man, the Great Spirit will listen good to you," Falling Star reminded him.

"Aye—aye, you're right, my friend." He reached for a lantern and lit it, then quickly donned his jacket as he made his way to the door.

"Where are you going?" Falling Star probed.

"To the church—to pray." Once outside, the tribespeople gathered around him, their lit torches illuminating the night. He forced himself to stay calm. "It's a girl—we have a daughter."

"And what of Golden Lady," Little Elk said.

"She is not well," he said, then added. "She bleeds too much." He sighed heavily. "I'm going now to the church to pray."

Little Elk's lips thinned. "Should I get Golden Eagle?"

"Aye," he said, hoping Gabriel's worse fears were not coming into play.

On the way to the church his resolve cracked, his heart aching for his love. Hot tears cascaded down his face, staining his cheeks and cooled by the night air. He ran to the front of the church, and placing the lantern aside, he fell to his knees at the altar. The light cast eerie shadows on the wall.

"God, Almighty, hear my prayer. I beg of You not to take away from me the woman I love. Please, I beseech You to spare my daughter from being a motherless child." When he thought of life without her, pain echoed through his body. He openly wept. "Why have You allowed me to experience this place of gladness—pure happiness and joy, if it was to be snatched from me. So long I have waited to love her, to be loved by her. I walked away once...knew my place...did what was right to do. But now she is my wife, the other half of my soul and the entire portion of my heart." He covered his face with his hands. "If You must, take me instead, for without her I cannot live. Please, dear Lord—hear me—hear my prayer."

He didn't know how long he knelt on the cold, wooden floor, before he felt a hand upon his shoulder. "I am sure the Great Spirit has heard you, Holy Man." He turned to find Rising Sun kneeling beside him. She placed her lantern beside his. "Does it not say in your holy book to trust all things to Him?"

He wiped his eyes with the backs of his hand. "Aye." He searched her face. "Is there any change in my wife's condition?"

"The doctor is doing all he can for her, and the Great Spirit guides his hands."

"Aye," he choked out.

"This night reminds me of when Sunny Eagle was a small girl. She was always finding and bringing home with her a wounded animal, a rabbit with an injured paw or a bird with a broken wing. And all day she would care for the creature, do all she could, her very best. But when night fell, and she had to go to sleep, she worried the animal would die because she was not beside it." Rising Sun smiled fondly. "Golden Lady would tell her to trust in God. He used Sunny to help the animal, but now the rest was up to Him." She searched his face. "If the Great Spirit cared so much for a woodland critter, would He not care then for my dear sister-in-law?"

He cleared his throat. "Aye, He would care immensely."

"Then there is nothing more for you to do but trust

in Him."

He reached for her hand, holding it tight. "I am blessed beyond all measure to have you as my friend."

"Sister, I am your sister now; we are family," she said.

"Aye, family," he agreed.

She picked up both of their lanterns and stood. "Come, time for you to go home."

When he walked into the house, Gabriel and Riley were there, little Ethan sleeping in his mother's arms. Looking at the child, he suddenly realized he had his own baby, and with all the excitement, he hadn't even gazed once upon his daughter's face.

In the distance drums could be heard chanting and singing.

"What are they saying?"

"They are praying to the Great Spirit for my mother's healing," Gabriel translated, his visage strained with worry. He began to pace as he spoke. "They are asking for her life's blood to replenish and nourish her once again, for she is their heart, the center all revolves around."

Riley gasped. "Mercy, they see her as their Queen Mother."

"Aye, and truthfully she is. When war captured their village, she led them to safety. Made sure they were fed, kept warm and dry. And when they had no place to dwell, her inheritance supplied the land on which new homes could be built. They were given another chance to stay together, to live in peace, because of her," he said, admiration for his wife warming his worried heart.

Both Owl Woman, looking tired, and Sean

O'Clarity emerged from the bedroom. His shirt sleeves were rolled up. In one hand he carried his black bag, his jacket draped over his arm, and with the other hand he wiped his brow. "The bleeding is controlled, and she's asking for the three of you." Sean pointed to Josh, Gabriel, and Riley. "But not too long, she needs rest. I will leave now, but I will return in the morning to see how she is."

"I will leave as well," Owl Woman said.

Dawn was also leaving as they entered the room, with the basin and soiled towels in her hands. "All has been cleaned," she whispered as she filed past them.

Amanda was dressed in a pink nightgown, her hair combed and falling in curls around her shoulders. Slightly propped against the pillows, she held the baby in her arms. His first instinct was to rush to her, but he stood back to allow her son the privilege.

She cast Gabriel a loving smile. "All is well, so you need not be so upset."

Gabriel's voice broke with his emotion as he fell on his knees beside the bed and took his mother's hand. "When I heard, I thought you were going to..."

"Nonsense, I am a prairie woman, made of strong stock. Now, no more worries. This is a joyous time." Angling the baby for Gabriel to see, she smiled. "Meet your little sister."

"Oh, she is beautiful," Riley marveled. "Look here, Ethan," she said, bringing her son closer. "This is your auntie."

Amanda's gaze met his. "Her father has yet to meet her as well."

Riley placed a hand upon Gabriel's shoulder. "Come, Gabriel. Let us give Josh a chance to be with his family."

Gabriel nodded, then leaned forward to place a kiss upon his mother's cheek. "I will stop by tomorrow."

Amanda smiled. "I'll be here; we'll all be here, where we belong. Oh, and Gabriel, go tell the tribe I am fine or else they will beat those drums all night long."

Gabriel chuckled lightly and placed a gentle kiss on his little sister's forehead. As he made his way out the door, he shook Josh's hand. "Congratulations." Then he added. "Take good care of my mother."

"I intend to," he whispered.

Now that everyone was gone, the house quiet, and his love alive and on the mend, he thought he might topple over from exhaustion. But he had yet to see his child. He sat on the edge of the bed, beside Amanda, and gently took his daughter into his arms. Her pink skin was flawless, soft to the touch, as was the pale fuzz covering a perfectly shaped head. Her little mouth was poised into a bow, and tiny hands rested on her chest.

"She's beautiful." Tears once again welled in his eyes.

Amanda smiled proudly. "She is, isn't she?"

"What shall we call her?"

"What do you think of Cassia? It was my grandmother's middle name, and if it weren't for her freeing my mother from a locked bedroom, everything would be entirely different."

"I like the name," he agreed. "But I would want her middle name to be Rose."

"Any special reason?"

"My mother's name was Eliza Rose, but everyone called her by her middle name."

"Cassia Rose Holmes," she tried out the name.

He smiled. "It's a perfect name for a perfect little miss who is the first child to be born in our now very legitimate township."

The baby woke and began to fuss.

"And our perfect little, Eagle's Landing native miss is hungry." Amanda unbuttoned the front of her nightgown to free an engorged breast.

Handing her the child, he watched as the baby suckled with ferocious greed. "The poor little darling is starving." He grimaced. "Doesn't that hurt?"

Amanda laughed. "Somewhat, but not as bad as when they start to get teeth."

He shuddered at the thought of being bitten in such a vulnerable and tender place. His reaction had his wife laughing again. He marveled in the sound of her joy, thankful to have her still...to see her face. He knew if she died; he'd die too. That's just the way it was. He wouldn't have been able to exist, because he would have been unable to breathe without her.

As he experienced for the first time his wife nursing their child, his spirit was aglow. Amanda's loving smile, as she gazed upon the angelic face of their newborn daughter, melted his heart. He began to tremble, as her expression reminded him of all the Holy Mother Mary and child paintings he'd seen. She wore the Madonna's beatitude upon her face, the serene, blessed visage of a mother's unconditional love. In having the privilege of glimpsing this moment, he suddenly realized he would be forever changed.

Her gaze fluttered to meet his and he lost himself in the depth of her eyes. "I love you with all that I am," he whispered, drinking in her beauty, quenching his perpetual thirst for her.

"As I love you." She caressed his cheek. "And as Cassia grows, she too will be aware of the wonderful father she has."

He turned his face into her palm and kissed it. "I am old enough to be her grandfather. Will I even be around when she is grown? Will I have a chance to escort her to the altar on her wedding day?"

"Death can come at any age," she reminded him. "I imagine thus the reason we need to make each day count, be thankful and blessed for every moment bestowed us." She cast him a reassuring smile. "I believe you will be around, my darling husband, for a very long time. And you will live to see our daughter bloom, as she turns into a fine and beautiful woman."

"Just like her mother." The love for his little family swelled his heart to huge proportions. Never in his entire life had he been happier.

When Doctor O'Clarity stopped by the next morning to check on Amanda, who was doing very well, he chuckled at Josh's disheveled appearance. "Aye, ye have the look of a man who knows not a full night's sleep."

He yawned. "How long does this go on?"

Sean arched a brow. "Till they marry and leave the house."

"Surely, you jest," he said.

"Nay, in some capacity, fatherhood tends to wreck yer slumber, as ye worry about the children, nay a matter what age they be," Sean warned.

"And folks are foolish enough to have more than one," he mused aloud.

"Aye, that we are," Sean said flatly. Then he pointed a finger at Josh. "But that shan't be the case for ye, my friend. Another babe would kill Amanda. So mind yerself until the lass is over her child bearin' years."

He raised a defiant chin. "Are you telling me to stay away from my own wife?"

"Aye, I would say that I am," Sean said with a frown. "Lest ye want to still have a wife."

He put a hand on Sean's shoulder. "I appreciate your concern, but it's not warranted."

Sean's frown deepened. "And why the hell not?"

"Because I know an alternative method." He grinned. "It's called the Apache way."

Chapter Thirty

Amanda was blessed for all the help she received during the month long convalescent time Doc O'Clarity issued her. Sylvie made a point of stopping by twice a week, preparing meals Josh could easily pull from the icebox and warm on the stove. Rising Sun stopped by daily to do the cleaning and washing. And Josh learned how to bathe, change, and dress the baby.

In fact, he was absolutely wonderful, carrying Cassia about like she was attached to him, the deep sound of his voice soothing her. She called the baby a little angel, Josh called his daughter a miracle, and the tribe's people called Cassia *The Last Bloom.*

After she fed the baby and placed her in the cradle for a daytime nap, Amanda would take one as well. It seemed Cassia was a night owl, and Amanda spent more time awake in the wee hours of the night, then she did in the day. But it was a perfect time to read her mother's journal, as the house was still—the town quiet—and Cassia snuggled in her arms. Picking up where she left off brought her to the night of her own birth.

*Thursday, September 24, 1846*

*I should be sleeping—like Ethan and my daughter—but as exhausted as I am from laboring to give her life throughout this day, I am too excited to close my eyes for even a moment. Perhaps, I fear, after waiting so long for her arrival, if I take my focus off her, she will disappear. But I also find it great fun to just hold her and watch the many strange expressions she makes while taking her slumber. She puckers her lips, wrinkles her nose, and flutters her eyelids. I wish she could tell me her dreams.*

*My precious daughter arrived at dusk. She has large blue eyes—the shade of mine, and pale peach fuzz crowning her head. We named her Amanda Cornelia (after her two grandmothers—Ethan's mother, Amanda and my mother, Cornelia). How we wished both women could be present to share this remarkable day.*

\*\*\*\*

*Friday, December 25, 1846*

*It is Amanda's first Christmas, and even though she is only three months old and understands nothing about the holiday, we have a gift for her from good old St. Nick beneath the tree...a rag doll, dressed all in red, that has a happy smile upon its face. Always I want happy things to surround my child.*

*Merry Christmas to you, my little darling.*

Tears welled in her eyes, as she remembered the rag doll—she named Lucy Jane. She carried it with her everywhere for such a long time. She knew she was named after her paternal grandmother, as her father often told and retold stories about her. But why was she never told of her middle name, Cornelia? Was the reminder too painful for Amelia or was it simply because Amanda never knew enough to ask? Several more pages were destroyed, and the next entry referred to the summer of 1858, when Josh arrived in Willow Creek, and his first Thanksgiving dinner with her family.

*Sunday, September 26, 1858*

*Our new clergyman arrived late Friday night, all the way from London, England. His name is Joshua Holmes, and he is a pleasant chap. He does seem to enjoy our company, though, as I am able to share with him his homeland, and Ethan shares Josh's love for books. Amanda gets on well with him, and enjoys the stories he tells. I think she both baffles and amuses the young Reverend. He is kind, patient, and understanding. One day he will be a loving husband and father. But he will not marry now, of this I am sure. For some reason I feel he will wait...for a long time...for a very special woman to be his bride.*

\*\*\*\*

*Sunday, November 21, 1858*

*Thanksgiving Day*

*I planned our Thanksgiving Day feast for today and invited the young reverend. My husband entertained us by telling the story of the first feast with the pilgrims and the Indians at Plymouth Rock. I made eel and roasted a wild turkey, to stay with tradition. Josh had a tremendous time. I think he feels right at home with our family.*

The next readable page in the journal was its last.

*Saturday, December 11, 1858*

*I woke up not feeling quite myself. I've a pain in my chest and feel feverish. Ethan went for Doctor Turner. He gave me something to make me rest—said I was working my fingers to the bone and sleep would help. I've slept away most of the day, yet I'm still feeling wretched. My dear Amanda made me a chicken broth, served it to me in bed. She's only just turned twelve, yet she is such an old soul—wiser than most children her age, and so very helpful. She means everything to me, my only offspring. Ethan and I have tried for years to have another baby, and nothing has happened. I ate as much of the broth as I could, but my appetite is poor. Tomorrow I hope to be back on my feet...I must! Christmas is only a few weeks away, and I have much to do. But for now I'll rest—just a bit more rest—and then I'm sure I'll get better.*

Amanda's tears fell freely down her cheeks. Amelia didn't get better. The next day her fever spiked. Joshua Holmes came to pray by her bedside. Even though her mother only knew Josh a few months, she trusted him.

She heard her mother ask him to send word to her family in England, and then made him promise to take care of her and Ethan if she didn't make it through. Josh agreed. And all these years later he was still keeping his word. There for her and her father—and then there for her after Ethan's death. And he was again with her now, fulfilling a promise to Proud Eagle. Never had he wavered, never would he abandon her.

She remembered Josh staying with her and Ethan

by Amelia's side throughout her mother's last night. At some point Ethan must have decided it was best to carry Amanda into her own bed, because that's where she woke—to the voices of Grace Thomas, Doctor Turner, their neighbor, Mrs. Eastman, and the Reverend…all comforting her father. She ran out of her room, her heart fearful, into her father's arms. He held her tight, and together they cried. And from that point on, Amanda was a motherless child.

When she raised her gaze to meet her father's, she noticed he was wearing around his neck her mother's wedding band hanging from a black cord. He wore it for years, as well as his own ring—handed down from his grandparents.

When Amanda turned sixteen, he presented her with Amelia's ring on a gold chain. She never removed it, keeping it always close to her heart. She added her father's ring onto the chain when he died. When she wed Proud Eagle they each wore the rings. Now she'd given her father's ring to her son. But she kept her mother's band. She wore it now on the ring finger of her right hand. Looking down upon it she remembered it on Amelia's hand. In fact, she remembered everything about her mother, thanks to the journal, as it brought her into full view. She may be gone—her American journey ending way too soon, but Amelia Bentley Gregory would never be forgotten.

****

April brought to Eagle's Landing nightly showers, sunny days, and new life blooming at every turn. Maggie Granger expected her first baby any day now, exactly nine months from the time she and Eli wed. Amanda was somewhat surprised the child hadn't been born sooner. Both Rising Sun's daughter, Dawn, and her daughter-in-law, Water Lily, were due to deliver their second children in November, only weeks apart from each other. And Muriel Dodd, the town's teacher, just announced she was expecting her first, due sometime in early December.

Without the pastime of reading her mother's journal, Amanda wrote more letters to Raven in Ireland and Sunny in England. To her great happiness, her two daughters decided to return to Willow Creek with their families for a visit, meet their new little sister, and celebrate Josh and Amanda's first wedding anniversary. Sunny and Rafe wouldn't arrive for three more days, but Raven and Braiton were scheduled to arrive at any time. In fact, Gabriel and Josh had left early that morning to meet them at the train station.

Vernon Washburn went along as well so he could place an order at the mill for more lumber—his furniture-making business was really growing. She stayed back, as there was much to do in the meantime. Fortunately Riley offered to take Cassia, freeing Amanda to accomplish her work quicker—including blueberry picking.

In recent months she had become quite fond of Michael, the oldest son of Mickey and Katie McCrea. He enjoyed learning to play the violin, and she relished teaching him. He also loved to help her pick berries. His most favorite part was eating the pies she made from the luscious fruit. She'd often reward him a slice or two, with a glass of milk, after a musical lesson. So, it wasn't hard to employ his assistance that afternoon.

She reached for her sun hat, a pail, and her father's pocket knife, handy for sawing away tiny branches, and slipped it into her shoe. When she lived with the Apaches, she always carried a dagger on her hip. You never knew when it would come in handy or be a weapon of protection.

The sun was high in the sky, the April day growing warmer by the minute when she and Michael ventured out to the far side of the creek, where the berry bushes grew.

"I don't think I'll ever be gettin' used to the heat o' this land." Michael scrunched down to pick the fruit she couldn't reach.

"It takes stamina, my friend." She plopped the berries she picked into a pail.

"And ye poor lassies, wearin' all o' those clothes," he said, shaking his head regretfully. "I'd be chokin' for sure, needin' to gulp for me breath. 'Twould be so much better for ye to be able to slip on a pair o' breeches, like us men folk."

She laughed. "You speak the truth, Michael. And one time, long ago, I did just that."

His eyes widened. "Ye wore men's breeches?"

"I did," she admitted. "Dressed up as a young lad so I could ride into a military fort and save my first husband."

"I've heard o' him from the Apache folk. He's the one they call Proud Eagle." He stood and stretched to reach berries atop of another bush.

"Reverend Holmes helped me," she continued. "Together we saved him from being hanged."

"You were a brave lass, then," he concluded.

"I was scared out of my mind, Michael. But sometimes you do what you need to do in order to protect your friends and family."

"Like dressin' as a lad?"

"That, and many other things." She shrugged. "Who knows, perhaps one day all women will wear breeches. Times change, and we are only three years away from the twentieth century." She handed him her pail. "This bucket will not hold another berry, but I've another one inside my home, on the kitchen table, we can use. Would you take this full one to the house, and fetch the empty one for me?"

"Aye, that I will." He scampered off on the errand she sent him.

She smiled as she watched him vanish around a cluster of tall shrubberies. For just turning thirteen, Michael towered over her; his burly form that of his father. Yet he had a gentle quietness about him, like his mother.

While he was gone, she scoped out another bush. Just as she was about to wiggle her way closer to the copse of greenery, a deep voice from behind startled her.

"And so we meet again, Golden Lady."

She turned to meet the beady eyes of her worst enemy. Standing before her was the white agent who terrorized her village; the one she knew compromised her daughter. Her knees trembled, her heart raced. Swallowing hard, she fought the fear rioting within her body. This wasn't the time to collapse into a dead faint, because just then, from the corner of her own eye, she caught Michael returning with the empty pail. She stepped to the left, hoping to block the intruder's view. With a wave of her hand, she made a motion for Michael to stop, then finished the gesture off to look as though she were just shielding her eyes from the sun.

"You are on private property, Denton Hall," she said as loudly as she could. She knew Michael to be a clever and resourceful young man. Hopefully, he would catch the man's name and sneak back down the path, going for help with the information. Gabriel and Josh weren't in town, but Falling Star, Rising Star, and Mickey McCrea could easily be found. Both warriors would recognize the name, realize the danger she was in, and come to her aid.

"I don't care much for other folk's boundaries; you should know that by now." He snickered.

She raised a defiant chin. "You have no jurisdiction on this land, so I will ask you to leave immediately."

His face contorted. "Not until I even the score with the bastard who's been askin' questions about me."

"What proof do you have the person you seek resides here?" She held her trembling hands behind her back. It would do no good for Denton Hall to know he frightened her to the very core.

He spit on the ground and moved closer. "I've got my sources. And the only way I know to flush the son of a bitch out is to take something belonging to him."

She backed away, preparing to run, but the hem of her skirt got caught on low branch. It was all the advantage Hall needed. In one fluid motion he was upon her. The last thing she remembered was the shocking pain of his meaty fist slamming into her face, before everything went black.

\*\*\*\*

The instant he halted the wagon in front of his house, Josh knew something was terribly wrong. Rising Sun—holding Cassia, Owl Woman, Riley—holding Ethan, and Maggie were waiting for them on the large front porch. One look at their frightened faces sent waves of terror through him.

Gabriel was the first to jump down from the wagon, making his way to his wife. "What is wrong, Redbird?"

Tears spilled from her eyes. "Your mother's been abducted by Denton Hall."

Gabriel's expression darkened. "When...where?"

"About two hours ago. She was picking blueberries with Michael McCrea down by the lower end of the creek." Riley gulped back a sob. "He came running with the news to his father. Mickey immediately rounded up Rising Star, Falling Star, and Eli Granger. All of them went out looking for her but didn't have much luck. They returned about ten minutes ago, concluding Hall must have had a boat and took her across the creek." She bit her bottom lip. "And nay a soul here has a boat."

"Ya don't need one." Vernon climbed down from the wagon.

Josh followed him, his terrified heart beating rapidly in his chest. "How will we get across the creek without one?"

"I know a way to the other side by horseback— gone there plenty of times huntin'," Vernon explained. "There was a small town about a mile in, on yonder side, known as Beaver's Bluff. It's deserted now, but at one time it was boomin', served as a weigh station for gold miners returnin' from stakin' their claims in California. They'd do some drinkin' and carousin' with the ladies of the evenin' before goin' on home with their fortunes." He laughed sardonically. "That's if they had much of a fortune left after a night in town."

Braiton and Raven joined them. He held their son, Casey by the hand, and she held their daughter, little Amanda, in her arms.

Raven was visibly shaken, her face pale. "Denton Hall is a ruthless scoundrel who will stop at nothing to get what he wants. He and the rest of the white agents destroyed our way of life when they took over our village."

Braiton moved to place an arm over his wife's shoulder, pulling her close. Softly he said, "Is he the one?"

Raven nodded and then broke down in tears, burying her face beneath her husband's neck.

Braiton's jaw muscles throbbed as he struggled to maintain his calm while he comforted his wife. "I promise we will find your mother and bring her back unharmed. Then he turned to Vernon. "We need to arm ourselves, mount up, and go after this bastard."

Maggie, due any day to give birth, made her way carefully down the porch steps. "Come now, lad." She took Casey from Braiton. "What say we get ye, yer mama, and little Mandy here, inside."

"Go, lass," Braiton said, bestowing a tender kiss upon Raven's lips. "I will find your mother."

Reluctantly Raven followed Maggie into the house.

"I think the men have gathered at the McCrea stables," Riley said.

Gabriel pressed a quick kiss to her forehead. "You go inside and take care of my sister."

"Aye, and you will be careful," she said, pleading with her eyes.

Gabriel nodded and forced a reassuring smile.

"And I will care for Cassia, holy man," Rising Sun

promised.

"Thank you, Rising Sun." Turning to Gabriel he suggested, "It will be faster if we all drive over to the stables in the wagon."

"It would be best if you remained here with the women." Gabriel climbed into the wagon's seat.

"The bloody hell I will." His tone left no room for discussion.

"Then, come, we have no time to waste," Gabriel conceded, reaching for the reins.

## Chapter Thirty-One

Amanda regained consciousness while lying on the hard, dirt floor of a small windowless, wooden shack. Both her hands and feet were bound with rope. Through the holes and spaces of the wall boards, light streamed onto her sore face. Her left eye was swollen shut and throbbed, as did her jaw. She sat up slowly, trying to focus through the dizziness and blinding pain pulsing in her head. Swallowing hard, she fought back the nausea threatening to choke her while shimmying over to a wall. Leaning with a shoulder, she strained to peek through one of the slits.

She spotted three men. One sat on the ground, his back propped against the trunk of a tree. He was thin, unshaven, his light brown hair fell to his collar, and he picked his teeth with the end of a small stick. The second man sat on a stump, rolling a cigarette. He was heavier, dark, and bald. The third man was Denton Hall. He stood beside the man sitting on the stump, wiping his forehead with a dirty, red bandana. All the men were armed.

She strained to hear what they were saying, a searing fear gripping her heart as her son's name was mentioned a few times, but they were too far away and spoke too low for her to really catch the entire conversation. However, she did pick up the fact there were more men than the three she could see. Laying her head against the wall, she closed her eyes—dread washing through her body. They knew Gabriel would come looking for her, and when he did...

She shuttered. How many would die today? Would it be her son, her husband, who she had no doubts would ride to her aid, or all three of them? As well as anyone else who tried to help in her rescue. Would Cassia be a motherless child or an orphan?

"Please, dear Lord," she whispered. "Don't let any of them find me. Let it just be me who perishes this day." As she had no doubt Denton Hall's intention was to end her life, if not immediately, eventually. Silently she prayed for strength to endure whatever her fate might be.

\*\*\*\*

Josh rode through the backwoods with Gabriel, Vernon, Braiton, Falling Star, and Eli Granger. Mickey McCrea and the other men stayed back at Eagle's Landing to protect the women and children, should more of Hall's minions come looking for trouble. As he and the band of men accompanying him to search for Amanda left, Mickey was barking orders to fortify the grounds in case of an attack.

The gun holstered to his side weighed heavy on his hip, a constant reminder he'd commit murder on this day, if it meant saving his wife.

"Have ya ever killed a man, Reverend?" Vernon said, bringing his horse beside Josh's.

"Aye, once," he reluctantly admitted. "The reason was much the same as it is now...to save Amanda. She was captured by the Chiricahua, and I rode with Proud Eagle and Falling Star to her rescue." The horror of that day, as it flooded his thoughts, mirrored the present situation.

Vernon took an audible breath. "I've taken an animal's life, as it's the way of survival out here. If a man's to put food on the table for his family, he's gotta be able to hunt, trap, catch whatever game he can for food." He shook his head. "But never have I taken another person's life...been the cause of someone takin' their last breath. I dunno if I can muster the courage to pull the trigger on a human."

"Aye, I feared the same," he whispered.

"How did you manage?" Vernon probed.

He cleared his throat. "When we came upon the Chiricahua's camp, we found Amanda stripped naked, her hands and feet tied to stakes. It was evident, if we couldn't rescue her from their clutches, that she'd be killed." He swallowed hard the emotion rising to choke him. "Proud Eagle knew my vow, as a clergyman, was *thou shall not kill,* and so he commenced to stress the urgency of my need to break that vow."

"What did he say?" Vernon said.

"Proud Eagle's voice carried the force of his own fear as he explained to me after the Chiricahua had their way with Amanda, they would peel back the pink flesh of her breasts and shove knives up into her; tearing apart her insides...then..." His voice cracked with emotion. "They would disembowel her."

"Jesus, Mary, and Joseph," Vernon gasped.

"Then Proud Eagle grabbed me by the lapel of my jacket, crumpling the material in his fist, as he went on to say he'd seen the hacked remains of the women tortured by the Chricahua. And if I didn't...couldn't stand with him, that's how Amanda's life would end." He heaved a sigh, that day playing out again in his mind as he continued. "I then told him I'd do whatever it took to save her. So he removed a dagger from his belt and slapped it into my hand. Then he asked me if I could slit a man's throat while he slept...sneak up behind him and plunge a knife into his back, and I said I could...I would...for her." He searched Vernon's face. "And I would again."

"There is no other choice in such a situation," Vernon said. "I would've done the same for my Emily, and now for Flora."

"Proud Eagle led the way, crouching and stalking his prey like a wild beast," he went on. "And I followed, my own silent steps taking me closer to the warrior I'd have to slay. I watched Proud Eagle and Falling Star, with one quick slash of their knife, slit the throats of the two men sleeping on the farthest end of the camp. And then on shaking legs, I darted to the third one, the man sleeping closest to me. My knuckles went white while I gripped the dagger with a sweaty hand. My heart pounded in my ears as I raised the knife and silently prayed, *forgive me, Lord, for what am about to do.* Then I quickly slashed the Chiricahua's gullet. Blood poured from the wound, staining my hand. My throat tightened, my stomach churned. Swiftly I snuck back to the safety of the trees and retched."

Vernon gulped. "How do you ever get over such a thing?"

"You don't. I've tried all these years to put it behind me by justifying the end to meet the means. I've done my penance a million times over, prayed, and recited Philippians 3:13—*Forgetting those things which are behind and reaching forward to those things which are ahead* over and over again. I've been haunted by day, have nightmares at night, done everything possible to bury such a tragic and traumatic event in the deepest part of me, but it never really ever leaves you," he said. "And I suppose it never will."

"And I reckon Amanda's kidnappin' today has brought it all back, like it happened just yesterday," Vernon sympathized.

Before he could answer, Gabriel pulled his horse up beside Vernon's. "It looks like the trail ends here."

Vernon, pale and visibly shaken, nodded. "The old town is to the left of that cluster of trees."

"Then ride now ahead with me, and show us the way," Gabriel said.

Chapter Thirty-Two

Amanda heard the shack's door being unbolted. She opened her eyes to find Hall's large frame stepping through the narrow passageway. Full light filled the tiny hut, blinding her.

"I'm expectin' yer kin at any moment to come ridin' in here. But they've got themselves a surprise. My men surround the place, all armed and ready to take the varmints down, just like we did yer Injun mate." He chuckled sardonically. "Ya didn't really believe the chief had a huntin' accident, did ya?"

His latter sentence sent her anger crashing through her body. "No, I knew better. Proud Eagle was an experienced hunter."

Hall moved closer, and she could see his face clearer—narrowed beady eyes; large, crooked nose; rotting teeth. His face was etched with disdain and evil. It was hard to believe a person such as he had a family, or a mother somewhere. What sort of a woman could give birth to such a monster?

"Not as good as me, since I'm the one who took that scum dog down," he boasted. "And after I finish off the rest of his kind and leave their carcasses to rot in the sun," he went on, his tone low and menacing, "I'm gonna come in here, raise yer skirts, and show ya what a real man is all about." He threw his head back and laughed. His sick mirth grated on every nerve in her body. "And when I've had my fill, I'm gonna slit yer throat. Then we'll ride to yer pathetic little shanty town and burn it down—be rid of the whole lot of ya, once and for all."

"You are a putrid and corrupt man," she spat through gritted teeth, cutting through the sinister cackle.

"And yer an Apache lover's whore, Golden Lady." He made his way out of the shack, bolting the door behind him.

Again she rested her head against the wall, a million things rushing through her thoughts. And then her mother's face came to mind—the way she smiled, eyes twinkling and the kindness of her heart shining through. Amelia was a willful woman, strong tenacity, didn't stop until she followed her heart. When Amanda closed her eyes again, she could hear the soft lilt of her mother's voice.

*"What is your heart's calling, my darling child?"*

*"To be free—save my son and husband—warn them—warn all of them in some way."*

*"Then do it,"* Amelia whispered.

*"I am bound, Mama...tied with rope."*

*"Think, Amanda...think how you might set yourself free,"* her mother's voice prompted.

She sat forward, her eyes popping open. "With Papa's knife," she realized aloud.

Pulling her knees to her chest, she reached inside her shoe and clumsily retrieved the pocket knife. Springing it open and twisting her wrists, she awkwardly sawed at the rope binding her hands. She sped up with the sound of gunfire in the distance, wounding her own flesh as she tried to break through her restraints. Her blood colored the rope, but she kept at the task of cutting the threads. Once her hands were free, she untied the rope binding her ankles.

Quickly she stood, and with the knife's blade, she chopped away at one of the spilt wallboards. If she could only hack apart enough wood, she could climb through the opening. With the sound of more gunfire exploding, her adrenaline spiked, and she went at the wall like a crazed animal. Once she could fit her shoulder through the opening she made, she pushed with all her might. The rotted wood cracked, giving her enough room to slip through, out to the other side. With the knife in one hand, and her skirt lifted in the other, she ran.

As she rounded the back of the shack, she surprised the thin man with the beard. His slight hesitation was in her favor. In an instant her Apache training kicked in, rules she'd been taught over and over. Strike first, move fast...came to mind. She threw the pocket knife like she'd been taught to throw spears and daggers. The blade flew the distance with her thrust, piercing the man through his right eye. He fell to his knees and howled in pain, ripping at the small weapon. She took advantage of his agony. Picking up a large rock, she began to beat him in the head with it. He swore, tried to grab her hands, but she kicked him in the side and pounded harder—faster—until his skull cracked. His blood was everywhere. But she didn't stop until he fell into a dead heap upon the ground. Then she threw aside the rock, grabbed her knife, wiped it clean on her skirt, and continued to run.

Josh emerged from the woods. Vernon Washburn and Falling Star were with him, the two firing at whatever they saw behind her. She kept running, daring not to turn around for even a second, the pocket knife gripped tightly in her hand.

Josh spotted her now, his face paling as she approached. Gunfire whooshed over her head, all around her, but she kept going. She was literally running across a battlefield.

"Get down, Amanda." He stepped farther out into the open.

"Go back," she shouted in return, sinking to her knees. "Keep your cover."

But he continued toward her and didn't stop until he reached her. With a strong hand, he pulled her to him, and together they ran toward the woods. Then, when only five feet separated them from gaining cover, she heard the cock of a gun directly behind her.

Josh pushed her forward. "Run!" He stood between her and whoever aimed the gun. But she didn't run. Instead she turned to face her husband. Behind him stood Denton Hall.

"Go," he whispered, before he turned and wrestled Denton Hall for the gun. Then the shot rang out.

Josh fell.

She screamed, falling to her knees beside him, cradling his head in her lap. "Oh, God, no!"

"Amanda," he choked out, blood seeping through his shirt. He'd been wounded in his left shoulder. "My life for yours," he said, wincing with pain. "I made the deal, now I must pay."

"No, no, no!" She rocked him back and forth. "You can't leave me. I won't let you, do you hear me?" Again she heard the cock of a gun. She glanced up to see Hall standing over them.

"Well, I'll let him—in fact I'll help him." He

aimed the gun's barrel at Josh's head. "Time to go to yer reward, preacher. And when I'm through with ya, this white trash slut of a woman, can join ya."

But before he could pull the trigger, gunfire blasted from behind her, hitting Hall in the neck. "That is for killing my father," her son's voice bellowed.

Another shot hit Hall between the eyes. "That's for raping my wife," a deep voice resounded.

Denton Hall fell dead in front of her.

Then Gabriel was beside her. "Josh needs help...we need to help him." Her whole body shook uncontrollably. Gabriel pulled her into his arms and held her tight. Then the other man, the one with the deep voice, came into view. She looked into his emerald green eyes. "Who are you?"

"I'm Lord Braiton Shannon." He placed a kind hand upon her arm.

Tears burned the back of her throat. "Then your wife is..."

"Your daughter, Raven," he broke in.

Weak and exhausted, her head fell against her son's shoulder. Gabriel pried the pocket knife from her bloody grasp, clipped it closed, and put it in his vest pocket. Braiton Shannon gathered Josh, who was as limp as a rag doll, and threw him over his shoulder.

Then Gabriel picked her up. "Come, my mother," He carried her away from the bloody scene. "Time to go home."

****

"How long have I been asleep," Amanda placed a hand over her throbbing eye.

"Only a few hours." Raven covered her with a quilt. "If your eye bothers you, I can fetch the

321

medication Doctor O'Clarity left for you to take."

She reached for her daughter's hand, holding it to her lips and kissing a knuckle. "No, I'm fine."

"Go back to sleep then...you need to rest," Raven coaxed, affectionately tightening her grasp on Amanda's hand.

But instead, she sat up to gaze upon her husband's face. Gabriel and Braiton had moved the parlor settee into her bedroom, placing it beside the bed, so she could be by Josh's side. That was two days ago. Doc O'Clarity was able to remove the bullet and stop the bleeding, but there was still the threat of infection. Amanda knew the risk to be a strong one—it was how Proud Eagle died. Would Denton Hall make her a widow once again?

Raven sat down beside her. "The holy man will pull through this, my mother."

She took an audible breath. "I pray you're right, Raven." For a moment they sat quietly, their eyes on Josh.

Then Amanda broke the silence, turning to look at her daughter. "Denton Hall admitted he was the one who killed your father."

Raven's lips thinned. "I hope his soul rots in hell."

"He compromised you, didn't he?" she whispered.

Raven nodded. "When did you know?"

"I had a strong inkling from the very start, that's why I sent you all to England—to protect you and Sunny further, and your father. If he knew what had happened, he would have fought for your honor and gotten himself killed."

"But in the long run, Denton Hall ended up killing Father anyway." Raven took an audible breath. "Why is nothing in this world fair?"

"That is a question, my darling daughter, people have been searching an answer for since the dawn of time. But the bad lots in life do eventually get their due, and justice prevails, like it did for Denton Hall." She reached over to rest an affectionate hand on Raven's arm. "Did you know it was Braiton's shot that killed him?"

"Yes, Gabriel told me, and I'm glad." Raven glanced at Amanda. "When Braiton first discovered I'd been taken against my will, he vowed...should he ever set eyes on the man who hurt me; he'd make him pay for his crime." Tears filled her eyes. "My husband has never gone back on his word."

"He is good to you, then—and the children?"

"Yes, extremely good and I love him with all of my heart," Raven said.

She wrapped an arm around her daughter and pulled her close. "It pleases me to hear this, Raven. And perhaps the reason for the way things turned out, the answer you seek, lies in the fact you were meant to meet Braiton. What will be, will be."

When Gabriel entered the room he gazed down at Josh. "He vowed he would give his life to save you and he has kept his word."

"I pray he hasn't, Gabriel. I prefer he lives," she said softly.

"I do as well," Gabriel admitted. "I understand it all, now...why father chose him." He cleared his throat of emotion and glanced over at her. "I came to say Rowena Cooper is here to see you, my mother."

She frowned, not recognizing the name. "Who might she be?"

"She is Hudson Cooper's wife, the shoemaker who is building a home here," he explained. "Mrs. Cooper is a healer, grows herbs, and she says she has a remedy for Josh, something to fight infection. But she will only give it to you."

"Something to fight infection; I pray it works." Amanda stood. She followed her son to the front door and extended a welcomed hand to the other woman. "Mrs. Cooper, I am so sorry I haven't met you sooner."

Rowena Cooper was a small woman, very thin, wore her black hair in a bun atop her head. Not overly pretty, but pleasant looking, with round, brown eyes filled with kindness. She looked to be a few years younger than Amanda.

"Please, won't you come in, have a cup of tea and a slice of blueberry pie?" Amanda sighed. "It seems my daughter and daughter-in-law have been baking up a storm."

"I do the same when I'm yancy, and I heard about the preacher, so I'm thinkin' ya all are probably mighty yancy about now," Rowena said. "But this ain't the time for me to be intrudin' on yer hospitality." She smiled. "Time enough to come, hey what?"

"Yes, we'll certainly have to get together soon," Amanda agreed.

"I'll be lookin' forward to it." Rowena looked down at the jar and small bottle she held in her hands. "I got here a tincture and healin' salve made from the herb *Calendula*, better known to ya as the pot marigold plant. If ya add the tincture to tea, it'll help settle the stomach and improve the appetite. When a body eats, it grows strong, strong enough to pull through whatever malady confronts it. And applyin' the balm, at least two to three times every few hours, to the wound will keep away infection." She handed the items over to Amanda. "And, of course, we'll all be keepin' the preacher in our prayers."

"Thank you so much, so very, very, much Mrs. Cooper," she said.

As soon as the woman left, Amanda handed the tincture to Riley. "Please, brew some tea and add to the cup a drop of this remedy."

"Aye, right away," Riley agreed.

Then she returned to the bedroom with the jar of salve. Her hands trembled as she removed the bandage covering Josh's wound. Gently she cleaned the area with a clean cloth and warm water, before applying Rowena Cooper's homemade balm.

"Please, dear God, let this work," she whispered.

Every time Josh stirred, she spoon-fed him a bit of tea. The only time she left his side was to nurse Cassia or use the privy. When Sunny and her family arrived, they stayed at Gabriel's house. Sunny had grown close to Riley when the two were in England, so they were happy to be together once again. And Raven remained with her, keeping the home fires burning, the house in order, so Amanda could care for Josh.

On the third night after the shooting, she climbed into bed with her husband. Leaning her head on his uninjured shoulder, she listened to his even, clear breathing. His lungs sounded good. There was no wheezing, no gasps of breath—no death rattle.

"You have always been there for me, Joshua Holmes." She placed the palm of her hand upon his heart. "Even when you were an ocean away, I felt your love and concern. Just having you upon this earth with me, has brought me peace and made me feel safe and secure." She sighed, her eyes filling with tears. "You, my love, are my heart's song."

"And you, my love, are my song's voice," he returned with a whisper.

She pulled back to meet his gaze, the tears slipping down her cheeks. "You're awake."

He winced, slowly bringing his hand to her face, wiping the tears away. "Aye, Mrs. Holmes, that I am." Gently he caressed her bruise. "Even wearing this black eye, you still magnificently bewilder me."

She smiled, silently thanking God and Mrs. Cooper. "You should see the other guy."

He arched a brow. "Dead, I presume."

"As dead as they come," she said.

"God have mercy," he whispered.

"Mercy is too good for him." She fingered the bandage on his wound. "But you are truly blessed. Getting shot at such close range could have...have..."

"Kept me from officially becoming a cowboy of America's Wild West," he interrupted with a humorous tone, trying to make light of it all for her sake.

"I think it is best you stick to preaching," she advised, thankful for the playful banter. It made her feel their lives were finally beginning to return to normal.

He arched a brow. "Aye, I'm much better at it, obviously. Perhaps carving a notch upon my belt would serve as a constant reminder to remain steadfast in my present position."

"And it will be your first and last notch." She pushed aside an inky strand of hair from his forehead. "When you were shot, you said something about making a deal—my life for yours and now it was time to pay. What did you mean?"

He sighed. "When you lay hemorrhaging after giving birth to Cassia, I ran to the church to pray for your life. I told God to take me instead."

"And so your deal was with God," she said, her heart expanding to enfold him strongly within.

"Aye, and when Hall shot me, I suddenly realized this was how it would happen, how I'd give my life for the one God saved." Then he frowned, "Except for the fact I'm still alive."

"Perhaps God decided you were needed here more." She traced his lips with the tip of her finger. "And I agree wholeheartedly. My aim is to do whatever it takes to get you well again." She planted a gentle kiss upon his chin. "How are you feeling now?"

"You mean right this moment?"

She pulled back to look at him and nodded.

He contemplated his answer for a moment, then said, "Hungry...very hungry."

"Well, we've plenty of food, as the neighbors keep bringing platters of this and bowls of that. I don't even know how we're going to eat all we've got before it spoils. So, whatever you crave, I'm sure we've got it. You need only to ask," she said.

He cast a roguish smile.

She giggled, catching his silent meaning. "Anything specific in mind?"

He pulled her close. "Why don't you surprise me?"

****

A week later they celebrated their one year wedding anniversary. Although Josh had to take things slowly, he was still up and about, enjoying the family. Now, as they were all gathered around the table,

Amanda took time to marvel over those loved ones surrounding her.

Her husband, well on the mend, held Cassia. Poor little girl, only three months old and was nearly made an orphan. But she and Josh would make it up to her. As it was, he cooed and talked to his daughter with so much love and affection, it made her heart melt.

Next to Josh, sat Gabriel—a strong, smart, loving man...chief, father, brother, husband, and her beloved son. Riley, his wonderful wife and an all-around genuinely good woman, held their son, Ethan, in her arms.

Then her daughter, Raven, sat close to her husband, Braiton. Two people couldn't be more in love with each other or as well suited, unless it was her other daughter, Sunny, and her husband, Rafe. Both young women glowed, as did the men who loved them.

Children's laughter filled the room, as Amanda was blessed with five grandchildren. Her heart beamed with pride as she gazed at each one: Casey, little Amanda—or Mandy as her parents called her, the twins, Peter and Amelia, all playing as toddlers should with wooden blocks upon the floor. And then, of course, there was little Ethan.

A knock at the door brought Gabriel to his feet, returning with Michael McCrea at his heels.

"Good day to you, Michael," she said. "What brings you our way?"

"I've come to tell ye, there are men out at the family plot, askin' for ye, Mrs. Holmes," he said.

Josh raised a brow. "Must be the stonecutters finally bringing Proud Eagle's marker."

"Then I better not keep them waiting." She reached

for her sun hat. Turning back to Michael she said, "We were just about to have dessert, your favorite blueberry pie." She cocked her head sideways. "Would you care to stay for a slice?"

Michael's eyes widened with the anticipation all males acquire for food. "Aye, I would."

"Mother, I will come with you," Gabriel offered.

"Me too," Raven said.

"And me," Sunny chimed in.

The four of them made their way to the family plot in silence, obviously each one was thinking of the man the headstone was for. This would be the first time they were all together to pay their respects and a final farewell to Proud Eagle.

After the men had positioned the marker upon its proper place and gone, she knelt beside the headstone and fingered the lettering.

*Here lies Peter Proud Eagle,*
*Beloved Husband, Father, and Apache Chief*
*October 5, 1842 to November 15, 1894*
*Rest In Peace Noble Warrior*

The four of them remained in quiet reverence for a long time before Raven broke the silence. "I always thought I would see him again."

"We should have been here for him, for mother," Gabriel commented, kneeling beside Amanda.

"That is exactly why Rafe and I decided to return to Willow Creek and build a home here in Eagle's Landing," Sunny said. "I miss my mother, missed her at my wedding and the birth of my babies. And I want Peter and Amelia to know their grandmother." She sighed. "Our plan is to visit after Brighton's summer season. Since we have turned Bentwood into a resort, we are needed there during that part of the year. But we could stay here from September to November, traveling back to England before we are too far into winter."

Raven gasped. "Braiton and I decided the same, but we would come from July to September."

Gabriel stood. "The two of you could build one big home, with enough room for both families to enjoy."

"What do you think, Sunny?" Raven said.

"I believe it would work out perfectly. The only time we would overlap would be the month of September, and that would give us time to visit and for our children to know their cousins," Sunny said.

Amanda stood to look at each of her daughters. "You all have made me very happy with this decision." She smiled warmly. "And since we are sharing plans, Josh and I have made a few of our own."

Sunny reached out to take Amanda's hand. "Oh, my mother, do tell."

"This time next year, when Cassia is old enough to travel, Josh wishes for us to visit London to see his sister, Marietta, and her husband, Jerome Cavendish."

"You will love my in-laws, my mother," Sunny said. "They are warm hearted, interesting folks who have made me feel welcomed and part of their family."

She inclined her head politely. "Then I shall look forward to meeting them. While in London," she continued, "I have a few friends of my mother's I'd like to look up—a Jacob and Katrina Jennings, and a lawyer by the name of Howard Rawlings." She frowned. "All of them have to be well into their eighties by now. Perhaps they're even deceased. But I'd like to give the search a try anyway, even if it's to find their families. If it weren't for the help they gave my mother when she needed it, I wouldn't be here today." She tilted her head sideways. "None of us would be here."

"Then Rafe and I will help you find these people," Sunny offered. "And I'm sure the Cavendishes or Aunt Kaylena and her husband, Lord Morgan Wade would not mind assisting your search. All of them know many influential people who might come up with solid leads."

"I will be sure to engage their help, then," she said. "Once we leave London," she continued, "we will spend time in Brighton, as I am anxious to see Bentwood and walk the grounds of my mother's childhood home."

"Riley and I could come along with you," Gabriel said. "I know my wife would love for Lucinda Collins to see Ethan and to visit with other loved ones at Collins Stead."

"You all could stay until September," Sunny suggested. "And then we can return to Willow Creek together."

Gabriel smiled. "I will have to talk further with Riley, but I am sure she will agree."

"Josh and I plan on leaving Bentwood in June, before your resort awakens," she said to Sunny. "And travel to Ireland," she said, meeting Raven's gaze. "I'd like to see your home and meet Braiton's family."

"And when we leave in July to return to Willow Creek, you can travel with us," Raven said.

Amanda smiled. "It all sounds wonderful to me."

"The large piece of land across from my home would be a perfect location for the big house you two wish to build. I can start to break ground tomorrow, so you all can oversee and draw out the dwelling's floor plan while you are here," Gabriel offered.

Raven and Sunny squealed with delight, taking turns to hug their brother.

"Come," Raven said, taking Sunny by the hand. "Let us go talk to our husbands."

The two ran off, hand in hand, like they did when they were little.

Gabriel chuckled. "Those two never change."

She smiled. "It's nice to know some things stay the same." Looking down at Proud Eagle's grave, she said, "Gabriel, when it is my time to meet our Maker..."

"Please, my mother, don't talk of such things," he interrupted.

"I must, Gabriel," she insisted. "Especially after the shootout with Hall. The whole situation has clearly made me see death can come to any of us at any time. When Josh is stronger, he and I plan on speaking to Edmond Dodd, whereby we'll draw up a document stating how we'd like our last wishes to be carried out. We've decided, should either of us pass away while Cassia is under age, we want you and Riley to be her legal guardians."

"I would have it no other way," he agreed. "And she will be loved and cared for as our own."

"I know she would," she said. "Next, I want you to make sure I rest to the right of your father's grave when my time comes. And Josh will rest on my right."

"Then you will lie in death as you walked in life," he commented.

She frowned. "How is that?"

"Between the rifle and the spear," he pointed out.

"Yes, I would say you're right," she mused. "Perhaps that's because it's exactly where I belong. When the good Lord means for us to do something...has a reason for us to be a certain way...or to perform a special duty, He will move heaven and earth to make it possible. It was always my destiny to live as I have. Often I didn't understand why, but God did. He had a plan. I was meant to lose my parents at a young age. And as sorrowful as that was for me, I would have never married your father, lived with his traditions, and given birth to his children, if my own parents had lived. If the white agents hadn't infiltrated our village, I would have never sent you and your sisters to England."

"I would have never met and married Riley. Raven would not be wed to Braiton or Sunny to Rafe," he reflected.

"And then your children would not have been born," she continued. "Proud Eagle's death made way for all that's happened this last year. That's why it's very important for future generations to know their heritage. They need to see how past events, and the people who lived them, have molded the world for them. And part of their legacy is to know me fully. So, I want you to make sure the name on my tombstone reads, *The Golden Lady—Amanda Cornelia Gregory Eagle Holmes*. That name sums it up, all that I am—all that I was."

"And *Peacekeeper* should be etched in there somewhere," he added.

She sighed. "Lord knows I've tried my best to bridge the gap between the white man and the Apache. Perhaps by the time I leave this world I will have accomplished such a task."

"Look around you, my mother. Can you not see you have done so already? Eagle's Landing is

Arizona's melting pot. All nationalities and customs are blending here in harmony. We are working together for the good of all who dwell upon this land."

She smiled at her son. "Yes...yes we are." She sighed again. "I'm glad we had a chance to talk. For days now this subject matter was weighing heavy on my mind."

"Whenever you need to talk, I am always ready to listen." He extended his elbow to her. "Now come, my mother, it is time to go."

She looped her hand through his arm. "What's the rush?"

He frowned. "If we do not leave soon, Michael McCrea will eat up all the pie."

"You never change, either," she teased.

They both laughed as they made their way home.

## A word about the author...

Roberta C.M. DeCaprio is a freelance writer of all genres in romance and woman's mainstream fiction. A prior "sexuality" columnist for *A.B.L.E.D. WOMEN* magazine, and former Assistant Editor for *INDEPENDENCE TODAY* newspaper, (both publications dedicated to the needs and rights of the disabled), Roberta has insight into the problems other physically challenged people face due to living herself with a walking impairment.

Author of a self-published book of poems, she has won awards for her poetry, becoming published in several anthologies. She is a graduate of the Writers Digest School and Cornell Cooperative Extension. During the years she was a member of the Romance Writers of America, she held office from 2002 to 2004 as newsletter editor for Capital Region, her local chapter of RWA, interviewing many published authors for the former monthly publication, *Capital Romance*.

A mother, and grandmother of two, Roberta shares her upstate NY home with many dearly loved pets and her artist husband. To view Roberta's backlist and read excerpts from her books, log on to www.robertadecaprio.com and check out her blog at www.thewordmerchantssociety.blogspot.com.

Other Roberta C.M. DeCaprio titles available from The Wild Rose Press, Inc.:

*A ROSE IN AMBER*
*THE GOLDEN LADY*
*ONE PERFECT FLOWER*
*A RIVER OF ORANGE*
*BORN OF PROUD BLOOD*

**Amanda sat beside Josh in companionable silence** as he drove the horse and wagon to Vernon Washburn's small cabin. The shower of emotions racing through her body set her on fire. Josh's touch, his declaration of love, and her acceptance of this admission brought to her senses an unexpected pleasure. And yet, how could this happen, how could she allow herself to hope for a life with him, to be happy again so soon after Proud Eagle's death? Wasn't she being selfish, fickle-hearted, or betraying her husband?

She reached up to pull the blanket Josh had draped over her shoulders, tighter. Uneasy thoughts bombarded her mind, as guilt scraped at her heart like the spines of a brush. But in truth she hadn't been deceitful in the least. You can't betray a dead spouse. Besides, Proud Eagle had sent for Josh, wanted the good reverend to love and protect her in his absence. She shifted in her seat and gripped the ends of the blanket close to her chest, where cold hands pressed against a racing heart.